STILL
NOT OVER YOU

By Jenny Frame

A Royal Romance

Courting the Countess

Dapper

Royal Rebel

Unexpected

Hunger For You

Charming the Vicar

Royal Court

Wooing the Farmer

Someone to Love

The Duchess and the Dreamer

Wolfgang County Series

Heart of the Pack

Soul of the Pack

Blood of the Pack

By Carsen Taite

Truelesbianlove.com

It Should be a Crime

Do Not Disturb

Nothing but the Truth

The Best Defense

Beyond Innocence

Rush

Courtship

Reasonable Doubt

Without Justice

Sidebar

A More Perfect Union

Love's Verdict

Pursuit of Happiness

Leading the Witness

Drawn

The Luca Bennett Mystery Series

Slingshot

Battle Axe

Switchblade

Bow and Arrow (novella in *Girls with Guns*)

Lone Star Law Series

Lay Down the Law

Above the Law

Letter of the Law

Outside the Law

Legal Affairs Romances

Practice Makes Perfect

By Ali Vali

Carly's Sound

Second Season

Love Match

The Dragon Tree Legacy

The Romance Vote

Girls with Guns

Beneath the Waves

Beauty and the Boss

Blue Skies

Stormy Seas

The Inheritance

Face the Music

Call Series

Calling the Dead

Answering the Call

Forces Series

Balance of Forces: Toujours Ici

Battle of Forces: Sera Toujours

Force of Fire: Toujours a Vous

Vegas Nights

Double-Crossed

Hell Fire (novella in *Girls with Guns*)

The Cain Casey Saga

The Devil Inside	The Devil's Orchard
The Devil Unleashed	The Devil's Due
Deal with the Devil	Heart of the Devil
The Devil Be Damned	

Visit us at www.boldstrokesbooks.com

STILL
NOT OVER YOU

by

Jenny Frame, Carsen Taite,
and Ali Vali

2020

STILL NOT OVER YOU

ISBN 13: 978-1-63555-516-5

This Trade Paperback Original Is Published By
Bold Strokes Books, Inc.
P.O. Box 249
Valley Falls, NY 12185

First Edition: July 2020

Credits
Editors: Ruth Sternglantz and Stacia Seaman
Production Design: Stacia Seaman
Cover Design by Jeanine Henning

CONTENTS

MY FOREVER GIRL

Jenny Frame

Chapter One

The morning was dark, wet, and gray, typical for an early Scottish morning, and it suited Braydon Murphy's mood. After a long night shift working as a maintenance electrician at a local bus depot, all she wanted was her bed and the oblivion of sleep, before the whole work cycle started again.

She leaned her head against the window of the bus and tried hard not to fall asleep. The bus edged along slowly through the heavy Glasgow traffic. Braydon looked at her watch. It was half past seven already, and if she didn't get back home by eight, she wouldn't get enough sleep before her day job started, but what was new?

Braydon sighed and watched the busy pedestrians walk along the pavements and cross at the lights in front of the bus. There was a time when she wouldn't have gotten out of bed for what she currently earned in a day from both her jobs, but now was very different.

As the bus crawled through traffic and time marched ever closer to eight o'clock, she knew she wasn't going to get enough sleep, but Braydon saw this as her purgatory. Punishment for her crimes that she would forever pay for.

Finally, she got to the bus stop near her rented flat and jumped off with her bag of tools over her shoulder. When she turned into her street, she saw a white Audi sports car sitting outside her building. It was her friend Kristen Alexander. They'd been friends since she was sixteen and played football together for the same team. They had gone to their first gay pub together, chased women together, until they both were persuaded by love to settle down, but that was a long time ago.

Kris had gone on to own a successful building company and had asked her more times than she could remember to work for her. Life would be easier if she did, but she had her pride, and after everything that she had lost, pride was about the only thing she had left.

As she approached the block of flats, Kris got out of the car.

"Mornin'—you look tired, mate," Kris said as she took Braydon's hand and gave her a hug.

"Yeah, it was a long night." Braydon didn't think that there was a time of day when she didn't look tired. "In you come."

Braydon buzzed herself in with the keys and led Kris into the building. She was on the first floor so before too long they were inside her flat. It was a small flat—one bedroom, a small living room, and an even smaller kitchen—but it was all Braydon needed.

She dropped her bag of tools and said, "How's Jan and Dani?"

"Good, keeping me on my toes. She's really into her football now and coming along with me to my games."

As lifelong Glasgow Celtic supporters, she and Kris had gone to matches together for years, but that had become too expensive a hobby for Bray since the divorce. She had dreamed of taking her own child to watch the games with her, but sadly, that would never be.

"Cuppa tea?"

"No, I don't want to keep you up, Bray."

"Don't worry, I'm having one anyway," Bray said.

"Okay, then."

Bray ignored the dishes piled up in the sink and made the tea. She was hopeless at keeping up with the housework, but since it was just her, living alone, she didn't care. It wasn't a home—she'd had a home and lost it. This was just a base to sleep before heading back out to work.

She brought through the tea and a packet of biscuits. When she put down the cups, she headed over to her computer and lifted an envelope with money. She hesitated before handing it over to Kris.

"This is the last one," Bray said.

Kris gave her a sad smile. "Yeah, I suppose it is."

Bray sat down and took her mug of tea in her hands. She tried to let the heat of the cup seep into her body, but it wasn't working. She didn't know how she would feel today, but now that it was here, she was honestly scared and felt her stomach churn with anxiety.

This debt, which she had been faithfully paying for four years, was the last tether holding her and her ex-wife together, and now she was being cut loose.

"An end of an era," Kris said. "Maybe you can work less now, start a new life."

Bray shook her head. "I had a life, a perfect one. I don't deserve another."

Kris sighed. "That was such a long time ago. Stop being hard on yourself. You've done your time, paid your debts."

Bray said nothing. She was never going to forgive herself. She still had nightmares about the night she was in a casino and Faith had called her in hysterics.

I should have been there.

"You know there's always a job for you with Alexander Building Services," Kris said.

Bray nodded. "You know I can't."

"Bray, you're my best friend. Stop being so proud—my company would be grateful to get someone like you on board."

Bray rubbed her face with her hands. She'd had her own thriving electrical business, often working alongside Kris's on big projects, doing well, making good money, giving her and her wife Faith a comfortable quality of life—then she'd fucked it up. She couldn't go and work alongside some of the guys who she'd had working under her on projects. Plus it would put her just too close to Faith.

Kris's wife Jan was Faith's best friend. Too close, too painful. Bray couldn't bear to hear about Faith's new life, new lovers—the thought made her feel sick. There had been no one for her since Faith. Faith was her angel—her forever girl, Bray used to call her, the only woman she'd ever loved—and because of Bray's weakness, she was no longer hers.

"How is Faith?" Bray asked. She couldn't not ask. After their divorce Faith had retrained as a nursery school teacher. She loved children and it was the perfect job for such a caring person. *And you destroyed everything you had together.* Guilt was a way of life for Bray, and she embraced that guilt, bathed in it in fact, because she felt she should be punished.

Kris took a drink of tea. "She's fine and not seeing anyone."

"I never asked if she was," Bray said.

"I can see the question in your eyes every time I see you. Why can't you move on?"

Bray stayed silent and stared into her teacup. She didn't want to answer that question out loud, but Faith was the first person she thought of in the morning and the last one at night. That and the guilt and pain of what she had lost.

When Bray didn't reply Kris said, "I've got some good news for you."

"Oh," Bray said, "what's that?"

"You know it's my fortieth next month?"

Bray nodded. It was her own fortieth in December this year. She was dreading it—not because she was worried about her age, but because of what she had expected to have by the time she was forty.

"Well, and this was Jan's idea, we're going to take a two week cruise to the Caribbean, and we're inviting all our friends. The cruise line has its own LGBTQ coordinator who's going to take care of our party. It's going to be amazing."

That was the kind of holiday she and Faith used to take when they had plenty of money. They had seen some amazing places, romantic places.

"I hope you have a great time," Bray said.

"You're invited too, Bray."

"You know I can't afford to go on a holiday like that." She was annoyed Kris had even suggested it. Did she want to make her feel worse?

"No, I mean, Jan and I will pay for your tickets."

"No way, Kris. I'm not taking charity."

Kris held up her hands. "Hey, hey, calm down. It's not charity—it's the simple fact that I want my best friend there to celebrate my birthday, like she always is. Do you remember my twenty-first?"

"Barely. You, me, Faith, and Jan went to that club called… Mandy's?"

"Yeah, I got absolutely hammered. I don't know how I managed to pull such a classy lady like Jan, convince her to put up with me—in fact, I'm still wondering. We hadn't been together long."

That was how she'd felt about Faith from the moment she met her. Bray was so punching above her weight, and it turned out that Faith had been too good for her.

"Go on your cruise. Have a good time. You can spend one birthday without me."

"Too late." Kris pulled a wallet out of her jacket. "The air ticket to Fort Lauderdale and your cruise ticket are already bought, so if you don't want to waste my money, then you'll come."

"What?" Bray stood up angrily. "You just paid for everything without consulting me?"

"Yes, because I knew you'd say no, and I want my best friend with me."

Bray started to pace anxiously. "I can't believe you did that."

She felt trapped. She didn't want to go on a holiday and pretend to be happy. How could she? Then a thought occurred to her.

"Faith isn't going, is she?"

Kris hesitated. "Eh, no. She can't get the time off, no one to cover her at the nursery. So what do you say? I know you have plenty of holiday time up your sleeve because you never take any. Food, drinks, they're all included, so all you need is some spending money. Please, come. It would mean a lot to me, mate."

What choice did she have? Kris was her best friend, and if Faith wasn't going to be there maybe she could handle it. She couldn't have coped with seeing Faith for two whole weeks. The heartbreak and the pain would be too much. People had always told her that time would ease the heartbreaking pain, but it never had. It got worse, in fact.

She sighed and said, "Fine, okay, but I'm going to pay you back for this. No matter what you say, Kris."

Kris jumped up and punched her softly on the arm. "This is going to be your holiday of a lifetime. Believe me."

❖

"This is the last one." Jan handed Bray's envelope to Faith as they sat at her kitchen table enjoying a cuppa.

The tired kitchen of Faith's old house wasn't much, but more than she could have hoped for after the divorce. She'd managed to get on her feet, with some help from her parents, who bought this old detached sandstone house at auction for her and refurbished one part to house her private nursery school. The rest of the house was waiting on more money and time to do renovations.

Faith took the envelope and felt a deep sadness. This was the last thing tying her to Bray, and now it was being taken away from her.

"Thanks, I'll give it to my dad."

"She's kept her word, hasn't she?" Jan said. "I mean, paid off her debts and never misses her meetings, so Kris tells me."

"So she's doing all right, with her meetings and handling her addiction?" Faith asked.

Bray was a gambling addict and had brought down their thriving business by borrowing money for her gambling debts and not paying the business's bills. They'd lost everything—their home, their business, their life together. But when the large family home they'd shared was sold to satisfy some of the debts, Faith's dad stepped in and paid the rest. Bray had vowed to Faith she would pay off every penny, and she had.

When Bray broke down and told her about her gambling problem, Faith was panicked, then angry, but then understanding. She would have helped Bray through her addiction and rebuilt what they had piece by piece, if Bray had told her everything, but she'd looked her in the eye and lied to her. That was something she'd never expected of Bray and found hard to forgive. Bray knew how important truth was to her after her disastrous first relationship, as a young woman. Bray understood—and still, she lied.

Jan continued, "She's still working her two jobs and keeping on top of her problems, I think, but doesn't do much else. Kris says she won't move on."

Faith's instinct was to wrap Bray in her arms and tell her it was all right, but there was too much pain. Too much history wrapped up in their failed relationship. Faith touched the gold locket she always wore around her neck.

"I'm glad she's okay," Faith said.

Then out of the blue Jan said, "Karen asked if I thought she should ask you out again."

Faith took a drink of coffee. "I don't think so."

"Why?" asked Jan. "You know she's had a thing for you since uni. She has a good job, nice looking, what's wrong with her?"

Inside, Faith knew the answer. No one would ever be Bray, but she and Bray would never be again. "I'm just not interested anymore. I have the nursery to run. It's my life now." When their family business was brought down by Bray's debts, Faith had retrained as a nursery teacher. Since the divorce, her nursery was thriving, and she now had her own staff of five.

"You have plenty of time for the odd date. Or maybe you're still in love with Bray?" Jan said.

Faith looked up sharply. "Of course I'm not. I've been divorced four years."

"Then why do you still wear your wedding ring and keep your married name?"

Faith looked down at her engagement ring and remembered the day they walked around the nicest jewelry shops in Glasgow looking for a ring, then going for lunch together afterward. It had been such a special day. She could still see the look of pride on Bray's face as they held hands in the restaurant, gazing at her new engagement ring.

Then came her wedding ring, the thing that made her finally fit in the world. She felt secure, more confident, all because of Bray's love, but she couldn't take it off.

"It's just so I don't get unwanted attention. I'm not interested in any romantic entanglements, and if people think I'm married, then they don't try."

Jan narrowed her eyes. Faith could tell she didn't quite believe her. "Hmm...well, you'll have the chance to spend some quality time with Karen on Kris's birthday cruise, so who knows, romance might be in the air."

"I doubt it," Faith replied. "You're sure Bray isn't coming?"

"We asked, of course, but she can't afford a cruise like that, and she wouldn't let Kris pay, would she?"

"No, she's too proud."

"There you go, then. I think this break is going to do you the world of good."

"You think?"

Jan grinned. "Oh, I'm certain of it."

After Jan left, she walked back into her living room and stood in front of the mirror above the fireplace. She opened the locket around her neck. In it was a picture of a smiling, proud Bray holding her in her arms.

How could she ever get over this?

Chapter Two

"Excuse me, sir…uh, sorry, ma'am, could you say that again?" Bray was getting frustrated. Not because she was misgendered, she was used to that. She was tall, well-built, and had a masculine look. But this was the fourth time she'd tried to give her American taxi driver her destination, and her broad Glaswegian accent was outfoxing him.

She tried to say it again really slowly. "I need to get to Port Everglades departures as quickly as possible."

The taxi driver put her last case in the boot of his car. "Port Everglades?"

Thank the Lord. "Yes, as quickly as you can. I'm really late."

The journey from Glasgow had been a nightmare. She'd traveled a day later than the rest of Kris's party guests because of her work schedule. Her manager was shocked when she'd asked for time off. Bray never took holidays, and she would have never taken this time if Kris hadn't guilt-tripped her into coming.

The flight from Glasgow had been delayed, and she'd arrived at her hotel in Fort Lauderdale in the middle of last night. She'd slept in and missed the cruise transport from the hotel. Now she had very little time to get to the departure building and get on board.

She got into the taxi, and they were driving at last. Her mobile beeped with a text. It was Kris, asking where she was now. They had already checked in.

"Shit, I'm so late." She said to the driver, "Can we go as quickly as we can, please?"

"Sorry?"

"Jesus Christ. Quickly?"

"*Quickly*, yes." He finally got it. "Are you French, ma'am?"

Bray had to laugh. Her accent was clearly so thick that she didn't even register as a native English speaker over here.

"Yeah, I'm French."

It wasn't long until they were in line to enter the vast dock departure area. When the large cruise ship came into view, she said, "Bloody hell. It's like a city on the water."

She'd never seen anything like it. It reminded her of the scene in Faith's favorite film, *Titanic*. All the hustle and bustle of the passengers arriving at the dock, little knowing what was in store for them.

Let's hope we have a better voyage.

When they were together, Faith made them watch *Titanic* all the time. Bray pretended to protest at watching the sappy movie again but secretly enjoyed holding Faith in her arms as she cried at the ending. No matter how many times Faith watched that film, she always cried, as she did at most sappy, romantic things. Faith was an emotional woman, and she loved that about her.

She secretly wished Faith had been able to come on this trip. It would have been awkward, but just to see her ex-wife and hear her voice would be amazing. Amazingly painful.

But that wasn't to be. It was going to be strange enough seeing some of the old crowd they used to hang around with. Since the divorce she'd cut herself off from the friends they had as a couple, except for Kris and Jan. It seemed easier that way. She didn't want to have any awkwardness, and Faith deserved to keep their friends. She didn't.

Bray finally arrived at the drop-off area of what resembled an airport terminal. She got out and paid the driver. "Thanks, mate."

She looked at her watch. Time was running out. She slung one bag over her shoulder and carried her suitcase. She hurried inside and tried to find her check-in quickly. The staff were eager to get her on board on time, so she was quickly put through all the relevant passport and ticket checks and finally walked over the enclosed bridge to the colossal ship.

She stopped as she stepped off the bridge into the main reception area of the ship and looked around in awe at the large opulent room. "This must have cost Kris a fortune for my ticket. I'm going to kill her."

High above hung crystal chandeliers, and the floor was highly polished marble. On either side of the room were four glass elevators. It reminded Bray of a very high-end shopping mall. All around her passengers chatted excitedly and staff pointed them in the direction of their rooms. This was a far cry from the wet and stormy streets of Glasgow.

She heard a voice beside her say, "Can I help you find your room, sir?"

She turned to face the young staff member, whose eyes went wide as he realized his mistake. "Sorry, I'm so sorry, ma'am."

Bray had to laugh to herself. Just wait till she opened her mouth, and the poor guy found out she was French too.

❖

Faith hung her last dress in the wardrobe. Kris and Jan had asked her to come up on deck to watch the boat leaving the pier, but she just wanted to get settled in and unpack. There would be plenty of time to stroll along the decks. Besides, it was a madhouse out there, with all the passengers trying to find their cabins and acquaint themselves with the ship.

She was happy to have a quiet, calm start to their trip. Faith walked to the bed and sat on the corner. This was a nice room. When Jan had asked her what kind of room she wanted, Faith decided to go for one of the nicer staterooms. It was larger than the standard, had a lovely bathroom, a large super-king bed, a sitting room area with a couch and TV, plus an absolutely gorgeous balcony.

Faith walked over to the balcony doors and watched as the ship pulled away from the pier. The balcony held a small table and chairs, and it would be wonderful to sit out there with a good book on her iPad and a glass of wine.

She intended to do a lot of that. Reading and relaxing. She was one of only a few of their party not in a couple and didn't want to play gooseberry, and so for the times she couldn't be around the pool topping up her tan, she wanted a roomy cabin and nice balcony to make her way through her long reading list.

It had been so long since Faith had a holiday, and she wouldn't have gone on this one if it hadn't been a special birthday for Kris, so she was going to make the most of it. Her nursery business was going well, after years of hard work, and she intended to relax.

"Yes, this is going to be perfect."

She went back to her suitcase and picked up the swimsuits she had brought. She was a bit nervous about wearing them as she hadn't worn a swimsuit in years. In fact, the last time would have been her last holiday abroad.

She and Bray had gone to Hawaii, and one of her best memories was sitting on the beach at the end of their holiday. Faith had snuggled up in Bray's arms and asked Bray how she'd feel about trying for a baby.

Typically loving and enthusiastic, Bray showered her with kisses and love. Strange to think that decision, which they'd made at their most loving, was the beginning of the end of their relationship.

"Enough. I need a change of scene."

Faith grabbed her handbag and phone and walked out her cabin door. She checked the cabin door was locked and put her key card in her bag. As she made sure her purse and everything she would need was in there, she heard a Scottish accent getting closer to her.

The voice made her heart stop beating for a millisecond. *No, it can't be.*

Faith was almost too frightened to look up, but she forced herself. This time her heart and everything stopped. It was Bray.

❖

"Here we are, ma'am. This is your suite."

Suite? This better not be an expensive room, Kris. She had already vowed to herself to pay Kris back. This ship and the trip were way too expensive for her to take from a friend. "Uh, thanks." Bray fished around in her pocket for a tip.

"Thanks, ma'am. My name's Tim. Anything you need, just let me know. There's a button in the room to call for service."

"Cheers, Tim."

Bray fumbled trying to get her key card into the lock when she felt someone staring at her. She looked up slowly and her stomach flipped. "Jesus Christ." It was her ex-wife, Faith. "Faith—you're not supposed to be here."

"Neither are you." Faith looked equally shocked as her.

"I...Kris said you couldn't come on the trip," Bray said.

Faith grasped at the locket she wore. She looked really stressed at her presence. "Jan said you couldn't come. I wouldn't have—I'm sorry, I need to get something in my room."

Faith went back into her room and shut the door quickly.

Bray finally managed to unlock the door and walked inside. She pulled off her jacket and threw it on the bed in frustration. "Fuck me. Kris, I'm going to kill you."

She started to pace up and down. This felt like a set-up. Otherwise what were the chances she'd be given a room right next door to her ex-wife's?

Faith had looked horrified when she saw her. She had to make things right. She had to make sure the next two weeks weren't going to be as awkward as that meeting.

She was going to have to talk to Faith. "Shit."

Faith looked beautiful. They'd been apart a long time, but seeing her just now, all the years melted away.

Bray slid her wallet from her pocket and pulled out the picture that never left her side. It was Faith and her, together. Bray was holding her from behind, her hands resting on Faith's baby bump. She had never seen anything more beautiful and never would. Faith pregnant with their son.

As much as it hurt to look at that picture, she gazed at it every morning, every break time at work, and every night before she went to bed. It reminded her of what she had lost, and every time she passed a betting shop or watched a betting advert on the TV, she remembered that picture and what those things had cost her.

Now her wife—ex-wife—was next door, and the past was catching up with her. Bray scrubbed her face with her hands. She knew she had to be the one to go and talk to Faith.

Faith hated confrontation. Always had, and Bray had always been her voice when any issues came up. She always felt good being that person for Faith, and when she wasn't anymore, it hurt.

She sighed. "Kris, I was going to kill you before, but now I'm going to do it slowly."

She took a breath and walked to Faith's door. She hesitated before knocking, but when she did Faith opened it slowly.

"Faith? Could I talk to you, just for a few minutes?"

Faith nodded and opened the door up for her.

"Thanks, Faith."

One weird aspect about no longer being her ex-wife's partner was using first names. She'd never called her wife *Faith* unless it was to outsiders. She always called her *darlin'*, and using her real name now felt strange.

Faith's room was virtually identical to hers, except Faith had a balcony. She could tell Faith had been crying. Her eyes were puffy and red, and her usual feelings of guilt just got a whole lot worse.

"Um…I just wanted to clear the air, before we go any further. I would never have said yes to Kris and made you feel uncomfortable if I'd known you were coming. In fact I didn't want to come anyway, but Kris bought the tickets before asking me and said I'd just be wasting her money if I didn't come."

"I understand," Faith said. "I wouldn't have come either. Looks like Kris and Jan decided for us."

"Yeah, looks like it. Well look, we're here now, and I don't want things to be awkward. We've got two weeks ahead of us. I promise I won't cause you any problems. I won't come to sit with the group at dinner or anything. I'll just keep myself to myself."

"You can't do that. It's your holiday too. You must come to all the group events. We're adults—I'm sure we can be civil to each other."

"Of course we can. I would never want to intentionally do anything to upset you, Faith. If me being at any of the group things is too much for you, just say, and I'll go, okay?"

"Thank you," Faith said.

Why did Bray have to be so accommodating? It was hard enough to see her again, without her being so accommodating and kind, but then she always was. That had never changed since they met. Only her truthfulness had.

There was a long silence, as if neither of them knew what to say.

A bit like their final days together before officially separating, Faith thought. Nothing about this wasn't strange, and it was going to be a really difficult holiday.

"I better head back and unpack," Bray said.

"Yes, I'm supposed to go upstairs and meet up with the others. I'll see you up there."

Bray smiled at her, but it was a sad smile, hardly surprising since there had been nothing but sadness in their life for years now.

Bray began to walk out the door, but stopped when Faith said, "How are you? Really?"

Bray looked back over her shoulder and said, "I'm fine. See you."

Faith could tell Bray was not fine. Bray looked tired. Their four years apart had taken their toll on Bray, as they had done her. She supposed both of them would never really be *fine* ever again. All they could do was to find ways of coping from one day to the next.

CHAPTER THREE

"Not in the face. If you're going to punch me, take it out on my ribs. Jan loves my good looks too much."

Kris had been sent down to hurry Bray up to join the group, and Bray was showing her displeasure. She was towering menacingly over Kris, who held her hands up in surrender.

"I can't believe you would do this to me, Kris. We've been friends since school."

"Jan and I were fed up from never having you both at birthdays, Christmas, you name the celebration. We wanted both our friends with us. We still love you both the same even if you two don't, and we thought enough time would have passed for you, after everything bad that happened."

"There will never be enough time passing from Faith losing our child," Bray said angrily.

"I didn't mean about the baby. Shit." Kris realized her mistake. "I know you'll never get over losing your baby, I mean you and Faith. But you can both be civil, and both spend time with us. We were never apart before you got divorced. Jan and I lost you both, it felt like."

Bray turned away and sat down on the corner of her bed and stared down at the floor. "Yeah, we can be civil. Faith is so gracious and polite that she would never cause a problem, but just being around her makes everything so painful."

"It's one holiday, mate. Forgive us. We just wanted our two oldest friends here with us," Kris said.

Bray let out a long breath. "Why next door to each other?"

"That must have been the cruise company. Same last name or something. Must have thought you were family."

Bray didn't quite believe that, but she couldn't hide in here for two weeks, and she couldn't stay mad at her best friend. "I still say you're a fucking arsehole."

"Absolutely," Kris said. "Complete arsehole, that's me. Will you come upstairs now?"

"Okay, you win." Bray stood up. "So, who's in the group?"

"There's Cath and Lucy, Beth and Jamie—"

"Jamie finally got Beth to go out with her?" Bray said.

Kris laughed. "Yeah, the longest crush in history, but Jamie finally got the nerve to tell Beth she had been in love with her since university. Beth gave her the hardest time and wouldn't go out with her for ages."

"Why?"

"Beth had a thing for her too but didn't think Jamie was interested. They could have had a lot fewer relationships with the wrong people if Jamie had been honest with her, but all's well that ends well. They're getting married next year. Then there's Dougie, Findlay, and Karen."

Bray snorted. "Talking of huge crushes, I can't believe Karen hasn't made her move for Faith in the four years we've been divorced. She did enough mooching around Faith when we were married."

"I won't say she hasn't tried, but Faith's never been ready for another relationship."

Bray didn't like the sound of that statement. "Meaning she is now?"

"Who knows? Now can we get upstairs to the lounge?"

Bray nodded and grabbed her wallet. She closed her eyes and looked back to the day her divorce was finalized. She remembered thinking that now she had given Karen the chance she always wanted.

Karen was in Faith's university course and, with a well-off mummy and daddy, looked down at Bray and Kris because of their broad Glaswegian accents and the council housing estates they came from. But Karen was friends with the rest of the gang, so Bray'd had to learn to get along with her.

They walked out of the cabin and Bray said, "I don't think Karen has ever forgiven me for marrying Faith."

"Yeah, probably. Jan says that Karen invited Faith along to watch her play footie, the day you met," Kris said.

They came to a lift at the end of the corridor and got in. Bray pressed the floor number and it set off. The day she met Faith, her football team were drawn in a Scottish cup game against Faith's university team.

"Do you remember that day? You met Jan and I met Faith?" Bray said.

"I'll never forget it," Kris said. "I often wonder what life would have been like if our team hadn't played Glasgow Uni. I don't think either of us would've mixed in those circles. I don't think we would have met our wives. Sorry, ex-wife for you."

"No, you were right the first time. Faith will always be my wife—in here." Bray put her fist to her chest.

❖

Faith and the rest of the group were gathered in the bar on the upper deck. There were blue skies and the sun was hot, scorching hot for someone coming from Scotland.

Faith was on edge and nervous. She was constantly looking around, waiting for Kris to arrive with Bray. It had been such a shock to see Bray.

Talking to her face-to-face had opened up a Pandora's box of emotions, so much so that she didn't know how she felt. If it was up to her, she'd go back to Scotland and hide in her home, so she didn't have to face the mix of memories and emotions that came with Bray.

She felt a presence beside her. It was Karen.

"It's beautiful isn't it? And a long way from Glasgow, thank goodness."

Faith turned to face her. "It is very nice, a nice break from routine, but I'll still be glad to go home to Glasgow."

Karen was a few inches taller than her own five foot three, had shoulder-length blond hair, and wore brightly colored shorts with a brightly colored T-shirt. Karen was more androgynous than butch. And since they'd arrived in Florida early yesterday morning, Karen had stuck closely to her.

"Glasgow has its merits, I suppose, but I'd go mad if I didn't get away to sunnier climes at least three times a year."

Karen Whitburn could be such a show-off, a generally decent

person but a show-off. The problem was Karen had always thought this was the right way to impress Faith, which couldn't be further from the truth. Karen was heir to the long-established Whitburn Biscuits and Cakes. Their brand was sold all over the UK.

Faith hadn't been aware of Karen's romantic interest in her until she started dating Bray, and Jan pointed out that Karen was acting badly toward her new girlfriend. In truth, she was never good at noticing flirting or interest because she didn't expect it. Then Bray came along and everything changed.

Karen cleared her throat nervously. "I asked Jan if she would pass on that I'd like to take you out—"

Bray and Kris arrived to join the group and Faith flinched, though she was grateful for the interruption. But then Karen slipped her arm around her waist and said, "Don't worry. I'm here."

"I'm not frightened of her, Karen. It's just hard—"

"Okay, okay. I just want you to know I'm here for you."

All conversation ground to a halt and Faith saw the whole gang look anxiously between her and Bray. She supposed that they were worried about picking sides. But Faith realized she wasn't worried at all.

Kris and Jan were right about asking Bray to come on the cruise. It wasn't fair that Bray had been cut off from these social occasions because of her. It wasn't fair, and Faith would just have to learn to cope with being in Bray's company again. In fact, maybe it would give her some closure—maybe it would give her a chance to lay some ghosts to rest and move on with her life.

"Hey, everyone," Kris said, "Bray is here."

Bray felt nervous. She could feel the awkwardness amongst her old friends at her arrival. Her gaze zeroed in on Karen's arm around Faith's waist, and she felt a dagger stab into her gut. But she supposed this was her punishment—she'd hurt Faith so badly and failed to protect her family. Now she just had to suck it up and take it.

Jamie was the first one to approach her and shake her hand, followed by her girlfriend Beth.

"Good to have you back with us," Jamie said.

"Thanks, I hear you two are getting married."

"Yes, and about time too." Beth gave her partner Jamie a soft dig to the ribs.

Next Dougie and Findlay walked over. Findlay gave her a big hug. "We missed you, Butch."

Findlay used his old nickname for her. He'd always joked she was the embodiment of a butch lesbian.

"Good to see you too."

Bray looked over his shoulder and saw Faith looking right at them. She wished she could tell what Faith was thinking, but Faith dropped her gaze when she saw Bray looking back.

Finally, Cath and Lucy greeted her. They both identified as femme, she knew, but Cath was very much an alpha female, with Lucy the softer, quieter of the two.

Cath gave her a strong handshake. "Good to see you, Bray. I—"

Just as she was about to speak, a member of the cruise staff walked into their little group. He was immaculately dressed, with short blond hair, and camp to the max.

"Good evening, everyone. I am Thomas, and I'm the LGBT representative of the cruise line. I and my assistant are here to help all the LGBT passengers on the ship, but primarily I'll be looking after your group and making sure everyone is safe and looked after, but most of all to make sure Kris has a very happy birthday."

Waiters appeared with trays of champagne and handed them around. "So welcome to the cruise of a lifetime, and raise a glass to Kris to wish her a happy birthday!"

❖

Bray hadn't had to dress so formally for years. She was a jeans and T-shirt kind of person, but for formal social occasions, she had to look a little smarter. Those kind of occasions didn't often happen to her any more, but dinner on the cruise would be formal most nights.

She gazed at herself in the mirror. "Will this do?" She had decided on smart blue trousers and an open-neck shirt with a smart suit jacket. "I look like a pretentious wanker."

She pulled off the jacket and threw it on the bed. "They'll just have to like it or lump it. This is as formal as I want to get these days."

Bray heard a knock on the door. It was probably one of the steward staff. They were certainly attentive, popping in and out to see if she had everything she needed.

"Coming," Bray shouted.

She opened the door and her heart thudded loudly. It was Faith, and she looked absolutely beautiful, wearing a blue floral print cocktail dress.

"Faith—"

"Can I come in?" Faith asked.

"Aye, come in." Bray was pleasantly surprised but panicked at the state of her room. She hurriedly picked up wet towels and discarded clothes from the floor. "Sorry about the mess. I wasn't expecting anyone."

Faith smiled. "You always were messy."

"Yeah, um…you look beautiful, by the way," Bray said.

Faith looked to the floor and said nothing. Four years hadn't changed her much—she never could take a compliment.

"I hope you don't mind me dropping in," Faith said.

"Of course not. What can I do for you?"

"Well, when we met up with the group this afternoon for drinks, things were awkward. Our friends didn't know how to be with us. Like they didn't want to appear to take sides or anything."

Bray nodded. She had felt the odd one out the whole time. "Yeah, it was. That's why I never came to any events since the divorce. I didn't want to cause anyone to feel uncomfortable."

"That's not fair on you. Perhaps after this cruise is over, you'll come to some of them again," Faith said.

Bray nodded but inside knew she never would. Not after the close intimacy she'd interrupted between Karen and Faith. She couldn't bear to see Faith with someone else. It might have been four years since they were together, but even if it was forty, Faith would always be Bray's wife in her heart.

Faith took a breath. This was hard, but she had to do this, so as she and Bray didn't ruin the holiday atmosphere for anybody else. "What I thought was maybe if we walked up to dinner together and showed that we're okay with the situation, then our friends would relax, and we could enjoy the rest of the holiday normally."

Bray rubbed her hands together. She looked on edge, nervous. The years apart hadn't dulled Faith's ability to read her mood. Bray struggled when handling negative emotions—it was one of the things that had contributed to the breakup of their marriage.

But here in this moment Bray was trying unsuccessfully to hide her uncertainty and worry, and it made Faith's feelings start to wake from their slumber.

"Isn't Karen going to come for you?" Bray asked.

"Karen? Why would she?" What was Bray thinking?

"Okay then. Sounds like a good plan. Hang on, let me just grab my jacket."

Faith could tell Bray wasn't comfortable in these clothes. She never had been a formal person, even wearing trainers with her suit on their wedding day. But that was just Bray.

"You look nice, Bray." It was almost an effort to use her name. When they were together it never passed her lips. It was always *baby*, or *sweetie*, and using the formality of Bray's name felt foreign to her.

"Thanks," Bray replied. "Do you think it's formal enough?"

"Yes. I know these kinds of events stress you out, but you're fine," Faith said.

Bray gazed at her for a few moments, then walked to the door and opened it for her.

I wish I knew what you were thinking.

When they started to walk along to the lifts, Bray offered her arm to Faith, then immediately apologized. "I'm sorry. I didn't mean to—old habits."

"That's okay," Faith reassured her.

Old habits indeed. Faith caught herself before she accepted Bray's arm. It was what they always did as a couple. It didn't matter if it was a long or short walk—she always took Bray's arm. They liked to be connected at all times. It gave Faith a feeling of security, something she had sorely missed.

They arrived at the lift and Bray pressed the button. No one else joined them, and so an awkward silence hung in the air. After a few seconds Bray said, "You got the last payment okay?"

"Yes, I got it. Thanks for sticking to your word and paying it."

"It was my debt. I wasn't going to have your dad think any worse of me. He was so good to me, and I let him down."

Faith wanted to say it was all all right, and none of it mattered, but there was too much water under the bridge.

"How are you really, Bray? Are you still going to your Gamblers Anonymous meetings?"

"Yeah, I've never missed a week in the four years since we—" Braydon's voice broke slightly. "Well, apart from these two weeks on holiday. But I have it set up with my friend from the meetings, that I'll phone him during our trip."

"That's really good, Bray. I'm proud of you."

"Don't be—I don't deserve pride," Bray said.

Faith was just about to reply when they arrived at their floor.

❖

Bray and Faith strolled through the crowds to the dining room. When they walked through the doors, Bray immediately felt out of place. Most of the male guests were wearing expensive suits, some in dinner jackets and bow ties.

Faith said, "There's Kris and the gang over there."

They walked across the dance floor toward the table. If there was going to be dancing, Bray was going to head to her room right after dinner.

As they approached the table, Bray saw there were only two seats left, one on either side of the table. Everyone was looking at them, probably surprised that they came together. Hopefully their friends would relax now that they saw she and Faith weren't going to tear each other's hair out. Quite the opposite actually.

Karen stood and held out the chair next to her. "I kept you a seat, Faith."

Everyone was watching. Bray knew Faith had no choice but to accept, but she still felt a twinge of jealousy.

"Bray, take a pew. We've got a lot of catching up to do," Findlay said. She took the seat between Findlay and Dougie.

At the top of the table, Kris stood up and said, "Friends, friends, I'd like to say a few words."

"Do you have to?" Findlay joked.

Everyone laughed, but Kris pressed on with her speech. "I want to thank you all for joining Jan and me for my fortieth birthday celebration. I'm especially grateful that my oldest friend, Bray, is back with us."

Bray felt her cheeks heat up. She looked over to Faith and found her looking back at her with a small smile. Her heart thudded. This was going to be two weeks of hell. Obviously time had done nothing to dampen the feelings in her heart. It would be so hard to be this close to Faith and yet so far apart.

Kris lifted her champagne glass and said, "To the best friends anyone could have."

The first course arrived, and Bray looked down at the huge array of cutlery and panicked. Beside her Findlay was busy chatting and hadn't started his food yet, so she couldn't get any hints from him. Bray hated this formality. It was a set of rules that she had never been taught, and it made her feel stupid. She looked up and saw Faith looking at her, holding up the correct fork for the first course. Nobody else seemed to spot Faith's maneuver. Bray picked up the small fork and mouthed, *Thanks.*

Then Faith winked at her and heat spread all over her body. She looked down quickly and started to eat her food so that Faith wouldn't see the want in her eyes. Why did she do that? This was really going to be torture.

The next time Bray lifted her gaze, she saw Karen with her arm around the back of Faith's chair, talking to her intently. Torture.

❖

Bray was first to leave the table after dinner. She needed some air and walked out onto the deck. She leaned against the railings and looked into the churning water beneath her. There had been an embarrassing incident after the dessert course, and she kept churning it over in her mind. Some of the ship's crew came around selling raffle tickets for big prizes. Apparently, they collected money to donate to a worthy charity on each of the islands they docked at.

Of course she had to decline. Giving money for a chance at a prize, even for a good cause, was too close to gambling for Bray. Usually she just made a donation when that sort of thing took place, and she'd tried to do that tonight, but of course Karen asked why, making a fuss about the whole thing. When she explained why, Bray sensed the embarrassment everyone was feeling.

People didn't realize how much a gambling addiction invaded every part of an addict's life. She had to constantly be aware of her surroundings and any actions that could open a door to the dark path again.

Bray closed her eyes, let the salty sea breeze brush across her face, and inhaled the fresh air. She felt a presence beside her and smelled a scent that she would always know, Faith's favorite perfume.

When she opened her eyes, she saw Faith standing beside her. "Faith?"

"I'm sorry if Karen made you feel uncomfortable."

Bray shrugged. "It doesn't matter. It's part of my penance, I guess, having to explain to people why I can't take part in a raffle, a competition. It happens all the time at work."

"I just wanted to say that you shouldn't feel uncomfortable, or embarrassed, because every time you say no, I can't take part, you're winning your battle. It's a positive thing—that's how I see it anyway. I'm proud of you."

Bray was quite taken aback. After all she'd put Faith through, she still had the grace to be supportive of her.

"Thank you. I appreciate that."

"Don't mind Karen. You know what she's like sometimes," Faith said.

I know what she's like all right. She's wanted my wife since I first met her. "Yeah, I know. Remember the first time we met?"

She heard Faith laugh for the first time in years and it made her heart lighter.

"How could I forget. Your football team came to play the uni team, and they were a bit shell-shocked, I think."

Bray couldn't help but smile at the memory. "Kris and I turned up with our rough-and-ready team. I don't think your uni team had ever played a real hell for leather cup game or a squad like us before."

Faith stepped closer and laughed again. "Yes, I think it was the waist-high tackles that were a shock to them."

Bray had gotten two precious laughs from Faith. Excitement bubbled in her stomach for the first time since she didn't know when.

"Football is a rough sport," Bray said.

"One girl broke her arm."

Bray smiled and put her hand on her heart. "Hey, that was a fair tackle. Remember Karen complained to the referee because of our team's bad language? I think that was a first in Scottish football."

"We were used to a more genteel way of playing. Lacrosse, rugby…" Faith said.

Bray turned around and faced Faith. Talking to her like this was like stepping back in time. Their chemistry was the same—she could still make her laugh.

"Did I ever tell you that Kris and I joined a university rugby team when we were about seventeen?"

Faith nodded and laughed. "Many times. You were both asked to leave because you were too rough."

"I see that as a badge of honor. I mean, imagine being too rough for rugby?"

"Everyone around me was booing you that day at the football game. But I wasn't. I'd never seen anyone like you."

Bray moved closer. "I looked up to the seats where you were and locked eyes with you. I never..."

"What?" Faith asked.

She couldn't go down that road. Bray couldn't expose her feelings, knowing that she would never have Faith again.

Bray turned back to look out at the sea. "It doesn't matter now."

There was an uncomfortable silence between them for a minute, and then Bray said, "You still wear your locket?"

Faith touched her fingers to the simple gold locket Bray had bought her. Jan had taken the picture of them inside it around the time they found out the sex of the baby. The photo was so perfect that Bray had to buy the jewelry so that Faith could keep her and their future son close to her heart.

"Yes, I'll always wear it. It was a perfect moment in time and I want to never forget."

Bray rubbed her forehead. "Yeah, I keep the picture—"

She stuttered and just as Faith was about to say something, they heard Dougie shouting behind them. "Come on, you two, the dancing's started."

"Are you coming, Bray?" Faith asked.

"You go ahead. I think I'll head down to my room. I'm really tired."

"Okay. Take care, Bray."

As she watched Faith walk away, probably into Karen's arms to dance, she cursed her luck and her addiction. It had lost her the best woman she had ever known. A woman who—after she had lied to her repeatedly during the latter part of their marriage, brought their successful business to the ground, and lost them their home, up to their eyes in debt—still was proud of her.

But she didn't feel pride. The guilt of not being there for Faith would eat away at her for the rest of her life. When Faith had miscarried at seven months, they were both devastated.

They had already decorated the baby's room, bought the best of everything to shower love and attention on their future baby boy, and then everything went dark. On top of grief, Faith suffered with severe postnatal depression.

Bray tried to ignore her own pain and be there for Faith, but she didn't know how to deal with Faith's declining mental health, and amidst her confusion and pain Bray retreated to the one thing that still give her that momentary high—gambling. In the end that was what brought down their family and what was left of their relationship. The guilt would never leave her.

❖

Faith could hear a slow number start as she and Karen had just finished dancing to the last song. When Karen smiled and slipped her arm around her waist, Faith pushed back.

"I think I'll sit down now, Karen. I'm tired out."

"Oh, okay. I'll go and get us some drinks," Karen replied.

When she got back to the table, Jan was chatting with Beth, while their partners, Kris and Jamie, chatted. The rest were dancing together. Both Jan and Beth smiled at her.

"I think Karen was hoping for a slow dance there," Jan said.

"She has latched on to me a bit, but no," Faith said.

"Why not?" Jan asked. "Karen might be a bit of a boast, big-headed sometimes, but she's a decent person at heart."

Beth added. "Besides, she's loaded. You'd have a really comfortable life."

"Money doesn't matter, as long as I have enough to live on—besides, I make my own money."

Jan grinned and said, "I think it's because of Bray."

"In a way it is. It would be disrespectful to start seeing someone in front of her," Faith said.

"Do you still love Bray?" Beth asked.

"I always will. When you're with someone that long, I think you always have a little part of you that's theirs alone."

"You two were perfect for each other," Beth said. "If only she had been open to you about her gambling from the start, life could have been very different."

Faith finished her glass of wine and thought about all the times she had picked up her phone to call Bray during the divorce, to call it off, and then stopped herself. Bray had broken her trust. She'd lied and Faith couldn't get over that.

"Divorces are rarely one-sided, Beth. I made lots of mistakes—I pushed Bray away. I know why you insisted on Bray coming on this trip, Jan, but too much water has gone under the bridge to resurrect anything we ever had."

Hadn't it?

CHAPTER FOUR

The ship had an amazing gym, Bray discovered. After not sleeping well the night before, churning over bad decisions in her mind, she decided she needed to tire herself out. If anything, she had to keep herself busy.

She was so emotional after talking to Faith last night that on her way to her room, she actually stopped outside the ship's casino doors and just looked in. She watched people cheer when their numbers came up, as others held their heads in their hands.

Logically Bray knew the only winner was the casino owner, but it didn't stop the pull toward the buzz, the high of gambling. The hunger to experience the dopamine hit, the thrill of betting never left you—you just learned ways to deal with it.

Bray had been betting since she was sixteen. She used to put on her granda's betting slip every week. Horses, football games, boxing. He would bet on anything, and as she began to realize through her recovery, he was an addict just as she had been, blowing his old age pension on the bookies and relying on Bray to make up for his losses.

At first betting was fun. Amongst the guys she did her electrical apprenticeship with, it was the norm, but as time went on it became a way to release stress. Those at her GA group wouldn't have advised what she did last night, but standing outside the casino doors looking in felt like she was punishing herself. Punishing herself was exactly what she wanted to do, because she had failed her family.

Bray put her bottle of water in the holder on the treadmill and programmed a slow start. The gym was fantastic, all the best equipment, and the treadmills looked right out over the ocean. It couldn't have been a more picturesque sight.

She had been running about five minutes and getting into her rhythm when someone stepped on the treadmill beside her. Bray glanced to the side and saw Karen punching in a program.

Fucking brilliant. *Can I not just have some stress-free time to myself?*

"Morning, Braydon."

"Morning." Bray tried to think of something else to say. "Nice gym, isn't it?"

Karen started to walk slowly. "Excellent, although I used an amazing one in LA when I was there on business. Four floors of every kind of equipment you could think of. I like to go to LA at least twice a year. The nightlife is brilliant."

"Sounds great," Bray said while rolling her eyes. Karen was such a bragger.

"Yes, you should go there sometime." Karen cleared her throat and said, "I'm glad I met you here this morning, Braydon, because I wanted a quiet word with you."

Bray was still jogging but looked to the side quickly. "What about?"

Karen continued her slow walk on the machine. "It's a little awkward, really, but I think it's best to talk about it with you so there's no bad feeling between us."

Bray knew exactly what was coming. "Go ahead."

"Faith and I are getting closer, and I feel like something could develop between us. I wanted to know if you would be okay with it—I don't want to step on any toes."

Bray could feel the jealousy and anger come to a simmering boil inside. Mostly anger at herself for making life turn out like this. She upped the speed on the treadmill and ran faster, trying to cope with her feelings.

"You're both adults—you can do what you want. She's my ex-wife. I haven't got any hold over her."

"I know, but still, I just wanted to give you the courtesy of telling you about it," Karen said.

Courtesy? What a joke. If Karen was so eager to do the right thing, she would wait till after the cruise and not try to get with Faith right under her nose.

"Yeah, well, you've done that, so it's fine," Bray said.

"Great." Karen stopped the treadmill and jumped off. "I think I'll go and pump some iron."

Jesus Christ, what an arsehole.

Bray increased the speed and ran so hard she was struggling for breath. Anything to try to get rid of the angry, jealous, sad feelings inside her.

"Hey, slow down. You're going to kill yourself." Kris took the treadmill beside her. Bray took down the speed to a fast walk and grabbed a long drink of water. "What did Karen say to you to make you want to run till your lungs burst?"

"Nothing." Bray wiped the sweat from her brow with her towel.

"Oh, come on, you can't hide your emotions from me. I know when you're angry," Kris said.

"It doesn't matter if I'm angry. I have no right to be."

"No right about what?"

Bray sighed. "She wanted to let me know that she and Faith were getting close, and would I mind, would she be stepping on any toes if she...got together with her on the cruise."

"What? She said that? She wants to seduce your missus right under your nose? That's taking a liberty."

Bray wanted to get off this cruise and go back home to Glasgow. She couldn't cope with this. "My ex-missus. Faith can do what she likes."

"Yeah, but, that's just not on. What are you going to do?"

She looked at Kris through narrowed eyes. "Do? What do you want me to do?"

"Fight for her," Kris replied. "We brought you two on this cruise to try to rekindle your relationship, and now you're going to let Karen just waltz in and try to win Faith's heart?"

"Now you admit it," Bray said angrily. "I didn't want to come on this bloody cruise, but you insisted, and now I have to watch Faith with someone else."

"I'm sorry, Bray, but Jan and I both thought you still had such strong feelings for each other. We wanted you to be happy. Why don't you tell Faith how you feel?"

Bray stopped the treadmill and grabbed her towel. "Because I don't deserve her. I fucked up, and now I have to live with the consequences." "But when you admitted to your gambling problem back then, Faith was understanding. She wanted to help you. It needn't have come to this."

"I lied to her. I looked her in the eye and lied to her because I was scared. I remortgaged the house and left us in even more debt than she thought. I'd never lied to her in my life because I know how much Faith values truthfulness. Her first girlfriend cheated on her repeatedly and humiliated her. I knew that and swore I never would deceive her, but I did, when she was trying to cope with grief and postnatal depression."

"It's all in the past, Bray. I'm sure Faith could get over that," Kris said.

Bray stepped down onto the floor and said firmly, "I can't. If Karen can win her over, then at least I know she'll be looked after. Something I couldn't and can't do."

❖

Faith made her way to the restaurant where the gang was having breakfast. Only Findlay, Dougie, Cath, Lucy, and Karen were there.

"Morning, Faith." Karen held a seat out for her.

"Morning."

"Everyone else is having breakfast in their cabin, I think," Dougie said. "Oh, there's Bray. Morning, Bray."

"Hi, everyone," Bray said.

Bray never looked at Faith once. She was feeling stressed, Faith could tell.

The waiter came around to take her order but Faith said, "Can I just have a black coffee, please?"

Bray said, "Are you all right, Faith?"

It touched Faith that Bray still knew all her cues. She loved her food, and if she didn't feel like eating, there was something usually wrong. "I just woke up with a bit of a headache, and I'm not very hungry."

The truth was she felt nauseous, but thought it was maybe being at sea.

Findlay said, "Are you all excited for our first day off the ship?"

That morning the ship had docked at Port Oranjestad, Aruba, their first stop in the Caribbean. Honestly, all she wanted to do was sit on her little balcony and hope her stomach would settle, but the group was so excited to start their holiday together.

"Yes, it'll be a lot of fun," Karen said as she edged a little into Faith's personal space.

Faith didn't know what Karen was hoping for, but even if she was interested in pursuing something with Karen, she would never do it in front of Bray. That wasn't fair. Faith knew how she would feel watching Bray get cozy with another woman.

Thomas came over to their table. "Hi, everyone. Just to let you know we'll meet here in an hour, then head off to our excursion. First, we're going to spend the morning in Aruba's national park, where a guide will show us the local animal and plant life. Then we're going to have lunch at one of the big hotels on the island before enjoying the sights and sounds of the casinos."

Faith looked up and met Bray's eyes. She'd forgotten Aruba was famous for its gambling. When Thomas left and breakfast broke up, she tried to catch up with Bray, who'd hardly said a thing over breakfast.

Faith finally caught up with Bray in the shopping area of the ship, which looked like a shopping mall. Bray had stopped in front of a shop and seemed to be window-shopping.

"Bray?" Just then, Faith felt a wave of dizziness come over her.

"Faith? Is there something wrong?"

"No, I just wanted to know if you were going to be okay with today's trip." She didn't need to mention the casinos—she knew Bray would know what she meant.

"Oh yeah, I'm not going ashore. I don't go anywhere near anything like that," Bray said.

"Could you not just go to the national park with us and head back to the boat after?"

Bray shook her head. "No, I'd be thinking about it all the time. At least the on-board casino is only open at night. Ashore, the opportunity to go would be a trigger, and it would just stress me out. Stress is something to avoid when you have an addiction."

"But you can't stay aboard yourself," Faith said.

Bray smiled. "Don't worry about me. You have a good time with your friends. Besides, you can be yourself without your ex breathing down your neck."

Faith didn't know what she meant. Bray's presence didn't worry her. True, it had when they first boarded. It was a shock to see her after all these years and it panicked her, but now they had talked a few times and it was fine.

"Bray, I don't feel like you're doing that, and this is your holiday too."

Bray smiled at her again and began to reach out her hand to her but pulled back quickly. "You'll have a great time. Don't worry about me."

That was the thing—Faith *was* worried about her. She felt so guilty and torn about leaving Bray here herself.

She started to speak but Bray cut her off. "How are you feeling? It's not like you to miss breakfast."

"I'm okay. Just a touch of seasickness, I think."

"Just look after yourself while you're onshore. Okay?" Bray said.

Going ashore was the last thing she wanted to do right now. Besides feeling guilty at leaving Bray here herself, she was starting to feel a little light-headed. But she couldn't let her friends down.

❖

Bray looked at her watch for what seemed like the thousandth time. After leaving the shopping area earlier she'd come downstairs to her room, flopped onto her bed, and put on the TV to pass the time and try not to think about Faith enjoying her date with Karen ashore.

She was never idle like this, being used to working two jobs and surviving on little sleep, and so before long she started to drift off. Sometime later she awoke with a start and a gasp. Bray looked at the time. One o'clock in the afternoon.

"Shit, I've been sleeping all morning."

Bray rubbed her tired eyes. Only she could come all the way from Glasgow to the Caribbean and sleep in her cabin instead of enjoying the heat and the scenery. She stretched out her tired limbs and thought she better go and take a walk on deck to get some fresh air.

She grabbed her wallet and headed out of her room. She made sure her door had locked and turned toward the lifts, but she stopped when she saw Faith walking unsteadily, her hand against the corridor wall.

"Faith? What's wrong?"

Bray hurried to her side and Faith clutched her, swaying with dizziness. "I feel ill."

Without a second thought, Bray lifted Faith and carried her to her door. "Where's your key card?"

Faith opened her bag and took it out. "It's here."

Bray opened the door and let Faith down. She touched her forehead. "You feel hot and clammy. Did no one come back with you?"

"I didn't want to spoil everyone's day, so I just told Jan I forgot something on the ship and would be back soon. Would you text her?"

"Of course I will. I knew there was something wrong with you this morning."

Faith suddenly put her hand to her mouth. "Oh no."

She ran into the bathroom and Bray heard her being sick. "Faith? Are you okay?"

Bray got no reply, but when the retching stopped, she asked again.

Faith just moaned in response, and Bray went in to her. She was reminded of all those times when Faith had been in a similar position when she'd been pregnant. How things had changed since then, but Bray's instinct to take care of Faith were undiminished.

She got Faith to her feet. "I'll get you cleaned up and into bed."

"No, Bray, you don't need to—" As Faith said that, her knees gave way and she fainted.

"Shit." Bray lifted her up again and carried her over to the bed. She would need to get a doctor. Faith started to come to as she lowered her into bed and pulled the covers over her.

"Bray—" Faith moaned.

"It's okay. Just relax and I'll get you some water."

Bray returned from the drinks fridge with the water and knelt down beside the bed. She helped Faith take some sips.

Faith cleared her throat and said, "You don't have to do this."

Bray smiled and stroked Faith's forehead. "Shh. I'll get the doctor, and then I can get Jan or Karen, if you'd feel more comfortable with one of them."

"Why would I want Karen?" Faith asked in a raw, husky voice.

Karen had made it sound as if she and Faith were already on the way to becoming an item, but maybe she'd overstated it a touch. "You relax, and I'll get a doctor."

❖

Faith pulled the quilt tightly under her chin while Bray saw the doctor out of her room. She felt shaky and her head was so sore, but the doctor had given her painkillers and something to calm her nausea. She appeared to have a simple forty-eight-hour stomach bug, and she was so glad to hear that. She didn't want to spend the rest of her holiday being ill on the cruise ship.

Bray returned and pulled an armchair from the living area next to her bed. "Can I get you anything else? Fresh water, open the balcony doors a bit?"

Faith said, "No, thanks. I feel too cold for fresh air."

"She was a nice doctor, wasn't she? She said that cruise ships are rife with bugs and germs, but a day or so and you'll be back on your feet." Bray sat down.

It was so nice having Bray with her. Bray had always made her feel safe and protected when she was ill, and it was something that she'd missed in the years they had been apart. But she couldn't expect that care anymore. It was unfair to Bray.

"I'm sorry you got stuck with me today, but I'm okay now," Faith said.

Bray's face fell. "You want me to go?"

"No, I just don't want you to feel obligated to look after me."

Bray leaned forward. "I don't feel obligated—I want to help. Anyway, once everyone's back, I'm sure Jan and Karen will be down to check on you."

Faith was puzzled by this constant referral to Karen. "Why do you keep talking about Karen?"

Bray looked down at the floor. "She seems to think you are becoming involved."

"What? When did she say this?"

"Well, at the meet-up on the first night she had her arm around you, and this morning at the gym she asked if I would be okay with her being with you on this trip, because you were getting closer."

God, this was *not* happening. She felt bad that Karen had harbored a crush on her since university, but she had made it more than plain over the years that they would only be friends.

"Bray, I'm not interested in Karen or anyone. I'm sorry she thinks so. I'll have a word with her when I see her. Besides, even if I was, I'd never get together with someone in front of you. We may not be together or love each other that way anymore, but it would still be cruel," Faith said.

Bray looked at her silently for a moment, then let out a breath. She appeared to have a weight lifted off her shoulders. Had this really been bothering her? More importantly, did Bray still have feelings for her like Jan thought?

❖

Bray had managed to persuade Faith to let her open the balcony doors to let some fresh air into the room. Shortly after, Faith fell asleep and had been asleep for hours now. Bray stayed in the armchair, dozing off now and then, but never leaving Faith's side.

Being so close to Faith and having nothing else to do made the memories of their life together come flooding back. The high of Faith telling her she was pregnant, and then the many lows that came along the way.

Bray scrolled through the album on her phone titled *Family*.

There were lots of photos and videos. Bray had been determined to capture every happy moment. If only she had known what was ahead.

She gazed at the pictures, each one at a different stage of Faith's pregnancy. Everything was so hopeful, so positive. A child was what they had dreamed of, and Bray had taken pictures of everything. Decorating the baby's room, building the new cot, scanning pictures, everything.

When they lost the baby and Faith was diagnosed with postnatal depression, Bray felt like she was losing Faith to the darkness that was surrounding her, and the pain of not understanding how to help made her seek solace in other ways. She had never been around anyone with mental health problems and didn't understand at first. Bray couldn't— or didn't know how to—say the right thing. They got into arguments, and she felt ever more distant from her wife.

Tears filled her eyes as she watched a video of Faith sitting on the floor of the nursery folding the new baby clothes she'd bought. Bray wiped the tears away quickly.

"Bray?"

Faith's voice made her sit up quickly. "Hi, how are you feeling?"

"Like a lorry has hit me. What were you looking at?" When Bray hesitated, Faith said, "If it's private—"

"It is private, but not from you." Bray handed her the phone.

Faith gulped hard as she flicked through the pictures. She stayed silent for a minute, then said, "There's some pictures here I don't have. Could we go through them sometime?"

Bray leaned forward and took Faith's hand. "Of course, they're half yours anyway, especially the ones when you were pregnant with our…"

Gazing into each other's eyes, Bray felt they connected on some deeper level. They had such a shared history that it was hard to keep emotional distance. They would always have this special connection.

Kris wondered why she wouldn't move on, but this was the reason. As Bray looked into Faith's eyes after four years apart, she knew she wouldn't ever love another woman again.

Faith pulled her hand to her chest and started to speak. "Bray, I—" But a knock at the door made them jump back from each other.

"I better answer that," Bray said.

She opened the door to find Jan and Kris standing there, worried expressions on their faces.

"Bray, I'm so glad you were here with her," Jan said as she walked past Bray and headed to the bed.

Kris followed her in and said, "How is she?"

"The doctor said she hoped it was a forty-eight-hour kind of thing, but she gave her some antinausea stuff and paracetamol."

Kris followed her wife to Faith's bedside. "You should have told us, Faith—we would have come back," Kris said.

"That's what I was afraid of. It's your holiday. I don't want you worrying about me. And besides, Bray was here."

Jan looked up at Bray, and she had the feeling Jan was studying her.

"Bray, why don't you get freshened up and go have dinner with Kris. You've been here all day."

Bray didn't want to leave, but it wasn't her place anymore. She couldn't say *I want to stay with my wife*, because Faith wasn't still her wife, and she needed to get used to that.

"Okay, but I'll pop in later, Faith," Bray said.

"Thanks for everything, Bray," Faith said in a weak voice.

Then she left, even though every fiber of her being was telling her to stay.

❖

"Thanks," Faith said, as Jan helped her sit up in bed.

"There you go, now drink some of this sweet tea. It'll do you good."

"I don't know if I can keep it down," Faith said.

"Just try. Little sips, okay?"

Faith took the mug and held it tightly. She did like the warmth seeping from the mug into her hands. She took a tiny sip, and it did feel so soothing.

"So when did Bray find out you were ill?"

"She was coming out of her room and saw me struggling back to mine, and she—" She hesitated, remembering the feeling of being taken in Bray's arms and experiencing the safety that she hadn't felt in over four years. She had struggled with anxiety most of her life, but when she met Bray, she found the safety and protection she had yearned for.

"She what?" Jan prompted.

"She took care of me. Got me into bed, called for the doctor, just took care of everything."

"Bray's a good person. She still cares about you so much."

"I do too. I'll always care about her."

Jan shook her head and sat back in the armchair. "I don't know why you two divorced. I mean, I know that even after the lying, the gambling, getting you into unbelievable debt, you still forgave her."

"I did. Addiction is an illness, and I would have stood by her side through it all, but I just asked her to come clean and be honest, and she lied."

"About remortgaging the house?" Jan asked.

"I thought we were starting again from scratch, and all the time the bank was hanging over our head. I couldn't trust her. When I read that bank letter, the bottom fell out of my world. I had just come through losing our baby and postnatal depression, and I couldn't cope with one more thing."

"Do you think maybe you could be friends again?" Jan asked.

"Friends? I think so. When I first met her on board it was a shock, but it's so easy to feel comfortable around her again. Plus, I'm so proud of how well she has done getting well, getting on top of her addiction while grieving."

"So you're glad you've met her again?"

"Yes, you were right to invite her—it was the adult thing to do. Bray deserves to have her friends around her without feeling awkward around me." The tea was starting to make her stomach roil. "Here, take my tea, going to be sick."

Jan took the tea and Faith hurried to the bathroom.

Bray had been thinking about Faith every moment since she and Kris left her. But she did need to eat and freshen up. Bray checked herself in the mirror. It was quite hot even in the evenings, so she opted for combat shorts and a T-shirt. This was much more her style than dressing for a formal dinner.

She checked her hair one last time and walked to Faith's room next door. She had that excited tingle that she always used to have when she would take Faith out in their younger days. Bray closed her eyes and tried to banish that feeling. Faith might have needed her today, but that was all it was. She knocked on the door and waited.

When Faith opened the door, Bray just wanted to gather her up in her arms. Her complexion was pale, and she had dark circles under her eyes.

"Come in." Faith's voice was raw.

Bray followed her in, and Faith quickly got back under the covers.

"How are you?" Bray asked.

"I stopped being sick in the afternoon, but I'm absolutely whacked. I just want to sleep," Faith said.

"Do you want me to go?"

"Oh no. I didn't mean that—just that I'm so tired. Sit down."

Bray sat in the armchair and said, "Do you need water? Anything from the shops upstairs?"

"No, thanks. I've got plenty of water. I need to hydrate—I know that. Did you have something to eat with Kris?" Faith turned the conversation to Bray.

"Yeah, I did. We went to the burger restaurant on board. Much more my scene than the dinners in the fine dining restaurant, even though they don't seem to understand the concept of no onions."

Faith laughed. "I know. I remember trying to cook two different meals every evening."

"It must have been a chore for you," Bray said.

"Not at all. I enjoyed it. You know how much I like cooking."

"You are a fantastic cook."

Faith pulled the covers more tightly under her chin. "You might be a bit biased."

"No way. I never ate properly till I met you. My granda and I lived on fish and chips, deep-fried pizza, and takeaway curries."

Faith laughed. "Only the Scots could take a beautiful Italian pizza, dip it in batter, and fry it."

"Hey, deep-fried pizza and Mars bars make me proud to be Scottish," Bray joked.

Faith laughed. Braydon was such a light-hearted, funny person. She missed that in her life. Bray always made her laugh. In fact, she'd laughed more since being on the ship with Bray than she had in months.

"Well, I enjoyed cooking for you." *In fact I miss it.*

Bray leaned forward and said, "Despite my feelings about evil onions and other things, you did get me to expand my tastes."

"Not by much, but you certainly were willing to try. Anyway, all this talk of food is making me feel ill."

"Sorry," Bray said.

"No, it's nice talking about the old days. I—" Faith hesitated.

"What is it?"

Should Faith say what she felt, or was it too dangerous? She decided to take a chance.

"When I was talking to Jan this afternoon, I realized something. When we split up, I didn't just lose my spouse—I lost my best friend.

I always thought there were too many raw emotions to ever see you again, and it scared me to face what we both shared and lost. That's why I was so panicked when I met you on the ship."

"Yeah, it was quite a surprise," Bray said.

"But I shouldn't have been. We have good history as well as bad, and the bad bonds us together more than anything ever could."

"What are you saying?"

Faith reached out her hand to Bray, who took it. "I lost my best friend, but maybe we could go back to being friends."

Bray looked down at their joined hands. Was Faith asking too much? Would it be too hard to be friends?

After a few seconds, Bray said, "I'll always be your friend, Faith. If you want me to be."

"I do. I want us all to have a good holiday, like the big pack of friends we used to be. We're at sea the next two days before we stop at Willemstad. Maybe we can enjoy the excursion together—with the rest of our friends."

"As long as you are up to it. It would be nice to have you back in my life, if that's where you want me to be."

"I do." Faith felt so much better, lighter almost, to have Bray back in her life.

Bray squeezed her hand and said, "Hello again, Faith Murphy."

"Hello again, Bray Murphy."

CHAPTER FIVE

Two days later the gang of friends was ready for their second excursion of the cruise, but Bray's first, to Willemstad, Curaçao. Bray was with Kris, Jan, Cath, and Lucy, already at a meetup point on deck, waiting for the others.

Bray had knocked on Faith's door and asked if she wanted to walk up together, but she was running late, as she always did. It reminded Bray of all the nights out they'd shared together, all the dinners, concerts, shows they were late for because Faith took so long to get ready. She smiled at the memory.

Bray leaned on the railing of the ship, closing her eyes and inhaling the sea air. Even though she hadn't been keen to come on this holiday, the sea air, the warm weather, and the thawing of her relationship with Faith were making it all worthwhile.

The past few days at sea, Bray had felt privileged to be of use to Faith. She had so much to make up for, and just to be around Faith again felt so good. She made sure Faith recovered from her stomach bug, brought her food that might tempt her appetite, and anything else she might need. Thankfully Faith had recovered enough to come on their excursion today.

Thomas was patiently waiting for all the stragglers, including another five women who were joining their party today. Thomas had recruited them to make sure none of the LGBTQ guests were left on their own.

Bray saw Thomas glancing anxiously between his iPad and around the deck. She texted Faith, *You better get your behind in gear. Thomas is looking really worried.*

Within a few seconds Faith texted back, *Five minutes maximum.* Bray chuckled to herself and replied, *So by five minutes maximum you mean thirty?*

Once again Bray was transported back to happier days. She'd be ready and waiting patiently to start their night out, and Faith would text, *Five minutes maximum*, but Faith's five minutes always took around thirty in reality. It was amazing how easily her rapport with Faith came back.

She felt a presence by her side. It was Karen, and she didn't look too happy.

"Mornin', Karen."

Karen let out a breath. "Good morning, Braydon. I don't know what it is about you, but Faith just won't move on."

"What do you mean?" Bray asked.

"I mean that I had a talk with Faith last night, and she's not ready for another relationship. I don't think she'll ever find someone to love or make a new life with."

Faith had mentioned she was going to have a chat with Karen and tell her she wasn't into her in that way. Karen must have visited Faith last night.

"What are you trying to say, mate?"

"I'm saying you either have to put up or shut up," Karen said.

Bray was lost. "I don't understand."

Karen turned and looked her dead in the eye. "Faith deserves happiness. She's a beautiful person. She can't or won't move on, so you either have to be straight and encourage her to move on or tell her how much you still love her, and make her forgive you, and make her happy."

Bray couldn't believe Karen was saying this. Karen had always annoyed her, but here she was telling her to get back with Faith.

"That's really generous of you to say," Bray said.

"Well, I care about her too much to see her lonely and unhappy."

"I know you've always cared about her."

Karen gave a hollow laugh. "I wasn't really subtle, was I?"

"Not really."

Karen patted her on the shoulder. "Make her happy, Bray, and if you can't, tell her to let you go."

Karen walked off, and Bray's thoughts went all over the place.

She imagined telling Faith she loved her and never letting go, but then the guilt kicked in. Could Faith ever forgive her?

Before she could attempt an answer, Faith walked up to her. Bray's heart thudded. The sun was glinting off Faith's hair, and her radiant smile warmed all the dark places inside her.

"I told you I'd only be five minutes," Faith said.

Bray tried to regain control of her body. "A bloody long five minutes."

There was that spark, the one that always made their relationship so exciting. It had never left. How was she going to encourage Faith to move on, when she wanted to be with her so badly?

Thomas's voice interrupted them as he called, "Okay, gang, everyone's here at last. Let's go!"

Faith felt so much better. She had been worried that she would miss another excursion, and she didn't want to miss this one because they were taking in the local food market, which wasn't too far away from the harbor.

She was still easily tired. The stomach bug had taken a lot out of her, and she found herself at the back of the group. Bray stayed close by, and when they turned into the busy market, full of locals and tourists jostling around the market stalls, Bray immediately came over and offered Faith her arm.

It touched Faith that Bray remembered she didn't like large crowds—one of her many anxieties—and wasn't going to refuse.

"Hold on to me," Bray said.

When she held Bray, she felt safe. Bray had always been her protector. She'd fight Goliath himself to protect her—Faith knew that—and she felt something once lost surrounding her once again. Safety and love. She had to physically stop herself from resting her head on Bray's shoulder.

Faith knew then she had never fallen out of love with Bray. She couldn't. Bray was everything, but that confusing, painful time after losing their baby had torn them apart.

"Are you tired still?" Bray asked.

"Yes, a bit."

"Thomas says we're going to split up shortly and look around the market at our own pace. Do you want me to stay with you or—"

"Yes," Faith said a little too quickly.

Bray had the biggest smile. "Great."

Faith was happy to see Karen up ahead, chatting to one of the single female guests who had come along with them.

"I see you had a talk with Karen," Bray said.

"Yes, she came to see me last night. She's not a bad person, Bray, and she deserved the truth."

"I know she's not. Annoying maybe, a boaster maybe, but bad? Nah. So what was the truth?"

Faith hesitated. The whole truth, that she had never gotten over Bray and never would, she would have to keep to herself, but she said, "Just that I'm not looking for a relationship. I have too much going on, and I'm not really interested in romance at the moment."

"Oh, okay," Bray said with a sad tinge to her voice.

Faith wondered for the millionth times if Bray had dated anyone seriously since they parted. She had never been one for jumping quickly into things. Bray took a lot of time to trust. She might appear big and tough, and in lots of ways she was, but only Faith knew what a soft-hearted person she was. A gentle giant with so much love to give.

Thomas brought the group to one of the food stalls where they were given samples of fried fish on a stick. Faith laughed when she watched Bray study her fish through narrowed eyes. She was never the most adventurous with food.

"It's not going to bite you."

Bray turned to her and said, "It's got a head. It's looking at me."

"Just pull away some of the flesh." Faith showed her how to do it and, before she knew it, was feeding Bray a piece of fish by hand. Faith realized what she had done without thinking when she felt Bray's tongue touch her fingers.

They looked at each other awkwardly, then Faith turned away. What was she thinking? She disposed of the remaining fish in the bin at the side of the stall and followed the group as they moved on, neither mentioning the fish incident.

The sights, sounds, and smells of the market were wonderful, as was the beautiful weather beating down on them.

Bray came closer and leaned in to Faith. "Look, a spices stall."

She knew how much Faith would love seeing the spices—she loved cooking. There must have been every spice under the sun here.

Faith grasped Bray's hand in excitement. Bray smiled and was happy they had gotten over the slight awkwardness they'd experienced at the fish stall. It was so easy to fall back into the closeness they once shared, and so she had done when she took the tips of Faith's fingers into her mouth.

"Hello, miss," the stall owner said, "would you like to try some hot sauce? Made fresh on the island."

"Oh yes, please," Faith said.

Faith was all smiles as the older lady gave her little mini cups of sauce with a disposable spoon. It was so nice to see Faith smiling again. There had been little for her to smile about for a long time, but here in this moment Faith appeared relaxed and as happy as either of them could be again.

Kris shouted her name, interrupting her daydreaming. Bray turned and saw Kris indicating that the group was moving on down the market.

"We'll catch you up, okay?" Bray said.

Kris smiled and winked at her. This was exactly what Kris and Jan had wanted, and as much as she had resisted it, Bray was loving being by Faith's side again.

"Taste the garlic one, Bray." Faith held out the little spoon and licked off some of the sauce.

"Wow, that's bloody hot."

"Should I get some to take back to the ship?" Faith asked.

"Yeah, if you like them."

Faith looked really excited. "Okay, I will."

Bray flexed her hand. She had to stop herself from slipping her arm around Faith's waist. This being friends thing was so hard.

As the lady behind the stall packaged up Faith's choices of bottles, a young woman walked up beside them, holding the hand of a young boy. The woman said, "Stay hi to your Auntie Anya."

"Look at you, big boy," the stall owner said with a smile.

"I'm five today, Auntie Anya!" the boy announced.

Bray saw Faith visibly stiffen. "Are you okay?"

Faith just stared at the little boy. She was obviously in some distress.

Bray paid for the sauces and took Faith's hand. "Come on. Follow me."

❖

Bray took Faith down a side street where she spotted a smart-looking bar and restaurant. She got Faith seated at a little private corner table. Now that they were face-to-face, Bray saw tears in Faith's eyes. She took one of the napkins and handed it over to Faith. "Hey, it's all right. Take deep breaths."

The waitress approached and she ordered two lagers-and-lime. When they were alone again Bray said, "Was it the little boy?"

Faith wiped her tears and nodded. "I'm sorry. Sometimes it just hits me. I think about what age our boy would have been. He'd be at school by now."

"I know. Every time I watch the football on TV, I think about Kris there at the Celtic game with Dani, and how we planned to go together when they both were old enough. I would have had such happy times with Callum." Bray's voice cracked, and she had to fight to keep control of her emotions when she said that name. When they'd found out they were having a boy, Callum was the name they had chosen, but he wasn't meant to be.

Faith squeezed her hand back. She felt bad for making Bray sad too. "He would have loved that."

"I didn't care, really, if he'd liked football, ballet, basketball, or Highland dancing. I'd still have been there, cheering him on."

"I know you would." Faith tried to lighten the atmosphere. "Remember the little Celtic football strip you bought him?"

Bray gave her a big smile at that memory. "Yeah, I remember. You were six months pregnant, but I had to buy it."

Just then the waitress came back with their drinks. Faith took a sip and said, "I haven't had lager-and-lime in years."

"Do you want me to change it?" Bray asked.

"No, it's nice, and refreshing. Especially in this warm weather."

There was a silence, and Bray didn't want Faith to be taken over by her pain. She wanted to distract her. "So, tell me about your nursery."

"Well, it's in the West End of Glasgow. A private nursery. Dad helped me buy and refurb the building."

Another thing Bray had to feel guilty for. Her mistakes had not only ruined her credit, but Faith's too, so that she had to rely on her father to start her business.

"It's really nice, and it keeps me busy," Faith said. "I love looking after children, and I suppose that's a way for me to channel that maternal instinct."

"You would have been the best mum. I'm sorry I let you down," Bray said.

"No, you didn't. How did you let me down?"

Bray sighed. "I wasn't there for you. I hid in the casinos and betting shops when I should have been with you."

"Bray," Faith said, "I pushed you away after the miscarriage. Grief and then postnatal depression crept up on me. You were out running the business, trying to earn us a good living, and I took my depression and anxiety out on you when I was struggling mentally."

Bray shook her head. "I should have understood. I should have looked after you and the baby. That was my job. I failed, and I failed you."

"Don't ever say that. You couldn't change anything. Baby Callum wasn't meant to be," Faith said.

Bray cleared her throat. "After, I crumbled watching you in pain, Faith, and I made matters worse by gambling our business and our house away."

"What happened after was your way of coping, Bray. I know that."

She would never forget the moment she saw she had five missed calls from Faith. By the time she got home, the ambulance was just about to leave, and Faith was wailing on a stretcher. Bray would never forgive herself for not being there.

All she could think of to say was, "I would handle things so differently now."

Faith looked her right in the eyes. "So would I, but we live and learn, don't we?"

Bray was meant to be cheering Faith up but in fact was making everything more emotional. She couldn't stand losing herself in all the guilt and hurt again. Then she remembered something Kris had told her, about an excursion at their next port. She had toyed with the idea of asking Faith, but then thought it would be too hard to be so close to her.

But now Faith insisted enough time had passed, and they now

could be friends. It would certainly change the highly emotional state they were in at the moment.

"Ah, some of the others are talking about doing some stuff themselves at the next stop. At Kralendijk, on Bonaire. I was reading about a tour that takes you out for snorkeling and water sports, and then some time on the beach. Would you be interested? I mean, I know you probably think it's a bad—"

"Like our holiday to Hawaii?" Faith interrupted with a big smile on her face.

When their family electrical business was doing well and growing each year, they had taken at least two holidays a year. Hawaii was one of their most memorable, because it was on the beach there that they'd decided to have a baby.

"Aye, I suppose. Would you like that?" Bray asked.

"I'd love it. Just to have fun and not think about things too much would be lovely."

"Are you sure you want to go with me?"

Faith rubbed her thumb along the back of Bray's hand. "Of course I do. There's nobody else I'd like to go with more."

Bray heart thudded, and her mouth dried up. She remembered what Karen had said about Faith not moving on. Did Faith still have feelings for her, really? She wanted to kiss Faith then, but could she survive another broken heart? Because she was certain Faith wouldn't want to rekindle what they once had. But no matter how hurtful this trip ended up being, she just couldn't keep herself or her heart from Faith.

"I'll book it when we go back on board, then. It'll be fun," Bray said.

"I can't wait." Faith's phone beeped with a message. "It's Jan. They're heading to lunch. We better catch up with them."

❖

A few days later the ship docked at Bonaire Island. Faith had been looking forward to spending time with Bray. Meeting Bray again reminded her of how much she missed her being in her life.

Today she wanted it to be like the old days when they had fun and there was no awkwardness. She heard a knock at her door and looked at her watch. She was late. Faith dropped her bag on the bed and opened the door. She couldn't help but giggle when she saw what Bray was wearing—Bermuda shorts with pineapples on them, with a matching Hawaiian shirt, open over a white T-shirt.

"You like me pineapples?" Bray grinned.

"I think there are few who wouldn't like them."

"You look beautiful, by the way," Bray said.

Faith looked down at her light blue swimsuit and floaty sarong. "I doubt I'll look beautiful compared to the young women in tiny bikinis on the beach."

Bray frowned. "No one could look more beautiful than you, so don't ever say that. Are you ready?"

"Nearly. Come in and wait. I slept in."

Bray wandered to the balcony and said, "You mind if I open the doors?"

"Not at all. You carry on—I just need to pack my beach bag."

Faith popped two towels into her bag and made sure to pack her suntan lotion and other bits and pieces. She thought about what Bray had said at the door, about her being beautiful, and once again was struck by the confidence and positivity Bray gave her, something she had been missing.

She'd never had confidence in her body. Her first ever girlfriend hadn't been the nicest of people, ridiculing her body, cheating on her—all to make Faith believe she couldn't expect better from a partner, and one of the main reasons she insisted on complete honesty from Bray. Faith was determined never to be made a fool of again.

She'd had higher standards for Bray, but then again Bray had always met those standards until her addiction took hold and lying became part of Bray's daily routine. But through it all, despite everything, Bray was always faithful to her, and she always made Faith feel better about her body.

"What are you thinking about?" Bray asked out of nowhere.

"Oh, nothing. Could you hand me my brush from the dressing table?"

Bray got it for her and said, "We better hurry up. We're to meet the tour guide in five minutes."

"Five minutes maximum," Faith said while hurrying into the bathroom.

"We haven't got five minutes maximum," Bray said.

"Two minutes then. I'm coming, baby. I—" Faith stopped dead and scrunched up her eyes. Her former term of endearment had just slipped off her tongue and made an inaudible clang in the room.

Why did I say that?

Bray had said nothing in return. Faith picked up a toiletry bag and walked slowly out of the bathroom. Bray looked unsure and a feeling of awkwardness hung heavy in the room.

"I'm sorry—force of habit," Faith said tentatively. "It just popped out."

"Hey, don't worry about it. I've had to make a conscious effort to call you *Faith* since we got on board. Your name sounds strange to my ear. You're not *Faith*."

"What am I?" Faith asked softly.

Bray opened her mouth a few times to speak, but no sound came out. She looked at her watch. "Bloody hell, look at the time. We better go."

Faith wished she could read Bray's mind at that moment. She put her toiletry bag in her large straw beach bag.

"Let me take that for you." Bray put her rucksack over her shoulder and took Faith's bag.

They walked out of the room and made their way up on deck. Bray didn't see any of their friends. It was probably too early for them, but she wanted to start their excursion early to pack in as much as possible.

Even though it was early, the deck was still quite busy. There were joggers making their way around a huge circuit, and others, like themselves, ready to start their day ashore bright and early.

Bray led the way down the ramp to the port area. She looked back at Faith and said, "Stay close."

Faith smiled shyly. She was obviously still feeling embarrassed about her slip-up earlier. Little did Faith know that the slip-up was music to Bray's ears.

When they got down onto the pier there were local vendors selling souvenirs and tour guides trying to sell trips around the island, but parked in a Jeep not too far away was a man holding a small sign out the window: *The Murphys*.

"I guess that's us." Bray had always wanted to ask Faith why she didn't revert back to her maiden name after the divorce. She couldn't help but feel that their shared name gave them a connection—a tentative one, but a connection all the same.

As they got closer, the man with the sign jumped out of the Jeep. He wore a bright shirt and shorts and a straw hat.

"Ms. Murphy?"

The tour guide was an African American man, and he spoke with what she thought was a New York accent.

"Yeah, call me Braydon, and this is my—" Braydon nearly made a mistake of her own, nearly referring to Faith as her wife. "My friend, Faith."

He shook their hands and took their bags. "I'm Trevor. Jump in, my friends. We have a lot to pack into today. I'm going to show you the beauty of Kralendijk."

"We can't wait," Faith said.

When they were all in the car, Bray said, "If you get stuck on our accent, don't worry. The taxi driver at the airport thought I was French."

Trevor laughed. "Don't worry—I used to work with a Scottish guy, back in a previous life. He talked super-fast, so my ear is well tuned."

"Are you from New York, Trevor?" Bray asked.

"Yeah, but I spent many years in California. I worked at a smallish computer company, made a few dollars, and decided to come here and live my best life. I love it here."

"What computer company? Do we know it?" Faith asked.

Trevor turned on the engine and winked. "Apple."

Bray laughed. "Oh, that small computer company. I think I might have heard of it."

Trevor smacked his hands together and said, "Okay, first up I'm going to take you to a nice café for breakfast and coffee, and then we'll hit the beach."

❖

Trevor parked the Jeep. Faith couldn't quite see the beach yet, but he said it was near.

He jumped out and took their bags. "First off, I'll take you to a nice, quiet part of the beach where you can swim, lie on the sand, get you acclimatized to the water. Then after lunch I'll take you to a part of the beach farther up the road, where you'll be doing a bit of snorkeling and water sports."

"Water sports?" Faith looked at Bray worriedly. She wasn't the most athletic of people. Bray of course was grinning at the prospect of fun like that.

"Don't worry," Trevor said. "You'll love it."

He led them down a sandy path, and suddenly the beach was there in front of them. Faith gasped and Bray said, "Bloody hell—I mean, wow."

Faith admired Bray's restraint, knowing she would tell her off for her language. Bray was rough and ready, and swearing was just how she spoke normally, until she met Faith. Faith gave her a hard time about her language, and it became their private running joke.

But on this occasion, looking at the dream beach in front of them, swearing was the only thing that made sense.

"Bloody hell, it's gorgeous," Faith said.

Bray raised her eyebrow and grinned at her. "Yeah, I think that's the only phrase to describe it."

The perfectly white sand stretched as far as the eye could see along the coast, and the water was the most beautiful light blue.

Trevor led them onto the beach and put their bags down. "I'll leave you two here for a couple of hours."

"This is amazing," Bray said.

Faith opened her bag and laid out her towel on the sand. Bray followed suit, and they sat down.

It was hot but nice, since it was still before noon. Bray took off her shirt, leaving her in her white sleeveless tee. Faith's eyes were immediately drawn to Bray's muscular arms. Manual labor had always kept Bray strong, and the black ink guardian angel tattoo only made her arm look more sexy.

Bray loved tattoos, and Faith knew there was one hidden on her chest, over her heart, with Faith's name on it. She often wondered if Bray regretted getting the name of her now ex-wife tattooed on her.

"So what will we do first?" Bray said excitedly.

"Lie in the sun and relax."

"Just lie here?" Bray said.

Bray couldn't stay still. During their time together, Bray would moan about having too much work and couldn't wait for her holidays to sit back on the couch and play her games system. Then the day would come, and she would have five minutes of sitting on the couch, then be outside remodeling the garden or decorating the house.

So Faith knew she couldn't keep Bray sunbathing too long. "How about we have a half hour sunbathing, to warm me up, and then we can go swimming?"

"Okay," Bray said, leaning back on her elbows and surveying the scene. It was a tropical paradise. She would never have believed a few weeks ago she'd be lying on a Caribbean beach with her ex-wife, who wanted to be her friend. Her life had taken a crazy turn.

Faith rummaged around in her bag, then rolled onto her stomach. She held out the suntan lotion to Bray and said, "Will you put some on my back and on the backs of my arms and legs?"

Bray gazed down at Faith's body and where she would have to rub the cream in deeply.

Oh, shit.

"Uh-huh, no bother."

But it was a bother. Faith's swimsuit had a very low back on it, just barely above her buttocks. Bray turned around and sat up on her knees. *Okay you can do this. Just stay detached.* Bray tried to imagine this was not her sexy ex-wife laid out in front of her, but as she held the lotion over her back, and watched it drip slowly and sensually onto her back, it was impossible.

"Is everything all right, Bray?"

"Uh-huh," Bray croaked.

She shook her head and decided to just plunge in. She spread the lotion all over Faith's back and began to rub it in. She found herself turning it into a massage, and when Faith moaned and said, "Yes, Bray. Just like that," she jumped and moved on to Faith's legs.

Bray was so turned on. She felt a fire low down inside her that hadn't been lit for so long. Faith was such a quiet, genteel sort of girl, and only Bray knew the desperate moans she made when Bray had made love to her.

It was almost too much to hear that sound again. Bray's heart was racing. She finished with Faith's legs and jumped up quickly. "I'm going to have a swim."

"Okay. I'll be in soon," Faith said.

❖

Faith dozed off while she was sunbathing. When she woke up, she turned over and looked for Bray. Faith spotted her a few yards farther up the beach, playing football with a little boy. The boy's mum was lying on a sun lounger, happy that her son was being kept occupied, by the looks of it.

She felt a wave of sadness come over her. That scene should have played out with their own son. Bray would have made a great parent. If only life hadn't been so cruel to them.

When she caught Bray's eye and waved, Bray gave the ball back to the boy and patted his head before running back over to her.

"You're awake at last. I met a little kid who wanted to play footie," Bray said.

"I saw that. You looked like you were having fun."

"Yeah, but I couldn't wait till you woke up. I didn't want to wake you because you looked so peaceful."

Bray's hair was still wet from her swim, and her tee was wet and stuck to the contours of her body. She looked so sexy. Faith knew deep down that Jan was right. No one would ever be Bray, and she would be the only woman Faith would ever love, but was it all too late for them?

Had the ship of their relationship sailed? The energy and attraction still between them was as strong as ever, but could they connect emotionally after all the hurt and pain that had come before? Faith made a decision in that moment. She wanted to find out.

Bray wiped her forehead with her hand. "Oh, man, it's bloody scorching now. You coming in?"

Faith laughed to herself at Bray's turn of phrase. *You can take the butch out of Glasgow, but you can't take the Glasgow out of the butch.* She stood up and brushed the sand from her swimsuit. "Let's go."

Faith then realized that she'd have to take off the protection of her sarong. The beach had filled up now since it was past noon, and everywhere she looked, she saw younger women with perfect bodies.

"Maybe—"

"No," Bray said firmly. "I know what you're thinking, and I'm not going to let you think badly of yourself. You're the most beautiful woman in the world, and I won't have your fears put you down."

Even when she was younger, she had fears about her body. Then Bray came along and spent their marriage chasing them away, not letting that bad voice inside her win. That was another thing she so missed since breaking up with Bray.

"I think you might be a bit biased, Bray."

"Take my hand," Bray said.

It was a leap of faith of a kind. Did she take Bray's hand and willingly take the confidence and protection that Bray offered?

There was no argument. She took Bray's hand, and with her other hand undid the knot of her sarong. "Let's go."

Bray squeezed her hand and said, "That's my girl."

Yes, I am. Always will be.

CHAPTER SIX

A fter lunch Trevor took them to a smaller cove, where they did some snorkeling. They had so much fun swimming with the beautiful fish that they didn't leave enough time for the water sports. Faith was secretly happy about that.

Once they had finished with snorkeling and swimming, Trevor got them each a bottle of ice-cold lager from the cooler in his Jeep. They clicked their bottles together.

"Cheers!"

Faith looked out to the sea and sighed with contentment as she listened to the sound of the waves rolling onto the shore. The little cove Trevor had brought them to was much quieter now as dusk was setting in slowly.

"I can't remember when I had as nice a day as this. Thank you for organizing it for us, Bray."

"Thank you for coming with me. It's not every divorced couple that could do this."

Faith looked into Bray's soft, open eyes. "Not everyone is us, Bray. Remember what you used to call us?"

Bray nodded and smiled. "Team Awesome."

"Even divorce can't stop us being Team Awesome."

They looked at each other silently for a few seconds, and then Bray turned away. "It's a long way from Glasgow, isn't it?"

"It really is," Faith replied. "When do we have to be back on the ship?"

Bray looked at her watch. "An hour. Trevor said he'd give us a shout in twenty minutes. It's funny, back home I'd have been starting my second job about now, and here I'm sitting on a Caribbean beach."

Faith frowned. "You have two jobs?"

Bray nodded. "How did you think I paid your father back so quickly?"

"I thought…I don't know. You were always paid well as an electrician."

"You don't just walk into jobs like that. When the business went, I left a lot of traders unpaid for the equipment Murphy Electrical used. Glasgow's not that big a place when it comes to business. Every job I went for, someone knew of someone who I'd left in the lurch."

"I'm sorry. I had no idea," Faith said.

Bray shrugged. "Kris kept asking me to work for her, as a foreman. A good job, but I couldn't do it. I know it'll probably sound ridiculous, but I've got my pride. Our company used to work alongside Kris's, and I just couldn't. Anyway, I always felt it was part of my punishment."

"Oh, Bray. There's no punishment. We were all punished enough, and not for anything you thought you needed to be punished for."

Bray felt embarrassed telling Faith this, but she had to. "Well, I got a job at last working as an electrician at a bus depot during the day, and at night as a cleaner at a shopping center."

Faith looked shocked. "Bray, you didn't have to do that. You could have taken longer to pay Dad back. He wouldn't have minded."

"I minded. I let him and your mother down as well as you and Callum. I promised them I'd take care of you, and I didn't," Bray said.

"Mum and Dad don't think that. They understand addiction," Faith said.

The embarrassment and shame that Bray felt was making her angry. Confronting those you let down made the shame intensify.

"I minded," Bray said with anger. She couldn't bear the shame she felt talking about this with Faith, so she jumped up and walked down to the shore. She felt tears come to her eyes, and she tried her best to gulp the emotion away. She had thought that giving Faith a special day, treating her the best she could, would dampen the pain and guilt that plagued her, but it didn't.

The waves flowed backward and forward over her bare feet. It would be relaxing if she didn't feel so bad.

Bray became aware of Faith walking up beside her, then felt her arm around her waist. Why was she being so nice to her? She didn't deserve it.

Faith said, "Do you know how many times I picked up the phone to call you, during our divorce, to try to work things out?

Bray's head whipped around in shock. "You did?"

"Uh-huh." Faith leaned her head on Bray's upper arm.

Why was Faith being so nice about this? "What stopped you?"

Faith sighed. "I couldn't trust you, and I couldn't trust myself. I was lost in a black hole of grief."

"How can you be so understanding? I ruined our whole life. What's changed?"

"You didn't. Our lives changed, but we're still here, standing on a beach together, with the waves rolling over our toes. What's changed? Time, and I've had some counseling."

"You have? Did you talk about us to your counselor?"

Faith nodded. "Yes. When I found out about you remortgaging the house, and that we were about to lose it, all I could see was the lie. I felt alone for the first time in our life together. You were my unshakable certainty. When our lives were falling apart after we lost the baby, you and my faith in you kept me afloat. To then know that I couldn't trust you made me fall deep into my well of grief and hurt, but I understand now you were terrified that telling me about the house would break us up. The grief of losing our baby made you terrified you'd lose me too."

"Yes," Bray croaked.

Her voice betrayed her emotion. Faith put her arms around her neck and pulled her into a hug.

"It's okay," Faith said.

Bray held her tight. "Forgive me, darlin'?"

Faith pulled back from the hug but held her arms around Bray's neck. "You don't need my forgiveness."

"I do."

Faith cupped Bray's cheek. "If you really need to hear me say it, then I forgive you. Anything you need, because I want you to be part of my life again."

Bray wanted desperately to accept that forgiveness, but could she let go of her guilt and fear?

"Faith, I need to—"

Just then they heard Trevor shout, "Braydon, Faith? Time to head back to your ship."

Fuck, Bray thought. She was just about to admit she still loved Faith.

Faith took her hand. "Let's go. We've got a whole holiday left to talk."

❖

The next day the cruise was at sea, and Faith was enjoying some sunbathing around the pool with Jan and Beth. Kris, Jamie, and Bray were in the pool. This large pool was for adults, and another large pool catered for the children farther up the ship.

Faith looked over to the bar and saw Karen sitting very close to the woman she had met on the excursion. She breathed a sigh of relief. Everyone was happy.

Jan sighed as they watched Kris, Jamie, and Bray splashing each other. "You would think this was the kiddie pool. So, how did your special excursion go yesterday, Faith?"

Faith couldn't help but smile. "It was the nicest day I've had in years."

"Really?" Beth said as she sat up quickly.

"I thought you looked a bit close when you came to breakfast this morning," Jan added, "so what happened?"

"Nothing really, but we talked and had fun—it was like we'd never been apart, like we had been transported back in time before anything bad happened in our lives."

"So do you think you might become close again?" Beth asked.

"It's difficult. Bray carries around a luggage load of guilt with her, but one thing I decided for sure is that I want to see where this could lead, because I'll never love anyone else."

"I told you, I told you," Jan said triumphantly.

Faith looked over to the pool, and Bray smiled at her and winked. Faith's heart fluttered. *I want you back, baby.*

❖

That evening Bray, Faith, and some of the others went to a special movie screening on deck. The movie screen was on the side of the ship's control tower, and the comfortable seats were lined up on deck.

Bray thought it was a truly magical experience. To watch a film while cruising along the sea in the Caribbean on a warm, balmy night was something unique.

She sat beside Faith, and halfway through the film, Faith took her hand. This holiday couldn't get any better. She had to keep checking to make sure this was real, that it was actually Faith holding her hand.

The movie they were watching was *Titanic*. She was sure the ship's crew thought it was funny to show a movie of one of the worst ship disasters while on a cruise ship. But it suited Bray immensely. As the later part of the movie unfolded, Faith pulled her closer and closer.

She could hear Faith's sniffles, and the sound made her smile. *Just like the old days.*

When the credits rolled, Faith tried to wipe her tears quickly. "Every time. Every time, I know what's going to happen, and I still lose it."

"That because you're a soft-hearted romantic. One of your endearing qualities."

Kris walked up to them and said, "We're going for a drink. Are you coming?"

"We'll catch you up," Bray said.

Kris grinned and winked at Bray. "Okay, take your time."

"My eyes and my nose are red and puffy. People will laugh at me," Faith said.

"Don't be daft." Bray cupped her cheek and looked deeply into her eyes. "They'll just think you're a soft-hearted sweetheart."

Faith searched her eyes and moved closer. "Instead of going to the bar, do you want to come to my cabin for a drink? We could exchange pictures? Wallow in nostalgia with a glass of wine?"

"As long as mine's a lager." Bray grinned.

Faith led them back to her cabin. There was a different energy in the air since yesterday, and even more pronounced tonight. An electricity, an excitement that Faith couldn't get enough of. On the lift, on their way down to Faith's cabin, Faith felt the urge to grab Bray and kiss her.

Faith opened up her door and they walked in. "Why don't you open the balcony doors, and I'll see what drinks the mini fridge can give us."

Faith got a nice mini bottle of rosé and Bray's favorite lager. She also picked up some Pringles and nuts and brought them out to the veranda table.

"You know they charge a fortune for those, don't you?" Bray said.

Faith grinned and handed Bray her bottle of lager. "It's not every day you have a lovely holiday with your ex-wife, is it?"

Bray laughed. "True."

"You wouldn't believe we hadn't seen each other in four years, would you?" Faith said as she filled her wineglass.

"Yeah." Bray took a sip of lager. "It was a long time apart."

Faith felt sadness in Bray's statement. "I think despite all the hurt and pain, deep down I was frightened this would happen."

"What would happen?" Bray asked.

"That we'd go back to being the best of friends, and I'd question all the reasons that we got divorced. I dreaded facing the fact that I'd made the biggest mistake of my life."

Bray's silence told Faith she didn't know how to respond to that. Faith wondered whether they still had a chance, or if that chance was long gone. She gazed at Bray, looking for some reassurance, some indication that Bray felt the same way. When Bray still didn't say anything, Faith's smile faltered.

After they finished their drinks and the snacks, they went back into the cabin. They sat on the couch and shared pictures and videos of their life together.

"Look at this one." Faith was laughing and turned the iPad screen to Bray. "Remember at our reception you lifted me up and swirled me around?"

Bray laughed when she saw the picture of her sweeping Faith off her feet. "You were so beautiful that day. Can I ask you something?" Bray said.

"Of course."

"Why didn't you go back to your maiden name when we got divorced?"

"Well…" Faith hesitated. "Lots of reasons, I suppose. It was easier than changing all my bank and billing information back to Bruce, but most of all it was because I didn't feel any different. I'm Faith Murphy."

Bray's heart started to pound. "Are you?"

Faith nodded. She was more certain than ever that she wanted to try again with Bray. Their love for each other had never dwindled, at least not on her part, but Bray didn't say much.

Bray flicked through the pictures on the iPad, and they came to Faith's pregnancy photos. The atmosphere changed, especially when they played a video Bray had taken of Faith in the nursery.

"Look at us. We were so happy," Faith said as tears started to fall down her cheeks.

"Can you send me this?" Bray said.

Faith nodded.

Unexpectedly Bray closed the picture app.

"What's wrong, Bray?"

Bray sat with her head in her hands. "I'm sorry. I'm sorry."

"Why are you sorry. There's nothing we could have done."

"I wasn't with you that night. I shouldn't have gone out."

Faith put her arm around her shoulders. "You couldn't be with me twenty-four/seven. Besides, I told you to go out that night. You'd been cooped up with me too long, and it was good for you to get out with Kris."

"Yes, but after we had a few drinks, I went to the casino. I didn't hear your calls. I should have been there with you."

Faith must have noticed her struggle because she cupped her cheeks and said, "You didn't know what was going to happen, and you couldn't have done anything anyway."

Bray couldn't talk, couldn't articulate what was in her heart. Love, fear, want, so instead of talking, she surprised Faith by kissing her.

Faith seemed surprised at first but then put her arms around Bray's neck, and she kissed her back.

Bray ran her fingers into Faith's hair and gripped it lightly. Kissing Faith again was surreal, but it was like all her dreams during the past four years had come true. Their kisses were becoming more frantic, and Faith pushed under Bray's T-shirt and scraped her nails down the small of Bray's back.

Bray moaned. "God, I've missed you."

Faith stood up and then pulled Bray up with her. "Make love to me, Bray."

Bray's heart nearly burst out of her chest. "Are you sure?"

Faith guided her over to the bed. "Yes." She felt more nervous than the first time they had done this, all those years ago. Faith turned around and presented the zip of her dress. Bray unzipped and Faith stepped out of it.

When she turned around, she lifted Bray's hand and placed it on her chest. Bray dragged the back of her hand across Faith's chest, down her sides and lower stomach.

"I remember every inch of you, darlin'. I've dreamed about you so many times since we split up."

Faith pulled Bray's T-shirt and encouraged her to take it off. When she did, Faith touched her in the same way. "I've dreamed of this too. You're the only one I want to touch me."

Bray looked hungrily through the black lace that covered Faith's breasts and quickly took off her bra.

Faith took Bray's hands and placed them on her breasts. Bray groaned, and the heavy beat inside Faith thumped harder. She popped open Bray's jeans, and Bray pulled them off, nearly tripping as she did it.

Faith sat down on the bed and lay back, bringing Bray with her. Bray's lips hovered above hers.

"I can't believe this is happening," Bray said.

Faith smiled. She couldn't wait to have Bray touch her. "Let's make it happen."

They took off their underwear as fast as they could, and then groaned as their naked bodies came together for the first time.

Faith had forgotten how her body, her need, and her want just came alive when Bray touched her.

They kissed passionately while Bray stroked her sides and her thighs, at one point pulling her thigh up over her hip so their sexes came closer together.

Faith already felt the urge to thrust. She needed Bray to help her climb to that orgasm that had been out of reach for over four years.

"Bray, touch me," Faith moaned.

Bray kissed her breasts, rolling her tongue over Faith's hard nipples. Faith felt shots of electricity flash down to her clit. She pushed Bray's shoulders down lower, hoping Bray would get to her clit quickly. On her way, Bray kissed all over Faith's stomach, but then she stopped dead. Faith looked down. She suddenly felt self-conscious about her stretch marks. Bray was tracing them with her fingers reverently.

"Bray?"

Bray looked up at her, and Faith saw tears rolling down her face.

"I'm so sorry, darlin'."

Faith realized what was wrong. The last time they'd made love was in the week just before they'd lost their son. After the baby was lost and postnatal depression had overcome her, she hadn't even wanted to talk about sex. She'd pushed Bray away. Now here they were, back in the same place, but their child was gone.

Bray hugged her stomach and cried, and Faith held her tightly and cried along with her. They had never done this. Never shared their deep, raw, emotional pain.

"I'm sorry, Faith."

"Shh…come up here."

Bray climbed up to Faith, and Faith wiped away her tears with her thumb. "I hurt too."

Bray screwed her eyes shut trying to stop the fresh tears that were overwhelming her, but Faith pulled her down into a kiss, and they both poured their emotion into it. Hurt, grief, love. Bray felt an overwhelming need to touch Faith and make love to her.

She reached down and squeezed Faith's sex. Bray could feel how wet she was. Without preamble she slipped her fingers inside, and Faith opened up to her with a groan.

Faith placed her leg between Bray's, and they both began to rock together. The tears, the hurt, the pain made their passion more desperate. Faith dug her nails into Bray's back as they got closer to release. Bray thrust her fingers faster to match her thrusts against Faith's thigh.

Faith started to shake and Bray felt the walls of her sex grasping her fingers as Faith's orgasm overtook her. That was enough for Bray, and when her orgasm came, she thrust her hips hard and pushed her face into Faith's neck with a strangled cry.

They were both shaking, holding each other silently. Then Faith said, "I love you, Bray."

But Bray was terrified if she said it back, it would hurt even more when Faith would inevitably leave her.

She kissed her instead and slipped between Faith's legs, so their sexes were together. She could feel Faith's wetness, how ready she was for more, and they rocked together, Faith wrapping her legs around Bray's hips, until they came together again.

CHAPTER SEVEN

B ray lay staring at the ceiling, the early morning sun starting to shine through the balcony doors. She should have been ecstatic. Faith was lying with her head on Bray's chest, her arm over Bray's stomach.

After all the emotion of last night, Faith had fallen fast asleep and never let go. Bray, on the other hand, couldn't. There were so many thoughts and feelings going around in her head, mainly about what would happen when they got back to the cold, wet, rainy reality of Glasgow.

They were floating in a tropical paradise, and it felt as if they were on a different planet. How would she ever cope with losing Faith again?

Bray kissed Faith's brow and stroked her bare back. She was scared.

Soon, Faith began to stir. She hummed and stretched, and then kissed Bray's chest. "Morning, baby. You're awake early."

"I'm used to getting up early," Bray said.

Faith leaned up on her arm and kissed Bray's lips. "That was the best sleep I've had since we split up. It's so good to be in your arms again."

Now, Bray told herself. *Ask Faith if this is what she really wants before you get any more involved.*

She looked into Faith's warm, loving eyes and tried to get the courage to speak the truth. "Faith? I need to say something."

Faith appeared to catch her serious mood and a worried look spread across her face. "What is it? You're not regretting last night, are you?"

"Of course not. I just wanted to say that I love you. I've never stopped. I never said that last night," Bray said.

Faith let out a long breath. "I love you too. It feels so good to say that to you again. I used to look at our wedding picture all the time and tell you I loved you. I never thought I'd get the chance to say it in person."

Faith leaned down and gave Bray the softest kiss, then stroked her fingers through Bray's short dark hair. Just looking at Bray made her heart skip. There was no one like Bray.

"Why did you never find someone else?" Faith asked. "I mean, four years is a long time."

Bray caressed her cheek with her fingertips. "You were and are my forever girl. No one else could ever take that place in my heart."

Faith couldn't stop the tears from welling up in her eyes at the mention of Bray's pet name for her. *My forever girl.*

"You remembered," Faith said.

"Of course I remembered. I called you my forever girl when we met, and if we never saw each other again, I'd still call you that." Bray wiped away Faith's falling tears with her thumb. "I'm a simple person, and there's only room for one girl in my heart."

"Even when she's old and gray?" Faith said.

Bray smiled. "Especially then."

Faith pushed her onto her back and kissed her deeply. She pulled away and said, "I want to remember every part of you."

She kissed her way down Bray's body and heard her say, "I'll do anything to make you happy, darlin'."

Faith awoke from sleep and grinned as she remembered who was spooned around her back. This morning and last night had been heaven, she thought, as she pulled Bray's hand to her chest. She looked at the bedside clock and saw it was two in the afternoon. They'd missed breakfast and lunch, and she didn't care one bit, but their friends would have realized they were together.

"What are you thinking so hard about?" Bray said.

"It's two o'clock. We fell asleep again."

Bray stretched. "It was the sleep of the gods. I can't remember the last time I lay in bed so long."

Faith turned around to face her. "Yes, it was great, but our friends are going to suspect we are together."

"Does that bother you?" Bray asked.

"Not at all. I think we just need to be clear and honest with ourselves before we face the others."

Bray sat up immediately, a serious look on her face. "Clear and honest," she repeated.

"Yes," Faith said, "after all we've been through to get back to here, I think we need to be. I don't think I could go through any more heartache."

Bray nodded. "Why don't we have fun and date for the rest of the holiday? Like we did when we first met. Then when we get back home to our normal lives, we can think about what we want to do next." It was the real life part that was worrying her.

"As long as we do it together," Faith said.

Just then Faith's stomach began to rumble. Bray laughed. "I think we better feed you."

Faith giggled. "I think making love makes me hungry. Why don't we be decadent and order room service?"

"Sounds fantastic," Bray said. She got up and pulled on her boxers, then picked up the menu from the coffee table. "Shit!" She ducked suddenly, startling Faith.

"What's wrong?" Faith said.

"I forgot we were docked in St. Thomas today. There's people on the dock looking in." She crouched and crawled her way back to Faith, who could not stop laughing.

"You'd have to have pretty good eyesight to see in here, and if they do, they'll get a gorgeous sight."

Faith wasn't joking. Time had not dampened her attraction to Bray. She was everything Faith had ever wanted in a partner. Manual labor gave Bray a strong body, but only Faith knew how soft her heart was.

"I'd rather keep my body just to you, darlin'," Bray said as she pulled on a T-shirt quickly.

Faith looked briefly at the menu, then realized this was their last excursion day before they went home. "Bray, we've missed most of our last excursion day. Everyone else will be ashore."

Bray shrugged. "We didn't have anything planned on St. Thomas till tonight. We were only going for a walk around the shops near the port."

"True. But I'm looking forward to tonight. Are you?" The whole gang was going on a tour of the St. Thomas Mangrove Lagoon in special glass-bottomed kayaks.

"Yeah, it'll be fun." Bray flopped onto the bed and put her arm around Faith. "Can I be your kayak partner?"

"If you're good," Faith joked. "Now let's get some food. I'm starving."

❖

"Whoa, this is amazing," Bray said.

It was pitch-dark apart from the lights around the perimeter of the kayak, and the moon and stars above. Bray sat in front of Faith in their two-person kayak, doing the paddling and steering.

The whole bottom of the kayak was made of Plexiglas so they could see the mangrove marine life below.

"Look at the stingray, Bray," Faith said behind her, as the gray shape appeared beneath them.

"I see it."

Their tour guide was standing on a bodyboard up ahead, holding a paddle and wearing a headlamp so she could keep an eye on them all.

"There's a few turtles down there," the tour guide said.

Bray felt Faith's fingers caress her back. "I want to see a turtle," Faith said.

Their friends had shot quite a few smirks, smiles, and winks their way when they met on deck for the excursion, holding hands and clearly together.

Kris and Jan had beamed from ear to ear. Faith had explained to them they were just taking it slowly, but that didn't stop Kris from smacking her on the back and saying, "I told you so, Braydon, didn't I? You were meant for each other."

Bray was on top of the world, and as long as she kept her worries about their future out of her head, she was enjoying making Faith smile again.

She heard Kris's voice in the darkness. "We've got two turtles over here."

She quickly paddled in their direction. "You'll see a turtle, darlin'."

They arrived over at Kris and Jan's boat, and Bray didn't slow down. Their kayaks bumped gently.

Kris shouted, "Watch it," then flicked some water at Bray with her paddle.

Bray laughed and flicked some water back, before Jan said, "Stop behaving like five-year-olds—you'll scare off the turtles."

"Look, Bray," Faith said. "There's one there."

The big turtle, seemingly oblivious to their watchful eyes, just moseyed slowly across the sea floor.

Faith handed Bray her video camera. "Quick, take some footage of him, baby."

Every time Faith used her old term of endearment, Bray lost a little more of her restraint and relaxed her vow to go slowly. It was like turning back time to the beginning of their marriage, when they had no clue about what sadness was lying ahead for them.

She took the camera, which was waterproof, and held it beneath the water.

"There's the other one coming behind it," Bray said.

"Oh, it's beautiful. Hi, Mr. Turtle," Faith said.

"Mr. and Mrs. Turtle, I think," Bray said.

They saw lots of beautiful fish and marine life as they paddled around. It truly was an amazing experience.

Bray felt so contented. She looked above her at the bright stars and the almost-full moon and felt awe. "Faith, look up at the sky."

"It's gorgeous. You don't get clear nights like that in Glasgow."

Then Faith touched her shoulder. "Bray, lie back a minute."

Bray looked over her shoulder. "What?"

Faith smiled. "Let's lie back and look at the stars."

Bray had a quick look to either side and saw the kayaks were paddling away from their position. She leaned back slowly into Faith's arms and looked up at her open smiling face.

"I should be holding you," Bray said.

"We all need to be held sometimes. Relax."

Faith lay back against the back of the boat, and Bray put her head in her lap. Faith stroked Bray's head and cheeks.

"The stars are so bright," Faith said.

The lapping of the water at the side of the boat added to the peaceful scene.

"I've missed this. Just you and me," Faith said.

Bray reached back to clasp her hand and brought it to her lips. "Me too."

"Do you think about Callum?" Faith asked.

"Yeah, I always think about him and the life he could have had."

Faith sighed. "I often think he'd be disappointed that we split up after he left us. I mean, I know that's silly—he wasn't even born yet. Maybe it's me that's disappointed in myself."

"You've got nothing to feel disappointed about. I'm the one who should be disappointed."

"Bray, I know you probably think that it's just because we're away from home or in such a romantic place, and we said we'd date and go slowly, but I love you, and I'd like to try again when we get back to Glasgow."

"What would your mum and dad think about that?" Bray asked.

"They'd be understanding. They always loved you."

"Until I let them down."

Faith sighed, "You didn't—"

They were interrupted by the tour leader paddling over to them. "If you'd follow me, please, we're taking the boats in now."

Bray jumped up quickly. "Sure. Lead the way."

They would have to have this conversation again soon. Faith thought everything was so simple, but life was never that simple.

Chapter Eight

Their next two days were at sea as the ship wended its way back to the US for the end of their holiday. Faith and Bray used the time getting reacquainted, and Bray was doing everything in her power to make Faith happy.

The gnawing fear in her stomach refused to leave her and grew more intense the closer they got to the real world, and the farther away from their dream holiday. The fear that Faith would realize what a mistake she was making when they got home. This holiday was filled with dreams of a better future, but Glasgow was where all the pain and hurt lived.

This was their last night on board, and there was going to be a big farewell ball this evening.

Faith was busy buying some souvenirs and last-minute items for tonight down on the shopping deck with Jan and Beth, so Bray went up to the pool bar for a drink. She found herself staring into her lager, wishing this feeling would go away.

Our her way up she'd passed the ship's casino. She wasn't tempted to go in, but she imagined how the thrill and anticipation of placing a bet would mask the churning feelings inside.

"There you are." Kris sat down beside her. "I phoned you, but it just rang out."

Bray patted her pockets. "Sorry, I must have left my phone in my cabin."

"What's wrong with you? You look miserable. You just got back with your ex-wife, the love of your life, and you're sitting here with a face like a wet weekend."

"I am happy." Bray ordered Kris a drink.

"Looks like it. Well, you must be doing something right because Jan says Faith is walking on air."

"As long as I can make Faith happy, then that's all that matters," Bray said.

"Mate, if there's something wrong or you don't want to get involved again with Faith, you can't string her along. She's had too much pain to have any more."

"I would never string her along. I love her with all my heart."

"Then tell me what's wrong," Kris said.

Bray sighed. "It's just all too perfect here, and I'm frightened that Faith is going to think this is a bad idea when we get back into the real world. And when you get down to it, I feel I don't deserve it."

"Bray, you've been given a second chance—don't blow it by letting your fears get in the way. Talk to Faith. The last time you didn't, and look what happened. Be honest."

But showing her fears and being honest were what made her scared.

❖

Faith had so been looking forward to tonight. Events like dinner dances always stressed her out since the divorce. In fact, she always tried to avoid them, but tonight she had Bray by her side.

She could hardly believe that she and Bray had found their way back to each other—and to think it would never have happened if their friends hadn't set them up. The only worry she had was that Bray had been really quiet tonight.

The gang enjoyed a last meal together, and then the band started to play. She sat holding hands with Bray, and they watched as Jan and Kris danced together. "Do you think Kris has enjoyed her birthday cruise?" Faith said.

"What, sorry?" Bray looked at her quizzically. "My mind wandered. What did you say?"

Quiet and distracted. A knot of worry started to form in Faith's stomach. Was Bray having second thoughts?

"I said, do you think Kris has enjoyed her birthday cruise."

"Oh yeah, she told me so when we had a drink this afternoon," Bray said.

"Let's dance. It's our last night on board."

Bray screwed up her eyes. "You know I don't like dancing."

"For me?"

Bray then smiled. "Anything for you."

Bray led them to the dance floor. They got a few looks from some of the older straight guests, but Faith didn't care. She wanted to cap off this wonderful holiday with a dance before they had to go back to real life.

Bray took her in her arms and started to dance slowly. She could tell Bray was tense—she could see it behind her eyes. She always could read Bray. The end of the cruise—was that what Bray was worried about? Going back to real everyday life?

They hadn't talked about what would happen when they got back to Glasgow. Faith just assumed they were back together and that their lives would meld together again. Maybe she was being naïve.

"You've been quiet. Is everything okay, Bray?"

"Quiet? Me? I'm fine." Bray kissed her quickly.

There was definitely something. "Bray, why don't we go. I don't want to share you with everyone on our last night. I want you all to myself."

Bray nodded and took her hand. "Anything for you, darlin'."

As they walked downstairs, surrounded by the music and the laughter of the other guests, Faith felt melancholy seeping into her bones. Bray was pulling away emotionally, exactly as she did before the divorce, but this time, she wasn't going to let Bray run. Faith was stronger now, strong enough to take on Bray's demons, if she'd let her.

Bray waited for Faith in bed. Faith had gone to change in the bathroom, leaving her with her thoughts, which were spinning at a million miles an hour. After her talk with Kris today, she had made the decision to tell Faith about her worries, but the timing was causing her stress.

Mainly because she was a coward. She was frightened to shatter the happiness of being with Faith again when all her worries, guilt, and shame still lived back home. Then Faith came out of the bathroom wearing a short silk nightdress. She was breathtaking.

"Wow, you look beautiful."

Faith slipped under the covers and onto her side to face Bray.

"Thanks. Now take your T-shirt off."

Bray smiled. When they were together, she always wore just a pair of boxers to bed, and Faith loved being close to her skin, being able to touch and stroke her as she wanted.

Bray pulled it off and threw it on the floor. Faith moved closer and put her arm around Bray's waist.

Faith sighed and said, "Just like old times." Then she pulled Bray close and hugged her. "I've missed this so much, baby," Faith said. "My bed's been empty without you."

Bray kept telling herself that now was the time. *Tell Faith the truth and have a fresh start.* But then Faith gently scratched across her back, making her shiver, and a fire came to life deep inside.

"I can't believe you're on a different flight home tomorrow," Faith said.

"It's because I didn't fly out with the rest of you. I'll be on the plane two hours behind. Be home in no time at all."

"Will you phone me when you get back to your flat?"

"Course I will," Bray said.

She pressed her face into the crook of Faith's neck and inhaled her beautiful scent. She tried to memorize it, in case she was never in this position again. Then Faith slipped her hand into her boxers and scratched her backside. The slow-burning fire inside turned into a blaze and she groaned.

At the sound of Bray's groan Faith tried to push her onto her back, but Bray didn't let her. She turned Faith onto her back and grasped the hem of the silk nightie.

"I wanted to make love to you," Faith said.

Bray shook her head. "All I want is you. Take this off."

Faith wriggled out of her nightie, leaving her naked, and Bray discarded her boxers.

"I want you to feel how much I love you," Bray said.

In fact, Bray wanted to do that and to memorize every inch of

Faith. This might be her last chance to love her the way Faith deserved. She kissed Faith's lips like it was her last time, and dropped kisses down her body. She took great care kissing all over her stomach, before kissing her way down to her thighs.

Faith opened her legs and invited Bray to kiss her again. Bray could see how wet Faith was and couldn't wait to taste her again. She kissed all around the sides of her inner thighs, then slipped her tongue between the lips of her sex.

Bray smiled inside when Faith's hips jumped at her touch. She traced the tip of her tongue all around her clit before gently grazing the tip of Faith's clit with the flat of her tongue.

Faith moaned and her hips rocked. "Bray, don't tease. I can't take it."

She gave a deep moan when Bray pushed her tongue into her opening and swirled it in a circle.

"Oh God."

She felt Faith grasp at her hair, and she returned to her clit and licked with more speed, but kept the touch light, just the way she remembered Faith liked it.

Faith's moans soon got louder and her hips thrust faster and faster. She was going to come soon, but Bray wanted to be as close to her as she could be. She stopped and made her way back up to Faith.

"What are you stopping for?" Faith said with exasperation. "I was about to—"

Bray smiled and stroked the side of Faith's cheek. "I want to look at you and remember this moment."

"But—"

Bray put a finger to Faith's lips. "Shh. Trust me."

She then moved her hand down to Faith's sex, and Faith groaned and then gasped when she slipped her fingers deep inside.

Faith wrapped her legs around Bray's hips, pulled her in closer. Bray thrust her hips along with her fingers and kept her eyes on Faith. This might be her last chance to love Faith, and she was going to appreciate every second.

Faith was breathing heavily and moaning. "You always know how to touch me, baby. Make me come?"

"Look at me, and I'll make you come, darlin'."

Faith did as she was asked, and when Bray felt the walls of Faith's sex start to flutter, she gazed at her lovingly and said, "I love you with all my heart. You're my forever girl."

Faith's body went taut and she cried out. She wrapped her arms around Bray and said, "I love you, baby. Will we always be like this from now on?"

Bray felt the fear flutter inside her. "I hope so."

CHAPTER NINE

The dawn of Saturday morning came too soon, and the ship docked in New York, their final destination. Bray and Faith had separated to finish up their packing before leaving the ship in an hour. The worry Faith had been feeling last night at the ball had been erased by Bray and the way she made love to her last night.

She'd lavished Faith with love, and Faith lost count of how many times she came. She felt pleasantly sore this morning. Tired but happy. She would have time enough to sleep on the plane. She just wished they were flying together.

She zipped up her last bag, and there was a knock at the door. "Come in."

It was Bray.

"You don't have to knock, baby," Faith said.

Bray looked really nervous and was carrying an envelope in her hand.

"What's wrong?"

Bray walked up to her. "I just wanted to give you this before we go ashore and everything gets crazy."

Faith took the letter and gazed at it. "What is it?"

"It's something I want you to read before we go any further with our relationship, but not here, not now."

"Why, what's wrong? You don't want us to work? What?" Faith was panicking.

"Hey, don't worry. It's not you. I love you." Bray caressed her cheek, then kissed her softly. "It's just something…I've been struggling to tell you how I feel. Just please, do me a favor and read it on the plane, and if you want to see me, I'll meet you tomorrow."

"Okay, if you insist. Where?"

"The park where you used to watch me at football training?"

Faith smiled, even though deep inside she was worried. But whatever Bray had difficulty telling her face-to-face, she was certain that nothing could change how she felt.

❖

Bray got off the bus and walked into the park. It was a dull gray Glasgow day, such a contrast to the Caribbean weather of blue skies and blue sea. She was exhausted. Between traveling home, and jet lag, and the anxiety about Faith reading the letter, she'd had no sleep.

Today was the day she would find out if she truly had a future with Faith, or not. She walked to a park bench and sat down, thinking about the countless times Faith had sat on this bench to watch her play football, no matter the weather or time of year.

Tears filled her eyes. "I had to tell her. I'm so sorry I wasn't there, Callum."

A voice behind her said, "Bray?"

Bray stood up quickly and turned around to find Faith standing there. "Faith?"

"Hi, I read your letter. Why were you scared things would change? I love you, Bray."

The tears escaped, and she wiped them with her jacket sleeve.

Faith walked forward and took Bray's hand. "Let's sit down."

Bray couldn't understand why Faith wasn't angry. She sat down and Faith didn't let go of her hand. "I couldn't bear the thought of losing you again," Bray said, "and I felt all the bad memories back at home would change things."

"Bray, I need you to let go of this guilt you're carrying around. You've paid for your mistakes, and I've paid for mine. I'm not blameless either."

Bray pulled her hand away from Faith and stared down at the ground. "Yes, you are. I was supposed to take care of you."

Faith put her hand on her back and rubbed it soothingly. "I was lost in depression and you didn't know how to cope with me, but if we are to make a new life, we have to promise to be open and honest, and you need to stop blaming yourself."

"I should have been there. I lied to you over and over," Bray said.

As Faith watched Bray break down, she realized this was the conversation they should have had before their marriage broke up, but neither of them had been capable of it at the time. But now Faith was.

"You lied because you had an illness, an addiction. But say you'd been at home with me that night in bed, watching a movie, anything? What could you have done? What happened wouldn't have changed."

Bray sat back in the bench. "Logically maybe that makes sense, but it doesn't feel like that."

Faith took Bray's hand again and put the other on her knee. "We've lost enough time to grief and sadness. Did you mean it when you called me your forever girl on holiday?"

"Of course I did. There's no one else but you, darlin'."

"Then marry me."

Bray had a look of shock on her face. "Marry you? Are you serious? After everything—"

"Especially after everything we've been through. I love you, Braydon Murphy. I never stopped being your wife, not really—we just need to fix the legal bit."

"Seriously?"

"Seriously. But only if we both forgive each other and let go of the guilt. Do you forgive me for pushing you away and hurting you, baby?" Faith said.

Bray screwed up her eyes. "You don't need—"

"Don't even say it. I do. There were two people that made our divorce happen, and two that can put our marriage back together. Do you forgive me?"

"Of course I do. Do you forgive me?" Bray asked softly.

"Yes, of course I do. Now nothing can come between us, and I don't want you ever to feel guilty again, okay?"

Tears rolled down Bray's face. "I'll always be an addict, Faith. You do know that. I might have ups and downs with it."

"I know that, and I'll help you through them. Life hasn't been kind to us, but we're still here, and I want to fight for a happy life with you.

There are no more secrets between us, and nothing can stop the love we have for each other. Will you fight for our future?"

"Always."

Their lips came together and sealed their bond.

EPILOGUE

Bray pulled her van into her driveway. It was six thirty, and after dropping off her apprentice electrician, she'd made her way home. She sat in the van and just gazed at the large sandstone house. She still had to pinch herself sometimes that this was her home now, and that she'd been given a second chance at life.

Faith's parents had bought her this hundred-and-fifty-year-old house at auction and added an extension for Faith to run her nursery business. Since she and Faith got back together, Bray had done a lot of work on it too, to make it exactly as Faith wanted it.

Bray vowed she would never forget how lucky she was. She was no longer catching the bus home from her night shift, just in time to start her second job. No, she was coming home to a warm, loving house and the woman she loved.

All of Faith's nursery children would have left by now, and Faith was probably cooking dinner. She couldn't wait to get in there. Bray got out of the van, opened the sliding door, and picked up her bag of hand tools. They were expensive, and she didn't like to leave them out overnight.

She slid the door closed and ran her hand over the company name on the side of the van. F&B Electrics. Much to her surprise, Faith's mum and dad had shown her as much forgiveness as their daughter had when they announced they were back together and had shown their confidence in them as a couple by giving Bray capital to start a new business. Since Bray had been declared bankrupt, Faith was legally the owner of the business, but Bray was just fine with that, because for the rest of her life, making Faith happy was Bray's mission. Business was going well enough for her to take on an apprentice, and she was determined to keep building.

Bray loved describing Faith as her wife again. Even after the divorce, Faith had always been her wife in her heart, but when she thought of her, it was with sadness. Not now.

She looked at the wedding ring on her finger, the exact same ring from their first time around, and smiled. Two months after they reunited, they'd remarried at the registry office. All their friends were there, even Karen with her new girlfriend. It was truly like a dream, getting a second chance to fix the mistakes she'd made first time around, and having Faith's family to support her.

Bray walked up the gravel driveway, past Faith's car, to the side door to the house. She put her hand on the door handle and paused to smile. She could hear Faith singing as she prepared dinner.

She opened the door and was hit with the warmth of the kitchen and the beautiful smells of onion and garlic cooking in the frying pan.

"Hey, Mrs. Murphy, I'm home." Bray walked into the kitchen and put her tools on the table.

Faith hurried over to her and kissed her. "Hey, baby, I missed you. How was your day?"

Bray put her arms around Faith's waist and kissed her back. "I love you, darlin'. We finished that rewire in the south side, and I got two more jobs booked in today."

"Great." Faith hugged her tightly. "I'm so proud of you."

Faith seemed to be in great spirits today. "What about your day?"

"Good. I left Kate in charge this afternoon. I went to the doctor's," Faith said.

Bray frowned. "You didn't say you weren't feeling well. What's wrong?"

Faith giggled and said, "Ask me what we're having for dinner tonight?"

Bray was confused. "What? Okay, what are we having for dinner tonight?"

"I had a craving for pasta and garlic bread," Faith said with a grin.

Bray was confused for a second, and then it hit her. When Faith was pregnant the first time, she had sent Bray out at all hours of the day and night to bring her pasta arrabbiata and garlic bread.

"You're pregnant?" Bray could hardly breathe.

"Yes! It worked," Faith said.

Bray punched the air like her team had just scored a goal and spun Faith around in a circle.

"Whoa," Faith said. "You'll make me dizzy."

Bray was just blown away. After their wedding, they began treatment at a private clinic to try to conceive, but they weren't under any illusions that it would be easy. But it had worked. "We thought it would take lots of tries."

Faith wrapped her arms around Bray's neck. "Well, it didn't. I think it's fate."

Bray cupped Faith's face. "This baby is going to be loved so much, and I promise that I will take care of you both. I've learned so many lessons since our first time."

Faith's smile faltered slightly. "What if I'm hit with depression again?"

"If you are, then we face it and get through it together. We're Team Awesome, remember?"

Faith laughed. "That's true. This is our second chance, Bray."

"And we're going to grasp it with both hands."

Bray kissed Faith's cheeks, then her nose. She then put her hand on Faith's stomach.

"You're my forever girl, and forever is going to be full of joy. There may be some tears along the way, but no matter what, there will be lots of love."

DOUBLE JEOPARDY

Carsen Taite

CHAPTER ONE

Today was supposed to be all about filling out forms to solidify a business arrangement, carefully planned and completely sterile in its efficiency. Today wasn't supposed to hold any surprises, but the one standing not six feet away was massive, monumental, mind-blowing.

I'd been here before. Well, not here actually, but at another courthouse, waiting in line at the clerk's office, forms in hand, ready to file the papers to obtain a marriage license. Not with the woman who was holding my hand right now, but with the one who was standing six feet away—Emma Reed—who was seemingly unaware I still existed. Right now, I kind of wished I didn't.

"Names, please."

The clerk's voice shook me out of my reverie, but when I finally focused, I realized she was calling the couple in front of us. I breathed easy again before I felt a hard squeeze to my hand.

"Are you okay?"

I tore my gaze from Emma and back to Ann Koen, the woman I was going to marry in less than a week. "I'm good. Yes. Why?"

"Because you seem a little distracted. Jitters?"

Ann gave me one of the condescending smiles I'm sure she thought was endearing, but which made me want to hurl. Not an ideal reaction to your future wife. I squelched my annoyance and smiled brightly back. "Nope. All good here." I turned as I spoke, to keep from drawing attention, praying Emma would finish whatever she was doing and leave before she spotted me. A second later I heard a familiar voice and knew my plan had failed.

"Hi, Katie. It's been a long time."

Way to be direct. It *had* been a long time. Eight years to the month, but who's counting? I cast a quick glance at Ann who was watching the two of us with the same penetrating stare she used in the boardroom, and I resolved to keep this reunion simple, quick, despite the fact Emma was even more good-looking than I remembered. I pushed past the guarded expression she wore and thrust out my hand like we were mere acquaintances instead of almost-marrieds.

"Hello, Emma. It's good to see you." I turned to Ann. "Emma is an old friend. Emma, meet Ann, my fiancée." I was so busy injecting distance and formality into the introduction, I wasn't quite sure if I'd seen Emma wince slightly at the word *fiancée*, but I was pretty sure she had. I'd considered trying to make it out of this situation without saying the *F*-word, but I knew Ann's predilection for telling everyone we encountered about our engagement, and Emma deserved to hear the news directly from me, since I was to blame for any wedding PTSD she might have. Which begged the question of what she was doing here, ostensibly alone, but before I could ask, Ann took over.

She stuck out her hand. "Good to meet you. You must be a friend from Katie's past because she hasn't mentioned you before. Are you here to get a license too?" She glanced around as if she could spot a fiancée wandering about looking for a mate.

Emma's eyebrows narrowed in confusion. "License?" She glanced at the sign above the clerk's window. "Oh no. I'm here doing some research on a deed for a client."

"Realtor?"

"Lawyer."

"Ah." Ann's tone had gone from mildly curious to total approval, and I recognized the shift for the snobbery it was, but even I had trouble hiding my surprise at the revelation.

"You went to law school?" I asked.

Emma's attention shifted back to me and the heat of it swept me back in time. "I did. I'm working at Dunley Thornton, downtown. Have been for a few months now."

While Ann chatted Emma up more, now that she found a reason to find her interesting, I digested the information that Emma had moved on with her life with no apparent residual ill effects from our last encounter. I knew I should be grateful, but my feelings right now were a swirled up mix of relief and regret, neither one sitting well on my already roiling stomach. I tuned back in to hear Ann say, "We should all get together for dinner. In addition to impending nuptials, Kate and I have mutual business interests that could benefit from outside counsel."

I hated when she used words like *nuptials*, but I refrained from shaking my head in frustration lest Emma witness my annoyance. I'd convinced myself that pretending to be happy would eventually lead to the real thing, and I wasn't ready to let go of that particular belief. But the idea of sitting through dinner with the former love of my life, watching Ann ply Emma for free legal advice, was more than I could bear. "Honey, I'm sure Emma is very busy and so are we."

"Too busy to catch up with an old friend?" Emma's smile told me she sensed there was more to this story. "Nonsense."

"Coffee then," I said, thinking quickly. Apparently, this confrontation was going to happen, but I'd be damned if it was going to happen in front of Ann. "You and I can catch up on old times, and then we'll schedule a real appointment with you, after the wedding."

Did Emma wince again when I said the word *wedding*? Maybe I'd imagined it, but I didn't dwell. That should be my mantra. *Don't dwell.* Because if I did, then I'd never be able to make the decisions that had to be made no matter how distasteful they might be.

"Coffee would be perfect." Emma gave me her card. "My cell's on there. I look forward to hearing from you." She shook Ann's hand and walked away. I studiously avoided watching her go, conscious that Ann was watching me the way she always did. Instead, I pretended to be studying the sign listing the requirements for a marriage license.

"She seems nice."

I kept pretend-reading the sign. "What? Oh, yes, I suppose she is."

"How do you know her?"

I heard the slight edge beneath Ann's friendly tone. She was digging, and I had to give her something or she would tunnel through my privacy to get answers. "We were in college together at Richards. She joined the Air Force after we graduated, but I haven't seen her in years, so something must've changed." I shrugged to signal it was of no consequence to me and hoped Ann bought my feigned indifference.

"Smart woman. Law is a much better field than the military. I mean, I think it's great to serve our country and all, but it's such a thankless occupation."

For the second time in less than an hour, my annoyance bubbled to the surface. "It's only thankless because we choose not to award it the same value as other careers."

"You're adorable when you're passionate," Ann said with her condescending smile just as the clerk called our names. "Let's channel some of that passion into this." She pointed to the window and stepped up to present the paperwork for our license. For a second, I stood frozen in place only able to watch her and wonder when my life had gotten so completely out of hand. When I was sure she wasn't looking, I glanced back toward the exit, wishing Emma would reappear and that my failed past could be rewritten, but I knew as surely as I'd known that fateful day, some mistakes simply couldn't be fixed.

I stepped up beside Ann and swore to the clerk that all the information on the forms was correct, and offered a silent prayer that this wasn't another one of those mistakes.

❖

"Are you going to call her? Huh? Are you?"

My best friend, Betty, wasn't known for being subtle or patient, and as much as I knew this, I'd still chosen to tell her about running into Emma at the courthouse, which probably said something about me, but I wasn't in the mood for introspection. Especially not with an impatient seamstress poking at me with a dozen pins. "No. Absolutely not. And put that card back in my purse."

Betty sighed and shoved Emma's business card into my bag. "But you said you would."

I waved her off. "It was one of those polite things you say. No one means it or expects you to really call. Especially not when I haven't talked to her since…" I let the statement hang in the air, certain there was universal agreement that it wasn't a good idea to go calling on the ex you'd dumped, especially not a week before your wedding to another woman.

"Huh." She frowned, and then took a long drink from the expensive champagne the owner of the dress shop had left for us.

I spent a few seconds resisting the urge to take the bait before I gave in. "What? And don't say *nothing* because clearly you have something you want to say."

"Is she still hot?"

Not the question I'd expected, and caught off guard, I blurted out, "Oh, so hot. Better than ever." I shook my head as if I could shake away the hotness in favor of acting rational. "But Ann's hot too."
"Different kind of hot. Emma was always *hot* hot and Ann is… well, she's more of an icy hot."
"That doesn't even make sense."
"Think about it. You'll come around."
I didn't confess that I'd thought of little else since Ann and I had run into her at the courthouse yesterday. But my thoughts weren't limited to comparing Ann's and Emma's physical appeal. I'd started a running list of all their traits, stacked side by side, which wasn't really fair to Ann since when it came to Emma, I was operating entirely from memory. It was possible she was no longer funny and charming and smart and honorable and…The possibilities were endless, but my little exercise in pros and cons was pointless. Ann and I were getting married in a week and nothing was going to change that. Too many people and plans hung in the balance.
"She's a lawyer," I blurted out.
"Well, that's a twist. What happened to the Air Force?"
The memory of Emma in her dress blues nearly caused my knees to buckle. "Pour me a glass of that stuff before you drink it all." While Betty poured, I let my mind wander back to the exact circumstances when I'd last seen Emma wearing that outfit—the last time I'd seen her before yesterday. "I don't know. I don't know what kind of law she's practicing. I don't know anything, including what I'm supposed to do with the information she's back in Dallas. For all I know, she's married with kids."
"Was she wearing a ring? And don't tell me you didn't look."
I hung my head. "No ring. But that doesn't mean anything."
"True. If you called her, you might find out."
"Not happening." I gestured at the yards of material enveloping my body. "I've got a pretty full schedule for the foreseeable future."
"Chicken."
"Am not."
"Are too."
In an act of stunning maturity, I stuck out my tongue.
"Looks like things are getting a little out of hand in here."
Damn. Ignoring the pleas of the seamstress, I turned and saw my

future mother-in-law filling the doorframe. "Hello, Mary." She hated when I called her by her first name, and I took whatever pleasure I could in doing so as often as possible.

"Would you like a drink?" I resisted adding, *You're paying for it after all*, since I'm sure she was acutely aware. Not my problem if she had to buy her daughter a bride. My only problem was being for sale in the first place.

It wasn't that Ann wasn't a catch. She was rich and good-looking, and her family was well-respected, but they didn't have a few crucial things they needed for world domination and I held the key. Hence the merger we were calling marriage. After the vows and cake and dancing, everyone would go back to their normal lives, but I would be the new wife of Ann Koen, and together our families would dominate the oil industry in the entire Southwest. Ann could check the *Acquire a Wife for Society Functions* box, and I could rest easy knowing I'd given up personal happiness for a practical and very necessary purpose. Romantic, I know, but I didn't have a choice.

Mary's only response was to pour herself a whiskey from the crystal decanter on the bar cart. The decanter looked heavy, like murder-weapon heavy, and I filed that thought away under the heading *If You Decide to Make a Break for It*. I wouldn't, though. Being a runaway bride once is bad enough, but twice? Not going to happen.

Mary circled the pedestal where I stood, hemmed in place by pins and measuring tape, micromanaging the tailoring. I knew it was her way of dominating the situation to ensure she had complete control. The sad part was that she did. Neither Ann nor I had decided virtually anything about these nuptials, from the diamond on my ring finger to the flavor of the cake. I doubted Ann cared about any of what she would call sentimental notions and I supposed the details didn't matter. This wasn't my first trip down the aisle, and nobody liked a picky bride on repeat. Besides, under Mary's careful direction, we'd have the best that money could buy. Everything would be picture perfect, literally, since *Texas Monthly* was doing a full spread on the romantic and business merger of our two families.

"All done," the seamstress said, brushing her hands and standing back to admire her work. "She's beautiful."

"Yes, yes, she is," Mary said, holding a fold of fabric between her fingers to make it clear she was talking about the dress and not me.

I called out to Betty, "How do I look?"

"Amazing as always. The dress doesn't look half bad either."

I spent a second reveling in Mary's frown of distaste, certain she'd prefer I'd chosen a more demure maid of honor for what she'd said numerous times would be a very dignified occasion. But Betty had been by my side when I'd run out of my first wedding, and I needed her to ground me or I'd never make it to the big day. "Sounds like everyone is happy. I better get out of this thing before I accidentally rip it or spill something on it."

Mary didn't take the cue to leave the room. "I'd like to speak to you alone for a moment." She shot a pointed look at Betty. "Family business."

I didn't hesitate. "Betty is family to me. Whatever you have to say, you can say in front of her." I didn't point out that she hadn't asked the seamstress to leave the room, likely because she considered her the help and therefore not important enough to consider at all. I stepped out of the dress and began putting on my regular clothes while Mary stewed, but I wasn't going to be bullied into talking to her alone.

"Very well then. I spoke with our attorney and he hasn't received the signed agreement."

I knew exactly what she was talking about, but I played dumb. "Agreement?"

"The prenuptial agreement." Her voice dropped on the word *prenuptial* like it was a dirty secret.

"Oh, that. I need to look at it again."

"Your family's attorney has already reviewed it and signed off."

I didn't bother asking how she knew that nugget of information, but I made a silent vow to throat-punch Randall Thatcher for his indiscretion. "If it's all the same to you, I'd like to read through it again myself."

"Please do. And I hope you aren't simply stalling in hopes that I'll give up on this issue. Because I assure you, I will not."

"I'm certain you won't," I said. I softened my tone. "Look, I know you find this whole arrangement unsavory and your family has more at stake than mine, but I'm committed to making this work and I'm not interested in hijacking your family fortune beyond what we've worked out. I've been very busy with wedding prep, but I promise, I will read through it again and have it back to you by tomorrow."

Mary's expression softened into something slightly less than bitch face. "Very well. Please don't forget. And don't forget about dinner tonight. It will be the first time you meet the extended family and I'd like you to wear the Valentino I had sent over. It will look lovely with the suit Ann has picked out."

I barely resisted rolling my eyes or laughing at Betty who was doing exactly that across the room. What was with Mary's desire to dress her daughter and her wife-to-be in matching clothes? When she finally left the room, Betty burst out laughing.

"What in the name of all that is holy was that?" she asked.

"She's used to being in control of anything remotely connected to her family."

"Ya think?"

"Ann says she'll settle down once the wedding's over."

"I wouldn't count on it. A dragon lady like that doesn't suddenly lose her love of setting things on fire."

I waved her off. "It's fine." It wasn't but pretending everything about this entire situation was normal was the only survival tactic I knew.

"I think you should have an attorney, not Thatcher, review that prenup."

"There isn't time. Besides, Ann assures me the language is boilerplate."

"And she has no motive to lie."

"Ann has plenty of faults, but dishonesty isn't one of them. Do you really think I'd marry a liar?"

Betty looped her arm through mine. "I don't. But I didn't believe you'd marry someone you don't love either." Before I could respond to set her straight, she pulled out her phone. "As your maid of honor, I'm taking control of this piece." She typed out a message and I heard the swoosh of it sending. "I just texted you the details for your appointment with a lawyer tomorrow. It'll take an hour tops and I insist."

I looked at my phone and read and reread the text that had just arrived, the name of the law firm nagging at the edges of my memory for a moment and then sinking in. "No, wait. This is Emma's firm. How? When?"

"I texted her while you were going back and forth with Dragon Lady. Emma has an opening tomorrow and so do you."

"Uh, no. Not a chance."

"It's the perfect opportunity for you to talk to her. Clear the air."

"You don't think the intervening eight years have been enough for that?"

"I'm pretty sure the silent treatment never cleared up anything."

"Whatever." I knew Betty well enough to know she wasn't going to let this go. "She knows it's me?"

"Nope. Which gives you the element of surprise. Make the most of it." Betty's smile was broad and I could tell she was quite pleased with herself. I should be mad, angry, furious she'd contacted Emma without my permission, but a small part of me was relieved. It was time I had a few minutes alone with Emma so I could properly apologize for leaving her the day before our wedding, even if I had to pay her hourly rate for the privilege of doing so.

CHAPTER TWO

When the receptionist called my name, I stood and smoothed my skirt. I'd spent way too much time selecting an outfit for my meeting with Emma, but since I was going all in, I might as well look nice for whatever was about to happen. I walked toward the receptionist's desk and she pointed me to a nice-looking woman in her forties standing in the doorway to the inner sanctum.

"Hi, I'm Rita, Ms. Reed's assistant. She asked me to apologize for keeping you waiting." Rita motioned for me to follow her. "Right this way."

"I wasn't waiting long," I said, nerves fueling the need to make conversation. "A few minutes at most."

Rita tossed me a smile over her shoulder. "Good. Would you like something to drink? Coffee, a soda?"

I was actually dying of thirst until I envisioned coffee cascading down the front of my light tan suit. "I'm good, thanks."

"Okay." She stopped in front of a door and knocked. "Go on in. She's expecting you."

I watched her walk away, wishing I was following her still, because now that I was standing in front of Emma's door, this meeting seemed like the worst idea ever. When Rita was out of sight, I considered making a break for it, but Emma popped her head out the door and nearly scared me to death.

"What are you doing here?" she asked.

I took a minute to catch my breath. "I have an appointment with you."

She narrowed her eyes in a move I recognized as thinking mode. "You're K. Koen?"

"Well, not yet. Betty made the appointment. She thought it would be good for us to talk and decided, at the very least, I could purchase an hour of your time."

Emma laughed. "I guess Betty hasn't changed. Well, since you're here, you may as well come on in."

I wasn't expecting to encounter easygoing Emma. I mean, I figured she'd been too caught off guard at the clerk's office to be anything other than polite *yesterday*, but her pleasant demeanor now that we were alone took me by surprise. "Are you sure? I mean, I totally get it if you never want to see me again."

She gestured toward her office. "I'm not the one who ran away."

She had a point. A good one. My personal discomfort aside, it was time to make things right. Or as right as I could make them. I walked in and sat in the chair she pointed out, taking a moment to glance around. Her office was nice sized and the walls were covered with framed diplomas and accolades from her military service. Apparently, Emma had spent little time nursing her wounds after our abrupt breakup. Last I'd heard, she'd deployed with her Air Force squadron.

"When did you go to law school?"

She cocked her head. "That's your first question?"

"I chose randomly. Do I only get a certain number?"

"You did say you were only buying an hour of my time."

"Fair enough. If we go over, I promise I'll pay."

"Okay. I applied about six months before I finished active duty and I graduated two years ago. Columbia. I started working for the New York office of Dunley while I was still in school and transferred here last month."

That explained why we hadn't crossed paths. "Pretty nice office for a two year associate."

"I do okay."

I was fishing and I knew it. The last time we'd spoken, ambition had been at the forefront of our discussion. Me in my wedding dress and her in her dress blues with a church full of people waiting across town. Not my best day and I didn't want to revisit it, but I owed her an apology at the very least. "I'm sorry."

"That I do okay? That I have a nice office?"

"You know that's not what I meant."

She leaned back in her chair and studied me while I struggled not to squirm under her stare and prayed her anger would be swift. But she didn't look angry. Contemplative, curious, but not angry. "Are you going to say something?"

"Once upon a time there were a lot of things I wanted to say, but it kind of feels like the window has closed." She sighed. "We were about to get married and you left me. You sent your father to explain, but he picked up the entire tab, so there's that." She shifted in her chair, a move I recognized as emotional discomfort. "Yes, I was mad and I thought I'd never want to see you again, but a lot has happened since I last saw you and it kind of puts things in perspective."

I don't know what I'd expected, but the complete lack of emotion of any kind—anger, relief, disappointment—wasn't it. I'd worked hard to suppress the memories of that day, but they always simmered close to the surface, a barrier to exploring anything deeper with anyone else. I'd tried, God knows, I'd tried. In my attempts to bury the memory of the greatest love I'd ever known, I'd actively sought out a replacement to fill the void, but no one measured up. No one.

"Now that we're both in Dallas," she said, "maybe there's room for us to try and be friends."

She said it like it was an afterthought. A casual tossing of a bone. Friends. What did that even mean for two people who'd shared a bed and their most intimate hopes, dreams, and secrets?

"She seems nice."

Once again Emma's words cut through my reflections. "What?"

"Your fiancée. Ann?"

I hid my surprise that she remembered Ann's name behind a fake smile. Apparently we'd just transitioned into the let's-be-friends part of our reunion where we discussed our significant others. "Yes, she is," I lied.

"When's the big day?"

"Next week. Saturday." I delivered the details in a flat recitation. What I really wanted to do was scream, *Why are you so blasé about this? Doesn't this make you angry?* But I detected no emotion from her, and I'd lost the right to ask for anything beyond the few minutes I'd reserved to make my apology.

"Your text said you wanted me to go over a prenup?"

I shook my head. "No. Betty made that up to get me in here. She thought we should talk. I mean, there is a prenup, but I'm good." Why did I say that?

"I'd be happy to look at it for you. I won't even charge unless you need me to rewrite it."

Why was she being so accommodating? I wanted her to yell, scream, show some emotion, but all I was getting were congratulations and *here let me help you*s. Maybe if she saw the prenup in all its legal glory, she'd get really pissed and give me the outrage I'd expected. "I…"

"Do you have it with you?"

"Uh, no…but I can email it to you."

"Perfect. If you still have my card, the address is on there."

"I do." I stood abruptly, ready to run, but determined to merely stride confidently from her office. I didn't have to follow up on the promise to send the email. I didn't have to see her again. I'd done my part by coming here and apologizing, and I could close this chapter of my life and move on.

I should feel relieved, but all I felt was sad.

❖

Later that night I met Ann at her favorite restaurant. She was big on eating out. She didn't like to cook and she wasn't interested in having her future wife be domestic. She assured me that once we were married and living under the same roof, we'd have help that would allow us to enjoy nice, home-cooked meals, but in the meantime, she was all about the no muss, no fuss dining out.

The hostess took us to our table and Ann pulled out my chair in a gesture some might find endearing and chivalrous. Once I was seated, she asked, "Do you mind if I order for us?"

I did mind. A lot. It was such a condescending question, loaded with assumptions about my ability to choose anything, let alone my own meal, properly. But I was tired and emotionally whipped after seeing Emma, and I didn't want to start a fight. If this marriage was about love and romance, I wouldn't be here, but it was a business arrangement and business arrangements often came with baggage. "That sounds good, thanks."

I barely listened while she rattled off questions to the server and placed our order. When she was done, she rambled about her day and all the important connections she'd made. She waited until after our meal was served before finally winding back around to the biggest business transaction looming between us. "Mother says you haven't signed the prenup."

"I need to read through it once more."

"It's fairly standard."

"I'm sure it is, but since I've never been married before and never been asked to sign one, it's not standard to me." I delivered the white lie with ease.

She smiled indulgently. "Good point. It's totally fine with me if you'd like to have an attorney go over it. Someone besides your family's attorney. I realize our union is primarily business, but it's personal too. I mean, you're going to be with me for the rest of your life. It's not a bad idea for you to be satisfied as well. What about your lawyer friend? The one we ran into at the clerk's office?"

Tangled up in her biz speak were some strings of caring, which made me feel guilty for not mentioning I'd already been to see Emma and she'd offered to review the prenup. But now that I had Ann's blessing, it would be all right to take Emma up on her offer, right?

If only I could turn back time a few short days so that we'd never run into Emma at the clerk's office. We'd been in the building that day for less than an hour. What were the chances we'd run into the woman I'd left practically at the altar, not to mention that she'd be an attorney who had now volunteered to review the prenup for the marriage I was about to make? I could hear Betty's voice echoing in my head, telling me nothing about these circumstances was random, but was I really supposed to believe Emma had reappeared in my life for some grand plan?

"You've barely touched your steak," Ann said, pointing the end of her knife at my plate.

"I guess I'm not as hungry as I thought." I touched my hand to my forehead. "I haven't been feeling well today. I'll get the rest of this wrapped up to go. I should call it a night."

"If you're coming down with something, that would definitely be a good idea. No sense both of us getting sick."

She was so sentimental. "Thanks. I'll call you tomorrow?"

"Perfect. If you're still not feeling well then, I'll meet with the wedding planner on my own. We'll simply be reviewing the seating arrangements one more time and I get the sense that wasn't really your thing."

That was a huge overstatement. I thought all the hours we'd wasted on the seating arrangements so far was a colossal waste of time and going back for more? No way. It was a wedding. You showed up, you wished everyone well, you sat, you danced, ate your cake, and then it's over. Why we should spend hours agonizing over who would sit where and why was beyond me. The back-and-forth made my head spin but saying so would only signal I was not completely invested in the festivities, and it was critical that I be completely invested or at least act like it until after this marriage was a lock. "Thank you."

She paid the bill and walked me to the valet stand, dutifully waiting until I was in my car before leaving on her own. The first thing I did when I got home was change out of my work clothes and tug on my ratty college sweats in an act of I'm-still-single rebellion. One night I'd stopped by Ann's house to deliver some papers and she'd answered the door wearing silk lounging pajamas—the kind you imagined old Hollywood starlets would wear. Who dressed like that?

I poured a glass of red, some random blend—Ann would've been horrified at the lack of vintage—and sank into the couch with my laptop. I had one of those email programs that merged all my email accounts into one giant inbox and right now it was an even mix of last-minute wedding details and semi-urgent business emails, both demanding my attention with equal weight. I fired off answers to the most urgent and flagged the ones that could wait until tomorrow. And then I came across one from emmareed@dunleythornton.com, and I froze.

Subject line: Thanks for stopping by

Open, noncommittal, and just vague enough to get me to open the message to see what lay within. I clicked twice and Emma's words filled the screen. *It was good to see you. It's been a long time, but I promise it was long enough* :) *If you want to send the paperwork, I'd be happy to look it over, but no pressure. Mostly, it was just nice to reconnect and close the loop. Glad to see you're living your best life.*

I read the message about twenty times, and on each pass I came up with a different interpretation. She hated me. She liked me. What was this *closing the loop* reference? She'd seen me again and knew

I was alive, meaning she could go on about her business? It was long enough? For her to have stopped wanting to hurt me back? And she was glad to see I'm living my best life? As if.

That last one made me a little mad, the kind that starts to burrow and then fester. I'd told her there was a prenup and she, of all people, knew how I felt about prenups. We'd discussed it at length, a long time ago when my parents insisted on one and I'd told them to shove it. Emma had been all, *hey I'll sign it because I trust you and I'm not in this for the money*, but I'd insisted there would be no agreement about money contingent on anything.

But that wasn't this. Ann and I were about to enter into the very definition of a marriage of convenience—all business, and that's exactly what a prenup was. Why was I resisting signing one with her?

I didn't know. I didn't know a lot of things lately, but I did know I couldn't resist replying to Emma and I knew I wanted to see her again if only to close the loop from my end because our little meeting at her office hadn't resolved anything as far as I was concerned. I typed and deleted three different replies before I spotted her cell phone number in her signature line. It was nine o'clock. Not late to me, but I no longer had any idea what kind of hours she kept. Would she still be up? If she was, would she think it was weird that I was calling? Why was it so hard to figure out a mind I once knew better than my own?

I punched in the numbers on my phone before I could overthink anymore. Would she even answer an unknown number? I didn't know anyone who would, but I supposed those people must exist or telemarketers wouldn't constantly be calling. If she didn't answer, I'd leave a vague message. I was composing it in my head when her voice came through the line.

"Hello?"

Her voice was clear and strong, not a sign of groggy fresh-from-sleep voice. "Emma, it's Katie. I just realized how late it is. I hope I didn't wake you."

She laughed. "Not even. I'm working on a brief and will be for the rest of the night. Anything would be a welcome distraction. What's up?"

"I got your email." I resisted mentioning her reference to closing the loop, especially since I couldn't think of a way to do it that didn't put a super sarcastic spin on the words. But how else was I supposed to explain why I'd called? I cast about for something to say when the only obvious thing popped in my brain. "I wondered if I could take you up on your offer to review the prenup."

"Okay." She drew out the word. "I guess you're in a bit of a rush since the wedding's next week."

"Uh, yes, I guess so." I wasn't sure how to take the fact she'd remembered.

"I can take a look at it tomorrow. Go ahead and send it tonight."

And now I felt stupid. "I should've waited until tomorrow to call you."

"Actually, it's better you called tonight. My tomorrow is a little crazy and I might be hard to reach."

"Work crazy or just plain crazy?" Why was I being so nosy? "Never mind, none of my business."

"A little of both, actually. I'll be in a mediation, but I anticipate lots of waiting around which will give me plenty of time to review the agreement. I should be free around seven—if you want to meet then, we can go over my notes."

I hesitated while I ran through my schedule for tomorrow, mostly to determine what I could shove aside to make this meeting happen. In addition to things at the office that needed my attention, I was meeting my mother and Mary Koen for lunch at the caterer's. I'd love to leave them both to attend to all the details, but it wouldn't do for me to act completely disinterested. Part of what Ann was paying for was all the doting, and it wouldn't do to kill this deal because I couldn't be bothered to fulfill all of my obligations, even if doting wasn't in my skill set.

In addition to the lunch, I was supposed to accompany my mother to her dress fitting later in the day. Something had to give if I was going to meet with Emma, and I made a snap decision to leave Mother on her own. It wasn't like she hadn't been to a tailor on her own before. Besides, Emma had never expected me to dote, which of course made me all the more willing to meet with *her* instead of the other vultures feeding on my free time. I shoved aside the idea there was any other reason to meet with Emma despite the flashes of how good she'd looked when I'd seen her in her office today. "Seven is perfect. How about dinner at the Tower Club?"

The few seconds of silence that followed had me on edge. I'd picked the Tower Club because it was close to her building, but it would give us a more relaxed setting than a sterile office. But maybe she wasn't interested in sharing a meal for what was supposed to be a business meeting. "Or I could come to your office. Whatever works for you."

"Dinner's great. I'll be working through lunch and likely starving by then. If you don't mind legal advice punctuated by chewing, I'm in."

"Perfect. I'll see you there."

I put my phone on Do Not Disturb and propped up in bed with the latest prospectus our accountant had prepared—or as I liked to call it, The Doomsday Report. Reading this was becoming harder and harder, especially after I learned the truth about how my father had kept the business afloat for as long as he had. When he died, he'd exhausted every available resource for funding and James Drilling was already taking on more water than we could bail out. I'd met with the company attorneys and reviewed every option from abrupt closure to restructuring in bankruptcy, but any choice would result in laying off employees and selling off key assets, and my father's actions precluded my ability to take legal steps to stave off the creditors. I'd given up everything for this company, and there was no way I was going to let it fade into oblivion. Not without a fight.

Enter Ann. Her family's business, Koen E & P, had been eyeing James Drilling for years as the perfect fit to complete their portfolio and monopolize the region, but Dad had steadfastly refused to cave in to their big-money offer, which involved gutting our company in exchange for taking over our book of business. Somehow, they'd come into possession of damaging information that gave them the leverage they needed to broker the deal they wanted. We'd spent weeks negotiating and finally settled on a good old-fashioned merger of our families, with me as the connecting link.

It wasn't the worst thing. On paper, Ann was a catch by any standard. She was a classic beauty as devoted to her gym time as she was to building her family's oil business empire. Since graduating from Wharton, she'd been in charge of operations for Koen E & P, and she knew the exploration and production side of the oil business like no one else. Since I knew drilling and service better than most, we were the perfect fit. On paper. We'd dated briefly about a year after I'd crashed and burned my relationship with Emma. There'd been no spark, and despite my father's urging, I'd broken things off after only a few dates.

She was arrogant and pushy and intolerant of anyone else's way of doing things, and those traits stuck with her to this day. She wasn't interested in getting married any more than I was, but the union would fulfill her family's expectations that she project the appearance of having settled down. We were destined to clash and as soon as we got through this wedding, we'd start to do battle over the way the business was run, but until then, I was minding my tongue, ever-conscious that one wrong move and this deal would fall through.

Was meeting Emma for dinner a wrong move? Maybe, but Ann had been the one who suggested I talk to her, and for now I was satisfied with that justification. Now it was up to me to keep it from going wrong.

CHAPTER THREE

Lunch at the caterer's was already off to a dismal start. Mom kept trying to assume her place as the mother-of-the-bride, but Mary wasn't ceding any ground as woman in charge of all things. When the caterer started directing all his questions directly to Mary, I could feel Mom fuming and I overtalked to deflect a fight. What I'd managed to taste was incredible, but I barely got to try a dish before one of the half dozen waiters hovering over the three of us swooped in to whisk it away. I was going to need a cheeseburger after this.

"You didn't like the lobster?" Mary asked me.

"It was lovely," Mom replied before I could answer. "All of this food is divine."

I mustered a smile. "Indeed, it is." I patted my stomach. "But there's so much of it—I'm trying not to get full before we get to the final course. And since I've had the final fitting, there's that."

My mother dabbed at her lips with a napkin. "I can't believe I haven't seen your dress."

"A good wedding should always have some surprises." The words were out of my mouth before I could stop them. I saw her frown form, but there was no sense apologizing since it would only draw attention to the fact I'd created a hell of a surprise at my last wedding by failing to show up for the ceremony. To be fair, my first attempt at a wedding had been a significantly smaller affair, and when I bowed out, I sent Betty down the aisle to make apologies. I heard later that everyone enjoyed the reception, aka we're going to eat your food and drink your booze because you dragged us out here and no one's tying the knot. "The dress is gorgeous. You're going to love it."

It *was* a beautiful dress, romantic even. Ann was going to love it and I wished I cared about the dress, about this food, about any single detail of the looming day, but I didn't. I cast about for something to say to illustrate some modicum of interest. "I like everything we've picked out for the reception. Mary, are you happy?"

She looked surprised I'd addressed the question to her, but she recovered quickly. "I'll be happy when we can formally announce the merger of Koen E & P and James Drilling, and so will you since you'll get your first bonus." She stood. "I'm glad you enjoyed the food. It's the best that money can buy and so are you." Her stare was pointed. "Make sure my daughter gets *your* very best."

She dropped the last words and turned and walked away. I glanced over at my mother. "Well, that was fun."

Mom placed a hand on mine. "I'm sorry."

"Don't be. I knew what I was getting into."

"I wish I could tell you not to. That we'd figure out another way. If only your father hadn't—"

"Died? Run up astronomical debt? Committed fraud and placed all of our futures in jeopardy?" I lowered my voice and took a breath. As much as I wanted to blame my mother for not noticing our lives were falling down around us, it wasn't like I'd noticed either. Neither one of us had thought to question my father's secretive accounting, and the result had been disastrous. Now I was about to marry a woman I didn't love to save the company I did, and the only person I could really blame was me. "My turn to be sorry. I know this isn't your fault."

"I should never have relied on him to handle everything, and I should've shielded you from his control."

Put that under reasons not to get married in the first place, or at least not for love. Maybe marriages like the one I was about to enter into with Ann were the only real solution. A business arrangement with the details set out clearly in advance. No room for second-guessing, no room for emotion to take over and blind us to the harsh reality of real life. Which brought me back to the prenup and tonight's meeting with Emma, who'd apparently completely gotten past the fact that I'd dumped her the day before our wedding, and gone on with her life as if we'd never been a thing.

If only I could do the same.

❖

Albert, the concierge at the Tower Club, greeted me the moment I walked out of the elevator and I have to admit I enjoyed the recognition as a regular enough not to want to sacrifice this creature comfort, despite the price. James Drilling's offices were several floors below, and this club had been my escape over the years when I needed to get away from whatever might be going on in the office. Of course, it was also good for business to be able to have a place to take clients to convince them we were a thriving concern, even when the appearance was far removed from reality. We'd been faking it for so long, I'd started to forget.

"Your dinner companion is already here," Albert said. "I took the liberty of seating her at your usual table." He cocked his head. "She looks familiar."

She would. Emma and I had dined here with my parents on a number of occasions when we were in college. Normally, I'd have no issue gossiping with Albert, but this hit a little too close to home. "She works for Dunley Thornton," I said, referring to the building next door.

"That must be where I've seen her."

"I'm consulting her on a legal matter, so if you could ask our server to be as unobtrusive as possible, I would appreciate it."

He nodded and I knew he would ensure we were not disturbed. The real question was, why was I asking for uninterrupted time with Emma when it was likely that if our past did come up, I'd like as much distraction as possible to keep from having to face the fallout of my poor decision-making.

Emma looked up as I approached, but before I reached the table, I felt a hand on my arm and looked up to see another familiar face. "Lily?"

"Hi, Katie," she said, pulling me into her arms. "I can't believe how long it's been. How are you?"

I shot a glance at Emma over Lily's shoulder and mouthed *I'm sorry* before Lily released me from her embrace. I'd known Lily Gantry for years, her family was old money oil, but up until the last year, she'd been out of the country. "I heard you married Peyton Davis. Does that mean you're staying in Dallas for good?"

"As long as Peyton is here, that's where I'll be." She smiled and the faraway look in her eyes evoked feelings I recalled from the distant past, and I barely resisted the urge to glance at Emma. "And from what I hear, congratulations are in order. You're marrying Ann Koen?"

We'd shared more than one conversation about Ann over the years, and there was no use pretending that Ann had suddenly developed traits that made her good relationship material, but I wasn't about to confide my reluctance to a friend I hadn't seen in years while standing in the middle of a crowded club, especially not with Emma, who Lily had met before, standing not twenty feet away. "That's right."

She ducked her head and lowered her voice. "Is everything okay?"

She knew. The question was how much. Was her knowledge confined to my family's financial troubles, or did it extend to the entire arrangement we'd struck with Ann's family? I didn't know and I didn't want to know, so I simply said, "Everything is great."

"Okay." She turned her head slightly to the side as if she was considering my answer and finding it lacking. And it was.

"Well, I'm meeting a friend for dinner, so I should probably go," I said. I didn't mean to look in Emma's direction, but you know how it is when you're trying not to focus on something.

"Is that Emma Reed?"

I could hardly deny it. I plastered on a too-big smile and spoke through my gritted teeth. "That's her."

"And that's the friend you're meeting." It wasn't a question, but it wasn't an accusation either. Lily nodded slowly, and her kind eyes were full of compassion. "I should let you go then."

There were so many things I wanted to say, starting with, *Take me with you*, but I didn't owe her an explanation for why I was having dinner with the woman I'd almost married, the week before my wedding to someone we both knew was a bad match. I settled on a vague pleasantry. "It was good to see you. Have a great evening." I started to walk away, but she called out.

"Wait." Lily reached into her purse and pulled out a card. "I'm working a couple of deals right now and I could use your insights. Give me a call?" She asked the question as she handed over the card. "My cell's on the back. I know you're probably swamped, but I promise I can show you all the details quickly and get you back to wedding planning."

I stared at her extended hand and flashed to the other day when Emma handed me her business card. Beware pretty women handing out business cards was the only thought I could muster. No doubt Lily was going to want to talk about how Gantry Oil could help bring James Drilling back from the brink, but I had no desire to explain the true nature of our plight to someone else, and certainly not a woman married to an Assistant US Attorney.

"I'm not going to bite you," she said. "But I would like the opportunity to talk about ways we can work together."

I didn't have the heart to tell her that in a few short days, I would no longer be anyone who had any power with regard to the family business. I tucked the card away and made a vague promise to call. I watched as she walked away, and I couldn't help but wish we could trade places. I'd heard the stories about her father almost ruining the Gantry family business with his questionable business practices, but apparently, they'd survived the storm and things were going well, unlike my own life which was spiraling out of control. Which brought me back to the reason I was here tonight: prenups and past loves.

Emma, ever the gentlewoman, rose as I approached the table, but her smile was guarded and I braced for whatever this evening might hold. I motioned for her to sit. "Don't stand on my account. Thanks for meeting me here. It's been a long day."

She settled into her chair but didn't relax her at-attention posture. "Was that Lily Gantry?"

"It was. I'm sorry I didn't bring her over to say hello, but I didn't…I mean, I…"

"You don't want everyone in town knowing your personal business any more than they already do?"

"That about sums it up."

"Makes sense. Besides, it's not like I run in the same circles as the Gantrys."

"She's pretty down to earth."

"I know, but I wouldn't even know her if I didn't know you." She gestured to my suit. "Did you come right from the office?"

I nodded. "Crazy day. Between work and the…" I realized I'd been about to say *wedding*. Could I not go for five minutes without sticking my foot in it? Apparently not. "Anyway, this place is so convenient."

"And you love it." She looked around. "It's changed a lot."

Her words were loaded with meaning and I knew she meant more than the club. "It has." I fiddled with my napkin, now wishing I'd never told Albert to keep us from being disturbed because I could use a big-time interruption right about now. And a drink. A stiff one. "Why are you being so friendly?"

Shit. The words had tumbled out before I could stop them, but now that I'd asked the question, I wanted an answer and I plowed on through.

"I keep waiting for the other shoe to drop, but you just sit there with your polite smile and offering to help and remembering things I like." My voice rose and I didn't try to temper my incredulity. "For crying out loud, I left you on the eve of our wedding. Why are you still speaking to me?"

I saw the storm build in her eyes, and I recognized the anger. It had never been directed at me, only at threats or injustices. Being illuminated in its dark shadows was disturbing and extremely uncomfortable and my first instinct was to run. Been there, done that. Had to stay put this time or the result would be the same—years of no contact—and I didn't want that as much as I didn't want to examine why. "Talk to me."

"You broke my heart."

Her words were quiet, and the only sign I'd penetrated her calm veneer was the slight crack in her voice. I wanted to pull her close and comfort her but seeing as how I'd caused the pain in the first place, I stayed put. "Go ahead. Get it out."

"There is no getting it out. There's only perspective. You did what you felt you had to do."

This was it. This was the moment I should tell her the truth, admit my weakness, my lack of trust. I cleared my throat and started to speak before I lost my nerve. "Emma, I need to explain."

She held up a hand. "Don't. You may need to explain, but I'm in a good place right now and absolving you of guilt isn't part of that." She hung her head. "After you left, I thought I would never recover, but then I was deployed. People died and I watched them bleed. Kind of put things in the proper perspective. I've changed. No one will be able to affect me that way again. You learn to get a tough exterior when you get burned like that."

I hated hearing what she had to say, but I was glad she'd said it. It certainly didn't clear the air though, instead pointing out the massive wall bricked between us. "So why did you agree to do this for me?"

"Because I can. Because there was a time we were friends. I never stopped caring for you. Just because I'll never let anyone get close doesn't mean I never want to speak to you again. I spent a lot of my life with you and I can hang on to the good memories and let go of the rest."

"You sound very zen." Always honorable. In the past, I'd given her a hard time for it, and I immediately flashed back to the day I learned she'd joined the military. I'd been wrong to give her such a hard time, but I'd been selfish then. Not unlike now. "I shouldn't have asked you to do this."

"Why? I'm good at what I do, and I have to admit, I offered so I would get the chance to talk to you." She shook her head. "Don't get me wrong. It's taken a while to get to this place. There might be a relapse."

"Fair enough. In the meantime, I appreciate this. I don't really want to go to a stranger with my personal business," I said, appreciating the irony, considering after all these years Emma and I were *practically* strangers.

"Understood." She folded her hands in what I recognized as a get-down-to-business gesture. "Are you ready?"

"Sure."

"Overall, it's a standard prenup, but there are a couple of lifestyle provisions that are pretty unusual. On the face of it, I'd advise you not to agree to them, and I think any other lawyer would agree."

I'd barely glanced at the prenup since I planned to go through with the marriage no matter what it said, but I was mildly curious about the unusual provisions. "What are they?"

She ran a finger along her notes. "Well, for starters, there's the one that requires you to attend a minimum of ten annual social functions together, along with a list of society balls, galas, and whatever." She pursed her lips which told me she was no more into big society functions than she'd ever been. I was right there with her on that but had always attended out of obligation, telling myself it was good business to court the whims of the rich and famous. "What else?"

"Um, well, there's language about being discreet in your personal affairs…"

She arched an eyebrow at me, but I didn't bite. I knew that she knew exactly what the phrase meant, but I didn't want to discuss how Ann and I had a built in an *it's okay to cheat as long as we're careful about it* provision to our union. "What else?"

A beat passed before she broke our shared gaze and resumed her back-to-business tone. "There's this one, that states you cannot work for any competing oil and gas company, or supplier or distributor for an oil and gas company, or…" She rattled off the rest of the clause and finished off with, "I assume you know if these provisions are deal breakers?"

"Everything is a deal breaker."

"Not following."

I was on the verge of telling her everything. About my stubborn father and how he'd wrecked the business and my future with it. About how Ann treated me like arm candy and how it made me feel cheap. But confiding in Emma about how I didn't want to get married—again— seemed the height of selfish and she didn't deserve that, so I simply said, "Do you have a suggestion for presenting them with a different option?"

She reached down and pulled out a stapled document. "I took the liberty of drawing up an alternative agreement. One that's a bit more fair to you." She flipped to the page she'd flagged. "I deleted the requirement that you attend all those functions and added a clause giving you the right to have an independent accountant review her assets, personal and business, on an annual basis. You should know what you're giving up if you choose to walk away."

I resisted the urge to respond to the loaded remark. "Thanks. You didn't have to do that and I'll gladly pay you for your time," I said, feeling a twinge of guilt that Ann's money would be going to pay for my personal protest of this whole fiasco. Emma cocked her head, and I anticipated her question. "You want to know why I'd sign one of these in the first place."

"I did think it was strange, considering…"

"I don't know. Maybe it's karma." I took a sip of my drink. Again, I resisted the urge to confide in her and shrugged off the question. "I appreciate your suggestions. What do I owe you?"

She pulled in her lower lip like she used to do when she was thinking, and I watched, waiting for her to name her price, but when she finally spoke, she took me by surprise. "Do you still have horses at the ranch?"

I hesitated before responding, leery of answering without knowing the reason behind her question. "Not as many as we used to, but we have a few."

"I need to brush up on my riding skills. We have a firm retreat in a few weeks at a working ranch. One of the senior partners makes a big deal about how if we're going to ride, we better be able to do the stuff where you clean the saddle and all that."

"Well, you might want to start by calling it the *tack*." I smiled to soften the remark. "Jed still works the stables and he'd be happy to show you the ropes. I'll send him a text in the morning." I drummed my fingers on the table and made a snap decision. "Actually, I could use a ride to relieve all this pre-wedding stress. Why don't I take you out? What about tomorrow?"

I watched her face, looking for any sign she was as excited about the idea as I was. I hadn't been riding in weeks, and I'd missed it. At least that was my justification for this invite. It was her turn to hesitate now, and I waited anxiously for her to politely refuse.

"Tomorrow is perfect. Ten?"

I wanted to ask a bunch of questions about the retreat, her boss, and why she hadn't ridden in a while, but my curiosity was quelled by the excitement that I would see her again. Tomorrow. A fact I was working hard to ignore. I pushed all the confusing thoughts to the back of my brain and mustered a polite, "See you then."

I could not wait.

CHAPTER FOUR

I had purposely picked the easiest bridle path, but I needn't have been worried since Emma was holding her own. After we'd ridden a short distance, I picked up the pace and smiled at the sound of her horse's hoofbeats as Emma urged him to catch up to us.

We used to ride together all the time, but I'd always been more at ease than she sitting six feet in the air on top of a large beast. As I eased into the familiar pace, I let my mind wander to one of those occasions, a few weeks before our ill-fated wedding date.

"You're beginning to look like a natural way up there," I said when we arrived at the clearing. I dismounted and looked up at her, admiring her confident bearing in the saddle.

"Not sure that's ever going to happen," she said. "Key words: way up there. I always feel so off balance."

The admission surprised me because Emma was consistently unflappable about every other aspect of our lives. She volunteered to sign the prenup, she'd agreed to let me stay in Dallas to deal with the family business instead of living on base with her while she was on tour, and she'd given in to the formal wedding in lieu of exchanging vows at the courthouse. At every turn, she'd compromised to accommodate my family, and not for the first time I wondered when the other shoe would drop and she'd say enough was enough.

Emma dismounted and we walked together toward the large pecan tree which we'd made our regular picnic spot. "Your father came to see me yesterday."

Her tone hadn't changed, but I braced for fallout. "Really?"

She nodded. "He doesn't want you to marry me, that's clear, but I think he's coming around. The whole prenup thing is weighing on his mind." She gathered my hands into hers. "You know I don't care about getting my hands on your stuff, right?"

I didn't need to see the earnest expression in her eyes to know the truth. Emma didn't care about material things. Since the moment we'd met, I'd known she had a higher purpose and when she'd enlisted, it had been clear she valued duty and honor above all else, maybe even me. "I do know that, but if we're going to do this, we're going to do it right. Equal partners in all things. What's mine is yours and vice versa. Agreed?"

She reached for my hand and squeezed it tight. "Agreed."

Two weeks later, I left her.

"You look pretty comfortable up there," I said, and I meant it. Emma had mounted with ease and now she handled Donovan like a champ. "I'm not entirely sure you needed this practice ride."

"I've kept up my riding, but I still don't have a handle on all the prep and post work. It kind of spoils the fun. I usually ride up at Livingston stables where they do all of that for you."

"Ah, you've become spoiled."

"I wouldn't say that. More like too busy to ride and handle the rest. If I had to do it all, I wouldn't be able to do any of it."

"Which leads me to ask how you have time to be helping me out for an as yet unspecified price?"

"Maybe I was just being nosy."

Although I was pretty sure she was kidding, it made sense. If I'd seen her with another woman, filling out paperwork for a marriage license, I'd have a ton of questions. The difference between us was my prior actions meant I had no right to answers whereas she had every right to specifics when it came to my personal life. Better to get this part over with as quickly as possible. "Ask me anything. I don't have any secrets."

"I doubt that."

She punctuated her words by smacking Donovan on the butt and galloping ahead, handling her mount like a perfect horsewoman. I stared for a moment, surprised and drawn to her athleticism and the words she'd spoken which implied she thought I still had something to hide. She wasn't wrong, but I was ready to clear the air between us and if that meant coming clean about why I was really marrying Ann, then I was prepared to do just that. I dug in my heels and galloped after her. I hadn't ridden like this, on a fun, free ride full of abandon, in a very long while. There just hadn't been time to do anything that wasn't related to saving the business, and even the wedding preparations—which should've been a fun and festive time—were only another chore, considering I didn't want to be getting married in the first place, let alone to someone I didn't love.

I pushed that thought away because it would only lead to dangerous territory. Once I started to think about why this marriage was a bad idea, I'd start picking away at the edges of it until it unraveled and fell apart, which would be a disastrous outcome for everyone in my life right now. Well, almost everyone—I doubted Emma cared either way about my marriage or my future with or without Ann, and that was entirely my fault and I was prepared to face the consequences of my own choices. As soon as I could catch my breath.

She was waiting under a tree in the clearing. Not just any tree, but the pecan we'd called our own. The one we'd carved our initials into in a silly adolescent gesture of love. She'd dismounted and was leaning against the trunk, looking relaxed and confident and way more beautiful than I'd ever remembered, which was saying a lot. I slowed my horse to a walk and used the last few yards of her gentle gait to let the past and present merge into a haze of what could've been.

Emma reached up to grasp my hand as I swung a leg over the saddle, and her hand stayed on my arm while I hopped to the ground. This déjà vu needed to stop before reality blurred into a mess of memories. I stepped back to put some distance between us. "You're wrong, you know."

"About?"

"I don't have any secrets. You can ask me anything." Why was I heading down this road when I knew where it would lead? The ride back to the stables wasn't going to be fun. But the truth was, I wanted to get this over with, clear the air between us, so we could…I don't know, but talking about it felt better than having some looming unspoken confession in the air.

"It's none of my business."

She started walking back to the tree, but I touched her arm to signal she should stay. "What's none of your business?"

"I get why someone like Ann Koen would want a prenup, a tight one, one that guards her family's fortune."

I was disappointed we were back to that, but it was my own fault for even consulting her about the prenup. *Damn you, Betty.* I started to offer some vague remark about how I didn't care about the money, but it wasn't true. The money was the only reason I was marrying Ann at all and I was determined to make sure nothing activated the terms of the prenup. Before I could come up with some neutral statement, Emma spoke again.

"But what I don't get is why you'd marry Ann in the first place. Do you love her?"

Two loaded questions, one easy to answer and the other much more complicated. I started with the easy one. "I don't love her."

Was that relief I saw flicker in Emma's eyes? What did it matter if it was? It was the first time I'd spoken those words out loud and trying them on for size made me not like myself very much. "It's complicated."

"Most things are, but that doesn't mean they can't be boiled down to a few simple truths. Care to share?"

I pointed to the ground beneath the tree. "I've got a blanket in my pack. Let's sit down."

"Okay."

Her tone was wary, but I was grateful for the cautious agreement. I had more than a blanket. I'd packed coffee and snacks. I don't know why, but it was what we'd always done in the past—rode for a bit and then took a break to connect. Some part of me craved that last part and prayed she would too.

I spread the blanket and invited her to have a seat. I held out the thermos. "Coffee?"

"Still brewing your own blend?"

"Is there any other way?"

She smiled and took a sip from the steaming cup. "Exactly the way I remember it. Some things never change."

"And some do."

She leaned back against the tree and crossed her legs. Nice long legs. Strong enough to grip the horse, run many miles, stand by my side whenever and however long I'd needed her. I missed those legs. I missed everything about her.

I shook my head. I couldn't, shouldn't be feeling this way because there was nowhere to go with these feelings and there hadn't been for years. I fished around in my brain and found the perfect mood killer. "Ann is not in love with me and I don't love her. Our wedding is purely business. I'm marrying her to save James Drilling and the jobs of everyone who works there." I braced for Emma's reaction, unsure what I expected. Her eyes flashed and I took it for anger. When she spoke, her growl confirmed my conclusions.

"Seriously? You think marrying someone you don't love is the only way you can solve your problems?"

Her stare was piercing, and I forced myself not to look away. "This problem, yes."

She shook her head in disgust. "You could file bankruptcy."

"We can't." I considered my next words carefully but decided to blurt them out before I could change my mind. "And please don't make me explain why because unless you're the company's attorney, I'd be divulging information that could be used against us in a prosecution." I looked away, ashamed of the admission even though I wasn't the one who'd placed the company in legal jeopardy. We'd explored bankruptcy after Dad's death, but the revelation that he'd raided the retirement accounts of our employees to keep the business afloat cut that search short. No judge was going to allow us to walk away from debt when it meant dodging legal responsibility for what essentially amounted to a fraud. "We can't." I repeated the words as much for my own benefit as Emma's.

"I guess some things never change."

Emma stood as she spoke the words, our little reunion oasis clearly over as far as she was concerned. She started to reach for my hand to help me up in what I was sure was an instinctive gesture of chivalry, but then she slapped it back to her side and I scrambled to stand and right things between us. "I've been holding out hope that one day you could forgive me."

"Maybe I could if I felt like you were no longer letting your family rule every aspect of your life. When will you learn your happiness is not dependent on them?"

"It's not that easy."

"It's not that hard." Emma looked down at the ground for what seemed like a long time before meeting my eyes again, and when she did, the sadness was glaring. "When I saw you at the clerk's office, there was a split second when…"

My entire body leaned in, ready for the next words, scrambling to prepare for whatever she was about to say. I couldn't read her expression—a mix of puzzlement and frustration, probably a brew of all the feelings my abandonment had stirred—and I knew I shouldn't be surprised at her reservation, her unwillingness to accept that I had changed, especially in light of my impending marriage to Ann. I deserved Emma's anger, her disappointment, her sadness. In fact, I wanted those things because any emotion at all meant there was at least a small part of her that still cared about me and I needed that right now. "Say it. Please."

"It doesn't matter." She pointed to her horse. "I need to get back. I can find my own way if you want to stay."

The message was clear. She'd never really wanted help with the tack, and now that she'd believed nothing about me had changed, she had no interest in anything to do with me at all. The nicest thing I could do for her right now, the thing I'd tried to do all those years ago, was to let her go. Maybe this time she would see it was best for both of us.

CHAPTER FIVE

We'd just arrived at the restaurant for our meeting with the wedding planner when my phone buzzed and I tried to surreptitiously check the screen before Ann caught me, but she had an eagle eye when it came to noticing what other people were doing.

"Who keeps calling you?"

I held up the phone and pointed at the three missed calls from the unknown number. "Not a clue."

"Block it. We've got too much to do for you to be constantly distracted."

I shoved the phone back in my purse, deliberately ignoring her command. I was giving up enough by marrying her in the first place and wasn't a big fan of being told what to do. Besides, part of me wondered if Emma was trying to call to hash through our encounter from the other day. Irrational, yes, since I had her number programmed into my phone so I'd know if it was her, but I held out hope maybe she was calling from somewhere else. Doubtful. More likely the call was from a telemarketer.

The wedding planner appeared at Ann's side and locked arms with her in a way I would find annoying if I were smitten with Ann. "Are you two ready to see the setup for the rehearsal dinner?"

I resisted pointing out that I'd done this before. No point in being hurtful even though my simmering resentment made me want to lash out at everyone. Funny, up until a week ago, I'd been resigned to my fate, happy even that I'd managed to find a solution to save James Drilling from certain demise and willing to make any sacrifice to save our legacy from doom.

Emma was the variable. Seeing her, spending time with her, had thrown me off course, had made me consider chucking this charade to pursue finding a love like the one we'd had before I'd blown it all to pieces. After years of looking for, but not finding, another woman like Emma and faced with our family's dire straits, it had seemed so easy to give up on happiness, but now the possibility had burrowed its way through my resolve, leaving me frustrated and wistful and sad.

Ann's mother had hired the wedding planner, of course, and everything was being done to her exact specifications, which meant our appearance here to approve the arrangement was only for show. I nodded politely whenever the wedding planner pointed out any of the details, and I smiled at Ann whenever I thought it was warranted. She seemed genuinely excited, but I suspected that had more to do with closing the deal between our respective companies than anything else. I'd been telling the truth when I told Emma Ann didn't love me, but I didn't really know how she felt and I hadn't cared enough to ask. It was likely she thought she loved me, but love to her meant possessing someone, controlling them.

"Are you bored?"

I zoned back into my current reality and Ann's question. "No," I said, glad to be able to answer honestly. Bored didn't come close to summarizing the growing angst of my many conflicts. "Not at all. It's just a lot to take in." I stopped talking to keep from saying this wedding was five times the size of my first one. She wouldn't want to hear I'd almost been married before and I had no desire to share this information with her, although I wasn't sure why. Prior relationships were a perfectly natural thing for couples to discuss, a threshold even before deciding to go further, commit, and risk the same mistakes. But nothing about this weekend's wedding was natural. Besides, it wasn't like we shared much of anything before we'd entered into this agreement. Feeding her nuggets of my past now felt odd and artificial, like reading the warning label after you'd already taken the pill. We were well along this path. No sense in deviating from the course at this point.

She squeezed my hand. "I'm sorry. It was selfish of me not to think about the fact your father won't be here to see you down the aisle." She placed a hand over her heart. "I mean, of course, I thought about it, but as part of logistics, not how that would make you feel. Forgive me?"

My mind went instantly to the day I'd identified his dead body, a task left to me because Mom couldn't summon the strength to see him as anything other than the larger-than-life presence he'd projected from the moment he'd met her. The room at the hospital morgue had been sterile, but I didn't have to enter, only look through a glass window while they wheeled the gurney into place. Despite the wounds, I knew it was him and I immediately doubled over, wracked with sobs, but my sorrow in that moment was completely eclipsed by the complete devastation that came days later, when I learned the extent of the disaster he'd left behind, including the lies he'd told years ago to keep me in the fold. Now, months later, I was left sacrificing my own needs and wants once again because of his actions. Would it ever end?

Ann grabbed my hand, and after telling the wedding planner to take a break, she ushered me to an alcove. "I have a surprise for you." She grinned like a giddy schoolgirl—not a look I was used to seeing on her. "I wasn't going to tell you this until Saturday, but I think it will cheer you up." She reached into her bag and pulled out a brochure. "I know we said we weren't going to take a honeymoon, but I booked us a trip to Italy."

I stared at the outstretched brochure and went numb. Apparently, I hid my shock well because she kept talking.

"I noticed the framed print in your room, and I talked to your mom. She said you've never been, but that you've always wanted to." Her smile was wide. "Anyway, I get that this wedding isn't what you would've planned, but it doesn't have to be just a business arrangement." She paused for a few beats. "No pressure, but whatever you decide, let's start this arrangement off right with the best hotel, the best wine, the best food. I'll make sure we make this the trip of a lifetime—better than you could've ever imagined."

I grabbed a chair and gripped it with my fist to hide the fact I was about to pass out. It had been easier to resign to this fate with the understanding it was all business for both of us—a buyout for me and a conquest for her. The idea Ann might start to want to explore actual feelings was outside the scope of our agreement, but I feared any reluctance on my part would crash my carefully constructed plan to save my company. I forced a smile. "*Everything* about this is different than what I could've imagined."

❖

"What did you tell her?" Betty asked after she'd ordered two double extra-dirty martinis from the handsome butch bartender who'd been checking her out all night.

"Can I just get a beer?" I asked.

"No. This is your bachelorette party, not a kegger," she said. "We're going to get smashed and we're going to do it quickly." She took the drinks from the bartender, handed over her platinum card, and told her to keep the tab open. "But not before you tell me exactly how this went down."

I followed her to the VIP table where a bucket of Cristal on ice sat waiting on the table behind the velvet rope. This entire production felt silly. I wasn't a Cristal kind of girl on any day, let alone the celebration of a wedding that was increasingly feeling like a straitjacket. I pointed at the bottle. "Any reason we couldn't just drink this?"

She took a sip of her martini and speared an olive. "That's for later. Trust me, you'll be glad we ended with the good stuff. It'll make for a much faster recovery time."

I rubbed my head, pondering whether I should make a break for it now while I could still walk. I wasn't a club person and I'd only agreed to come out because the alternative was sitting at home counting down the minutes until I lost whatever freedom I had left. Oh, and Betty was a colossal nag and I'd promised she could be in charge of my bachelorette party in exchange for her role as my best woman, if you could call this a party since it was just us.

"I see you looking for the exits."

"Sorry. I'm not in a party mood."

"I get it. Let's pretend we're back in college and we just finished finals. We have the summer to look forward to and we don't have to marry anyone we don't want to."

"Wow, you really are into fantasies, aren't you?"

"Little bit, yes. Now, what did you tell her when she flashed those tickets to Italy?"

I sighed, realizing my stalling was over. "It was a brochure, not tickets. Nobody gets paper tickets anymore."

She punched me in the arm. "Quit stalling."

"I told her my passport expired."

"And she believed you?"

I shrugged. "It's not like I've been doing a lot of world travel lately. I'm not even sure I know where my passport is."

"I'm surprised she didn't name-drop someone at the State Department who would hand-stitch a passport book for you by tomorrow."

"Said the woman who knows everyone."

"There's a big difference between knowing everyone and acting like you know everyone." She pointed at her chest. "I bet I could get you a new passport in time."

"I'll keep that in mind if I ever need one."

"You lied. Katie James, when did you start deceiving people? That's not like you at all."

She was right. Honesty was my trademark trait, except apparently when it came to women I was about to marry. "I went horseback riding with Emma yesterday." I took a big gulp of my martini to keep from babbling any other random admissions and waited for Betty's reaction. Several seconds passed without a word, and besides a tiny furrow to her brow, I got nothing. "Aren't you going to say anything?"

"I'm not sure what you want me to say. Happy trails?"

I hunched over the table wishing I'd kept my mouth shut. "I don't know."

"Did you have fun?"

"Sure, right up until the moment she told me off for letting my family run my life and galloped back to the stable without me."

"Ouch. Tell me everything."

Between sips of the briny drink I spilled every detail of the ride from the easy way we got along to the argument over why I was a jerk who'd agreed to marry a woman to save my family's business. "That's it. She could not think less of me."

"You have to tell her."

I thought about feigning ignorance and asking, *Tell her what?* but Betty and I would both know I was lying. "It doesn't matter anymore."

"Maybe not, but do you really want her to go the rest of her life thinking you're an asshole?"

"No, but I doubt she cares what I want, and I don't blame her."

"Tell her."

"Let it go." I pointed at our nearly empty drinks. "You're killing my buzz."

"A buzz is all you'll ever have if you don't take my advice."

I wished I could see things her way, but the fantasy that I'd tell Emma the entire story around why I'd left her all those years ago and she'd come running back to me was just that—a fantasy. The cold hard reality was the truth would likely drive her farther away and I'd be left more lonely and without the assistance Ann's family had promised as her end of the bargain. Wasn't going to happen. I raised my glass. "I guess I'll have to rely on this to keep me warm at night."

Betty started to respond, but stopped when a voice from behind me said, "Katie James, twice in one week."

I turned around at the sound of the familiar voice to find Lily Gantry standing with a striking woman at her side, who I guessed was her wife, Peyton Davis. "Hi, Lily, great to see you again." I held out a hand. "You must be Peyton. I'm Katie and this is my best friend, Betty Abrams. Nice to meet you."

After we all exchanged pleasantries, I invited them to join us.

"We wouldn't want to interrupt your party," Lily said.

Betty jumped in before I could respond. "She wouldn't let me throw a real party, so you'd be doing me a favor by filling out this little gathering. If you stay, she'll look back and have better memories than just the two of us raising a glass."

"Please join us," I said. "Betty's right. A big party isn't really my thing, but I'd love the company. It'll keep Betty from harassing me into silly games."

"You two must be good friends," Peyton said.

"The best." I squeezed Betty's hand while she waved the other one for the waiter and asked for more glasses for the champagne.

This was the second such party she'd thrown for me. The first had been a big affair as befitted our role in Dallas society. A stretch limo packed with acquaintances from all the right families, ready to dine at the most expensive restaurant in town before heading to the most exclusive clubs, hoping their photos would wind up on the society pages of the Sunday papers. Lily would've been there, but she'd been away at school in Europe. The thing I remembered most about that night was missing Emma, wondering what she was doing while I was drinking expensive champagne and dancing with Betty and a bunch of women I barely knew but who had to be part of the party because of who their parents were. I was so distracted wishing Emma was with me, that once everyone was drunk, I ducked out of the party and took a cab to her apartment.

"Aren't you supposed to be out enjoying your last bout of freedom?" Emma asked after opening the door.

"Freedom is overrated," I said. "Besides, once we're married, I'll be free to bug you whenever I want."

"Oh, really?" she said with a grin.

"Are you going to invite me in?"

She made a show of looking over my shoulder out. "Where's Betty?"

"Back at the club with the rest of the entourage. I imagine they'll be out until brunch." I put my hands on her chest. "If I don't get out of this dress soon, I'm going to come unhinged. Can I borrow a pair of sweats?"

She laughed and tugged me closer. "I love it when you want to slum with me."

"Make me a snack while I change?"

"You got it." As she walked toward the kitchen, she called out over her shoulder, "They're clean. I just put them away."

I grinned as I walked into her bedroom, loving how easily she read my mind. I rummaged through her dresser drawers until I found the pair of Air Force sweats I loved, the ones that had faded from wash and wear and were softer than their moniker implied they should be. She always complained she never got to wear them because I stole them, but I knew she liked the way they looked on me and would never deny me these or anything else. Her generosity was her only weakness. Aside from the sweats, I did my best not to exploit it.

"Where are you having the ceremony?" Lily asked, her voice shaking me out of my trip down memory lane.

"At The Mansion. Saturday night." I almost tossed in a casual *You should come*, like it was a backyard BBQ instead of a fancy formal wedding. Anyway, I knew Ann had purposefully excluded anyone with the last name Gantry from attending as Gantry Oil was a mortal business enemy. "It's a small intimate affair with only a few hundred of Ann's closest friends." I laughed to cover my sadness. Somehow, I'd managed to push all the details about the day itself to the back of my brain to keep them from scaring me out of going through with this disaster of a plan, but there was no backing out now, especially considering how much work had gone into the plans.

"I'm sure Ann's excited," Lily said, without a trace of duplicity.

"Someone has to be," Betty said, downing the rest of her champagne. I punched her in the side. "What?" she said. "It's true."

I willed my face not to turn red and turned back to Lily. "Betty has no filter, but I'm sure you knew that already."

Lily laughed. "That's what best friends are for." She winked at Peyton, leaving no doubt she considered Peyton her best friend. Ann and I would never be like that even if the circumstances for our wedding had been much different.

Peyton stood. "I think we could all use something a bit stronger to drink. Betty, join me at the bar?"

Betty looked my way and I nodded to show her I was okay to be left alone. I waited until they were out of earshot before blurting out, "It's an arranged marriage." I studied Lily's face and could tell she was trying to hold in her reaction, which wasn't good. I rushed to explain. "I mean, I did the arranging, but it was for a very good reason." Now that I'd rushed to explain, I was all out of words unless I wanted to admit my father's transgressions. Most everyone knew the obvious stuff, but the secrets I was sacrificing my freedom to hide left me to question how eager I was to tell them here, even if telling meant I could explain what seemed like such a crazy action on my part.

I met Lily's kind eyes and knowing look. "You know."

She placed a hand on mine and nodded. "I know your dad ran into trouble. I don't know what kind and it doesn't really matter. He was your father, and even though he's gone, he left behind a family and a business that keeps that family afloat. It's not important that I know the rest, but here's what I've learned. Secrets can kill, but only if you keep them close. Exposing them can set you free. Trust me, I have firsthand experience."

I didn't know the specifics of her situation, but I did know her father had been all over the news when the local US Attorney had raided his offices and tried to connect him with the Cartel a few years ago. And, like everyone else who ran in our circle, I'd heard the stories about how her birth mother, who'd been thought dead, suddenly reappeared in her life and her dad had had to confess she was his blood relative despite the fact he'd always told people she was adopted. The stories were intriguing and strange, but I'd never judged. Was it possible she wasn't judging me now? I could tell by the warmth in her eyes, she wasn't.

"I don't have a choice. Believe me, I've explored a bunch of options, but none of them work. I wish it was as simple as selling the company to a worthy buyer or finding an investor who would give us time to get things under control, but there's more to it." I let the implication hang in the air with all its foreboding, wishing I could say the words out loud if only to have someone to talk to. I hadn't even told Betty about the crime because I didn't want her to be burdened by the knowledge.

Lily gestured to Peyton and Betty who were a few feet away, carrying two whiskeys each. "Let's table this tonight and have fun, but I'd like to talk more. Maybe there's a way out you aren't seeing since you're in the middle of this. You have my number. Promise me you'll keep an open mind. There's always a solution, and sometimes the anticipation is worse than the reality."

At that moment, Peyton and Betty set drinks in front of us, saving me from answering. I wrapped my fingers around the thick glass and lifted its weight to toast this night, these women. How I wished this was really a celebration instead of a mourning of the life I could've had. As I sipped the first bit of the amber warmth, my only thought was for the person I would want to be celebrating with and how quickly I could get to her.

CHAPTER SIX

I paced the sidewalk outside Emma's apartment building, but no matter how many times I walked back and forth, I couldn't seem to work up the nerve to go inside and knock on her door. What was I even doing here? Unfinished business was the best excuse I could muster, leaving open the question of hers or mine.

I didn't like the way we'd left things back at the ranch, and I'd spent way too much time focused on the words she'd almost said but hadn't. My mind buzzed with questions. Had she been poised to say seeing me again after all these years was a relief because now she could express her anger in person, or did she have different feelings to express? Lingering feelings that left her reminiscent of us in our best days—the same kind of feelings I'd been having since I'd seen her. I tried to shake away the thought, but the emotional hook was in deep. Whatever she'd been ready to say, I needed to hear, and I was convinced if we didn't talk it through, I would never be able to move on, and moving on was essential if I was to make it through this wedding. Before I could talk myself out of my plan, I dialed her number and willed her to answer.

"Shouldn't you be out doing wedding things?"

Her voice was soft as silk, and but for the touch of sarcasm, it was exactly what I needed right now. I was desperate to hear more of it. "Actually, I've been at my bachelorette party. I managed to escape before anything embarrassing happened."

"And you decided to call me?"

I heard the question in her words, but I decided to go all in. "Actually, I'm standing outside your building." I waved in case she could somehow see me from her window, lurking. "I totally get it if you're busy or if you want me to go away."

"Go to the lobby. I'll let the front desk know to send you up."

She clicked off the line before I could determine if she was annoyed that I'd shown up like this, but it was too late now. I pressed the buzzer to the outer door and explained to the disembodied voice I was there to see a resident. When the door clicked open, I pushed through and made my way to the desk where a bored-looking skinny guy asked if I was Katie. "Elevator's that way." He pointed. "She's expecting you."

I spent the five-floor ride contemplating how this was not at all the kind of place I expected Emma to live. It was sleek and modern and fancy. Emma was more of an old-fashioned cottage with a big front porch kind of person. Or at least she had been when I knew her. I supposed time and being jilted could change a person's outlook in all kinds of ways.

When the elevator stopped, I checked the signs and strode toward her door, determined if I was going to do this thing, I might as well dive in. The door swung wide as I raised my hand to knock and for an instant time froze. Emma wore the Air Force sweats I used to steal from her dresser drawer. For a second I thought they might be a new pair, but then I recognized the hole on the sleeve from the time I snagged it on the nail by the door in her old apartment where we'd used to hang our keys. I sucked in a breath. She'd always looked better in those sweats than I had—fitter, finer. My thoughts wandered to other ways Emma outshined me. While I stayed at home and pledged my misplaced loyalty to my father's mishandling of everything, Emma had gone to war, and then plunged right into law school. She was the epitome of a focused and disciplined soldier, and I was still muddling through, wondering where things had gone off track while life happened to me. The buzz of alcohol evaporated and was replaced with the realization I had no business here, on her doorstep, intruding into the order of her life with the chaos of my own.

"Are you coming in?" she asked.

"I should go." I spoke the truth, but I couldn't make my legs move. I willed them to work, but I was frozen to the spot. To our unfinished business.

She stood back, holding the door ajar with one arm and gesturing inside with the other. "You're here. You may as well come in." She left the door open and walked back inside. I watched her back and knew I should leave, but I couldn't. No, that wasn't right. I didn't want to, but what I really wanted wasn't ever going to happen. I wanted to turn back time and redo every moment of my life since the day I'd lost her. But I doubted she wanted that too. Still, I had to clear the air. If I was going to start a new life, however dreadful it might be, I needed to find some kind of closure on the old one and it needed to happen now.

"I'm sorry."

She turned. "It's okay. I wasn't asleep. Actually, I was about to make a snack. Are you hungry?"

I ignored her question, determined to do what I'd come here for without the distraction of snacks or the way the sweats hugged the muscles in her legs. "I am sorry, but not about showing up on your doorstep tonight. I mean, I am sorry for showing up unannounced, but I owe you an apology for leaving you on the day of our wedding. I can't believe it's taken me all these years. I came to find you later, to try to explain, but you'd shipped out and I didn't know where you were. I know I could've tried harder to find you, but I didn't know if you'd want to hear from me. Then days and weeks and months passed, and the more time that passed, the more I started to question if you'd want to hear from me at all or if I should just leave you alone and let you be happy with someone else since I'd fucked up so badly, and I didn't think you'd ever forgive me." I paused to catch my breath and stared across the room at her. She was standing still, her jaws locked and her eyes narrowed. I braced for blowback, but the first thing she said was, "Sit down."

I followed her instruction, showing her I had some discipline, and I waited for the fallout.

"Did you really come here on the night of your bachelorette party for your wedding to another woman to finally apologize for leaving me eight freaking years ago?"

Oops. My great idea didn't sound so good when I heard it out loud, but it was too late to turn back now. "Can we agree I have a horrible sense of timing?"

"We can absolutely agree on that."

I listened closely but couldn't get a read on her tone. I'm not sure what I expected—anger or dismissal probably—but there was a firm acceptance underlying her words that hinted she'd already made peace with my betrayal and I was only picking at a closed wound. I stood. "Well, that's what I wanted to say. I'll let you get back to your evening."

Three steps to the door, she barked out, "Katie James, sit your ass down. Right now."

I barely recognized the commanding voice she'd rarely used and had never been directed at me. In all the years we'd known each other, Emma had never raised her voice to me, but maybe this evidence of her anger was what I needed to feel like I'd atoned for the hurt I'd caused. I returned to the chair, ready to take whatever punishment she wanted to dole out.

She paced the room and with each pass the energy in the room rose, and not in a good way. But I kept quiet, waiting, but not patiently. I'd about decided she was going to wear a hole in the floor when she finally stopped.

"I meant what I said when I told you that you broke my heart."

This time, her voice cracked with the admission, confirming what I'd known all along. I'd hurt her. Badly. I'd figured the pain would pass in time, but the anguish in her voice told me the hurt lingered on. Or had it only resurfaced because we'd come back into each other's lives? I reached out a hand, but she stepped back and started pacing again.

"All these years, I convinced myself I was over you. I had to be over you because you were over me. You were, right? If you weren't, you wouldn't have left." She paced some more. "I've spent all this time wondering why, reviewing every moment of our relationship, looking for clues. I knew you were your father's daughter, and I would always have to compete with the family and the business for your attention, but I was convinced you loved me more than you loved the lifestyle I might not ever be able to provide, no matter what your father said. I swore when I saw you again, I wouldn't let you get away without giving me a real explanation. One that made sense. And then there you were, getting a new marriage license like it's the most mundane task in the world. Like you do it every day. Like it doesn't mean anything. And then I find out you're marrying a woman you don't love for a family whose approval you will never truly have? Were you so desperate for their love you were willing to give up on us? That's not the woman I knew and definitely not the woman I love." She shook her head. "Loved."

Too late. I'd heard it. Could she really still have feelings for me, after what I'd put her through? After all this time? She wouldn't if she knew the truth. This was it. The moment I should tell her everything, but when I opened my mouth, the words boiled down to one simple admission. "I will never love anyone the way I loved you."

"Is that supposed to make me feel better?"

I wanted to shout my own truth, but it wasn't true, and it wasn't real, and it never had been. I shook my head at the realization my actions tonight were, once again, all about me. Coming here was designed to make me feel better without any regard to how dredging through our past might cause pain for Emma. "You've never been anything but loving and honorable, and you deserve only good things. That's not me. It never was." I stood again, determined to leave this time, before I could do any more harm. "I'm going to go now. I won't bother you again."

I walked to the door, slowly at first, kind of like I expected her to stop me again, and I was disappointed when she didn't. I turned the knob and walked away, hating myself and my life, and wishing I could rewrite the past.

❖

I slammed my hand against the nightstand, hoping to hit the phone and turn off the incessant beeping. Morning had come way too quickly, but it was right on track with how fast my life was spinning out of control. In two days, I'd be Mrs. Koen, and nothing could stop me from hurtling toward that dubious destiny.

Once I had the phone in my clutches, I stared at the screen, noting the multiple texts. Betty had sent several to ask if I'd made it home all right. Ann had sent several texts saying she wanted to go over some details, her tone growing more terse when I didn't respond. I remembered the vague but pointed portion of the prenup that mentioned discretion in personal affairs and knew she'd flip out if she knew I'd decided to show up on my ex's doorstep instead. Even if we weren't in a real relationship, my job was to play the role, and spending the last half of my bachelorette party at Emma's could be construed as a deal breaker for our agreement.

I texted Betty first to let her know all was well, but I purposefully avoided answering her follow-up about what I'd been up to. I composed three different texts to Ann, deleting each one because it was either too vague or contained too much detail. I finally settled on a simple, *Turned in early and missed your text. See you at my mother's this afternoon?*

Mom had insisted on hosting a tea for us. It wasn't really for us. It was for her to show her society friends that her daughter was marrying into a rich family, thereby granting her the cachet to reenter their exclusive circles following my father's death. Of course, if her condescending crew knew about the destruction he'd left in his wake, they probably would've closed their doors to her no matter who I married. Oh, Emma, aren't you glad you dodged all this drama?

I'll be there, Ann replied and added a bride and a smirk emoji. Not her typical fare, but apparently the closer we got to the wedding, the more she was buying into the fake romance. Whatever.

I took my time in the shower, like I could wash away all my worries, but by the time the hot water ran out, I wasn't feeling any better. Emma's words kept ringing in my head. *You broke my heart.* The echo shadowed and slowed my attempts to move forward.

I trudged to the closet to find the appropriate clothes for a society tea and swept the hangers back and forth until I located a suitable dress. I reached to the top shelf for the shoes that would go with and wound up knocking another box down, spilling its contents onto the floor. When I bent down to clean up, I recognized the mess—I'd added to it not long ago, although I hadn't taken the time to sort through the rest. I gathered all the scattered bits and settled on the bed to cull through my past.

Our wedding invitation. Mine and Emma's. We hadn't wanted anything super fancy, so we'd gone with a conservative jet-black design on white linen stationery. The invite promised a ceremony followed by a hosted dinner and reception at the Dallas Arboretum. Emma loved the arboretum and I'd been happy to oblige since it held plenty of sentimental value for me. It was where we'd gone on our first date and it was the scene of our first kiss, weeks later. Besides, I could deny Emma nothing. Then.

I sorted through the other papers. The copy of our marriage license. The one that had never been signed by an officiant, never been filed with the county clerk. I didn't remember that I'd kept it or why, but now I studied it, contemplating the difference a couple of signatures could make.

Memories flooded back and I reached for another paper I knew was in the box. I pulled out the envelope, addressed simply to Emma Reed. I'd given the short, terse letter to my father the morning of my wedding day, and he'd promised to deliver it to Emma—his idea to spare me the ugly confrontation. I didn't find out he hadn't done his part until the week after his death, when I found the unopened envelope in his personal safe. I'd placed it in this box with the rest of my past life, never dreaming all of it would bubble to the surface once again. But it had, and it was time for me to stop denying how easily I'd let Emma go and how quick I'd been to misplace my trust.

> *Emma,*
>
> *Today was supposed to be the best day of my life. I was convinced love would find a way to bridge our worlds, and no amount of physical distance could come between us.*
>
> *I was wrong. It was foolish of me to believe the good could last, that you would stay true when you started your new life without me. I only wish you would've had the courage to spare me this disgrace. I hope she makes you happy.*

I'd written more—line after line of angry accusations, spurred by the photos my father had shown me of Emma and the other woman. Soft gazes, a gentle embrace—nothing tawdry, but my father had assured me the investigator had provided him with a full report on Emma's indiscretions to accompany the photos. The me of today would've insisted on reading every word of that report, never letting someone else's interpretation substitute for my own, but back then I'd been so indoctrinated in the creed of family loyalty, it never occurred to me to distrust the patriarch of our little dynasty. Talk about being wrong.

It wasn't until Dad was dead and buried that I learned the truth. I'd hired a locksmith to break into the personal safe, discovering a reverse treasure trove of distasteful secrets. Among other things, I found the second set of financial records that revealed the fraud Dad had perpetrated against our business, my unopened, undelivered letter to Emma, and the full report from the investigator he'd hired to investigate my future wife. That last revealed more of my father's fraud.

> *Taken out of context, the photos appear to show an*

intimate relationship, but I found nothing to support the contention that the subject is engaged in any inappropriate behavior. Close surveillance and reliable sources inside the OTS at Maxwell AFB confirm that other than the occasion captured in the photos, which was a birthday party at a local bar, the subject and the other woman in the photos do not see each other outside of their regularly scheduled training activities, and any perceived intimacy is merely the type of close camaraderie that exists among peers who are submerged in an intense training program.

I hope this information allays your concerns.

I tossed the letter aside. I'd read it dozens of times when I first found it, unable to process how far my father had been willing to go to come between me and Emma. First, he'd tried being as unpleasant as possible to her, and then he presented the unreasonable prenup that she'd willingly agreed to sign. When his initial tactics failed, he resorted to faking a cheating allegation, but as much as I detested him for his efforts to break us up, I couldn't deny my own role. Young and insecure, I'd been so quick to believe him when he said Emma had been cheating on me, and to compound it all, I'd been too cowardly to confront her myself.

I set aside the letter I'd written to Emma on our wedding day and the investigator's report and picked up a pen.

Dear Emma,

This letter is way too late and it's absolutely not enough to make up for the pain I've caused you, but you deserve to hear the truth.

I poured my heart out, telling her everything from the beginning seeds of my insecurities in her decision to join the Air Force, to the confession of how I'd failed to trust her when it mattered most. I laid bare every detail of what led me to leave her the day of our wedding and hoped it sounded more like a sincere apology than a list of excuses. I even told her the truth about my father's fraud—a gesture of trust, I suppose. I ended with:

You were the best thing that ever happened to me and I don't believe I'll ever love anyone the way I loved you. My hope for you is that you find someone who will love you for who you are and have the same strength of character that you possess. You deserve to find true love. You deserve happiness. I'm sorry I wasn't able to give you either of those things, but I believe that you will find them.

The lobby of Emma's apartment building was open when I swung by on my way to the tea, and the same bored-looking skinny guy was working the front desk. I handed him the envelope and walked out the door, certain this chapter of my life was closed for good.

Chapter Seven

Mmy pickup bounced its way up the dusty dirt drive to the headquarters of Gantry Renewable Resources, a sister company of Gantry Oil. The sign a few hundred feet back told me I was at the right place, but the only building in sight was a small trailer with a Jeep parked alongside. Figuring whoever was inside could direct me to the right place, I parked and started toward the trailer when Lily Gantry stepped out of the door.

"You came," she said with a broad smile.

"I did. You seem surprised."

"I might be. I know you've got a lot going on right now."

Understatement of the year. Of course she was talking about the wedding. Ann had groused when I told her I had to duck out this morning and her mood got worse when I wouldn't say where I was headed. I'd managed to smooth things over with a vague suggestion that I was on a surprise errand, the implication being it was related to her. I made a mental note to pick up some token gift on my way home as cover. Telling her the truth about where I was today would invite too many questions, and suspicions that I was up to something. I wasn't really. I mean, I was curious about what Lily had to say, but mostly I was hiding out from the entire Koen clan that was descending on Dallas for what Ann hoped would be the social event of the season. I was already dreading seeing them all tonight at the rehearsal dinner, so I was counting these few hours of freedom as a bride's luxury.

So here I was, curious about Lily's several overtures to tell me more about my options, but not putting much stock in anything to save me from the fate I'd chosen. "At this point the wedding planner is doing all the work. I think all I have to do is show up, look pretty, and say all the right things."

Lily smiled indulgently. She'd been to enough big society weddings to know what I meant. The bride was merely a centerpiece—it was all the flowers, the food, the festivities that would make the social page in the next day's news. She locked arms with me. "I'm glad you're here. Ready for the tour?"

"Sure." I followed her to the Jeep and climbed in. She drove down a barely discernible road for a bit until the wooded area gave way to a large meadow lined with giant steel wind turbines. To our right was a large hangar and in front of it, on the ground, were rows of turbine blades. She pulled over and motioned for me to follow her to the hangar.

"Wow," I said, pointing to the ranks of three-pronged rotors. "The turbines look big installed but seeing these blades on the ground really gives you perspective."

"Go ahead, stand right up next to one."

I did and was blown away to find it was almost twice my height. "How many of these do you have? How do you assemble them? Are you leasing this land?"

"Come on." She led the way into the hangar, pointing out various stations, explaining the construction of the windmills along the way. I was captivated by her knowledge and enthusiasm. "This property is the back half of Circle Six, Peyton's family's ranch. We've installed a hundred twenty-three turbines here, and we have hundreds more in locations in other parts of Texas and various other states."

"Wow."

"This is only the first phase. I want to have ten times that amount in the next five years."

Her ambition was intoxicating. "Is that doable?"

"With the right partnership, it is. Which brings me to why I wanted to talk to you." She opened a door and led me into a small office furnished with an old metal desk and two mismatched chairs. "Have a seat. I realize these aren't the finest digs, but this office isn't used much except to receive materials, and to log inspections and repairs. We have a crew that monitors the turbines and tabulates their output, but we don't get many visitors so there's really no point in dressing up the place."

I nodded, feigning patience, but inside I was dying to hurry her along to the point of my visit.

"I guess you want to know why you're here."

"Yes. I do."

"We're going to need a substantial increase in personnel and equipment to maintain our growth and I'd like to discuss how Gantry Renewables can merge with James Drilling to corner the market in Texas wind turbines."

I let out a big breath. Well, shit. I didn't know what I'd been expecting—some business from Gantry Oil thrown our way or some other friendly overture to help out a fellow businesswoman—but a partnership? Hadn't been on my radar at all. Of course, Lily didn't know all the details behind the financial straits we were in. "I appreciate the offer. What you've done, what you're doing with renewable energy, is amazing. I admire you and under any other circumstances, I'd love to be in business with you, but I've already agreed to merge our company with Ann's family business. I'm sure you understand."

Lily leaned back in her chair and studied me until I grew uncomfortable under her gaze before she said, "I don't understand."

"Excuse me?"

She raised a hand. "Look, I get that your business is in trouble, and I want you to know I have no intention of taking advantage of your position to try to scoop up a good deal. I will admit I'm taking advantage of your situation to suggest this as a way for you to diversify and me to benefit, but I want us to go into business together because I know you and I respect you. Relationships are more important to me than balance sheets. Which brings me to ask—and I realize this is probably not an appropriate question for me to ask on the eve of your wedding—why on earth are you marrying Ann Koen?"

Maybe it was the kind, gentle expression in her eyes. Maybe it was the underlying anguish I detected in the tone of her blunt question, but whatever it was, I burst into tears. Big, messy sobs that wracked me through and through. Lily moved her chair next to mine and pulled me close, letting me literally cry on her shoulder until I was spent.

I pulled away and dabbed at my eyes which I was certain were red and puffy. "Damn. I'm sorry."

"You have nothing to be sorry about," she said. "I'm the one who should apologize. Clearly, you're feeling a lot of things. Do you want to talk?"

"No. Yes." I balled my hands into fists, conflicted and concerned I'd already said too much by virtue of my overly emotional reaction. The tears had been cathartic, but I needed more. "I don't want to marry Ann. I'm only doing it to save the family business." Lily started to speak, but I shook my head. "You're going to say I have options, that if I go into business with you, I can save my company from being dismantled for parts, but I promise you there are reasons that won't work."

"And Ann knows those reasons?"

"Yes. If I break off our…arrangement, she'll ruin James Drilling and all of this will have been for nothing."

"It sounds like you're carrying a heavy load. Is there anyone you can talk to?"

The only people who knew the full extent of my predicament were my mother, Ann, and her family. Betty knew I was marrying Ann as part of a business arrangement, but out of fear for her lack of a filter, I hadn't told her anything about my father's fraud and how his misdeeds precluded other options for saving the business. I met Lily's eyes and saw empathy and kindness. Lily's father had been investigated for money laundering, yet here she was, storming the energy business, unwilling to let it hold her back. Our lives were a study in contrasts. If only I'd married Emma all those years ago, left the family business to be an Air Force wife, had the strength to question my father's motives in having Emma followed in the first place and the bravery to confront her personally. In the face of Lily's fortitude, I felt small and weak, and in my weakness, I could no longer keep my secret.

"My father drained the company retirement fund." I blurted out the words, and once I started talking, I couldn't stop. "Some of it he spent trying to grow the business, but a lot of it he squandered trying to keep up appearances—new cars, expensive restaurants, diamonds for Mom." I told her everything. How I'd had an internal audit done on the books after he died because I couldn't find the funds. How the auditor had delivered the news and suggested we hire a lawyer to defend against possible lawsuits and criminal prosecution once the news got out. How the Koen family lawyer had approached me to say the Koens had obtained inside information about the fraud, but they were willing to keep it quiet in exchange for a business arrangement that included marriage to Ann in some sort of weird family dynasty maneuver. I told her about how I'd given up on love after my first attempt at marriage and figured entering a union for solely practical reasons would be easy, but the closer we got to the wedding, the more I realized exactly how much I was giving up.

"Emma."

Lily had only to say Emma's name and all the feelings came rushing back. Love, pain. Love, regret. Love…No matter what came after, there'd always been love between us, and even all these years later, I believed there was a part of Emma that still loved me, despite what I'd put her through. The hardest part of marrying Ann tomorrow was knowing how much I loved Emma and always had.

"When I saw you together at the Tower Club," Lily said, "I thought maybe there was a chance you'd get back together."

"No. Not a chance. That was just…" I cast about for a way to distill what we had been into what we'd become. "A lawyer consulting with a client. A meeting between two people who used to know each other. And I'd probably be fine with my decision to marry Ann if I hadn't run into Emma again after all these years."

"Okay. Sure."

"What?"

"You've been very honest with me about everything related to your business, which I appreciate, by the way. I'm sure you know I'm familiar with the delicate balance of family and business, with a father who crosses lines he shouldn't. But experience has taught me this—if you love this woman, together you can find a way out of any difficulty."

I let her words sink in. She wasn't talking about Ann, but what did she know about any feelings I might have for Emma or she for me? Besides, it was too late for me and Emma. I was getting married tomorrow and too much hung in the balance for me to run away a second time. I stood. "I need to go."

We rode in silence back to where my car was parked, and while I appreciated her not pushing the points she'd made, I missed the comfort of our conversation, and the realization left me feeling very lonely. When Lily hugged me and wished me a happy wedding day, I blurted out, "You should come. You and Peyton. I realize it's silly to invite you at the last minute, but I could use another friendly face in the crowd." I left unsaid that she would be the one friend present who could truly appreciate the toll this whole ordeal was exacting from me, which suddenly seemed very selfish. "I'm sorry, you probably have plans already, or better things to do than dress up to attend a loveless wedding."

"We'll be there."

Her firm response gave me comfort as I spent the next hour driving around the countryside, stretching my freedom to the last minute, before I finally turned my car back toward the city. I barely had time to change before I had to be at the rehearsal dinner, and as I walked through the doors of the restaurant, I realized I'd completely forgotten to pick up a gift for Ann, something to allay her frustration that I'd been MIA most of the day. A week ago I would've cared more about keeping her happy, but now all I felt was the sour taste of regret. Screw the gift. I was already giving enough.

CHAPTER EIGHT

I stood in front of the mirror in the bedroom of the luxurious hotel suite Ann had booked for me to use to get ready for the wedding ceremony, an hour from now. After the reception, a car would whisk us away to the airport for two weeks in Italy, a romantic trip I'd dreamed of taking someday, definitely with my wife, but never with her.

I stared at my reflection, desperate to reconcile the perfectly coiffed woman in the white dress with the tangled knot of nerves lurking underneath her polished veneer. No matter how hard I tried, I didn't recognize this version of myself. Yes, I'd made some dumb decisions in my life, but what I was about to do was next level. If so many other people's livelihoods wouldn't be affected, would I walk away, or was the rope that tethered me to the fate of my family legacy so strong, I could never break free?

But my decision to stick it out and try to save James Drilling was about more than other people's jobs and keeping up appearances. When I'd chosen to trust my father and leave Emma, I'd thrown all my energy into this business, thinking I was building a life for a future family of my own. Silly, really, since I'd given up my one true love, and any other woman, any other family, would never measure up. Which left me with the woman in the mirror who was about to give up her own hopes and dreams, and I didn't much like what I saw.

The door burst open behind me and my mother glided into the room. "Katie, you look gorgeous. I'd hug you but I don't want to crumple your dress. Are you excited?"

Ugh. She should've known I wasn't, but she'd let herself get swept up into the festive atmosphere, conveniently forgetting this marriage was arranged and our family's legacy was the dowry. "Have you seen Betty?"

Mom looked over her shoulder. "She was outside talking to the rest of the bridesmaids, but she said she'd be right here."

I hoped so. I'd sent her off a short while ago, begging her to get Ann's cousins as far away from me as possible before the ceremony began. Ann had been curious and disappointed when I told her I only wanted Betty to stand with me. She wanted a big wedding and had narrowed her list of bridesmaids down to five willing sycophants. When she'd come up with the solution of having some of her cousins join my bridal party for balance, I gave in as I had on every other detail of this farce of a ceremony because I simply didn't care about anything other than getting through it.

"I brought you something old," Mom said.

She reached into her bag and pulled out a plain gold signet ring. I recognized it as the one my father had always worn on his right ring finger. It had been handed down from three generations of James men. It wasn't particularly valuable, but it stood for family and tradition, and I'd always expected it would be mine someday, but I recoiled when she thrust it toward me.

"What's the matter?"

"I don't want it."

She frowned. "He would've wanted you to have it."

"What he would've wanted is no longer important to me." I questioned the truth of my words, but I wasn't prepared to take them back. Some would argue I was selling out to preserve his reputation as much as my own legacy. My relationship with him had always been complicated, and death only made it more so because only one of us could fix what was broken now. But my role in making things right didn't include a wearable reminder of why I was in this situation. Maybe I should wear the ring as a reminder I should keep my own counsel, because trusting him had cost me everything.

No, that wasn't fair. Young and naïve as I'd been, I could've, should've questioned more—when he told me Emma was cheating, when he insisted he had a plan for the future of James Drilling. No one was to blame but me, and the sooner I owned my part in my unhappiness, the sooner I could start work on a way to correct the course. I pointed at the ring in my mother's hand. "Keep it, don't keep it. I don't care, but I will not wear it. I am my own person, and whatever happens from here on out will be because of my hard work, my sacrifice, not some tradition or legacy that may or may not be real."

Mom stuffed the ring back in her purse, a disappointed expression on her face—the kind that would usually have me scrambling to fix her mood—but I felt nothing.

"Wow."

Mom and I both turned toward the door. Ann was wearing a striking custom-cut black tux, and no one could deny she made a picture-perfect partner. Mom stepped in front of me and shook a finger at her. "What are you doing here? It's bad luck for you to see the bride."

I managed a laugh. "Mom, she's a bride too. I'm pretty sure the bad luck cancels out." I could only hope. "But seriously, Ann, I didn't expect to see you until the ceremony."

"Can you blame me for wanting to have one last look before we make this official?"

I wanted to give her the benefit of the doubt, assume she wasn't actually talking about me like I was a roast she wanted the butcher to display before he wrapped it up for her to take home, but my stomach soured and I knew my gut was right. "Give us a minute?" I asked my mother.

"Of course. Guess there's no harm now."

I waited until she left, and then invited Ann to join me at the dining table in the kitchen area of the suite. "I assume you have something you would like to discuss."

"Thank you for finally signing the prenup. My lawyer told me you gave it to him yesterday. He'll file it along with the signed marriage license." She grinned. "I've deposited a bonus to your bank account as a gesture of goodwill. Use it for whatever you want." She reached out and clasped my hand. "We're going to get along just fine."

I stared at her hand and dug deep for some emotional reaction to what I'm sure she envisioned was a thoughtful gesture, but all I felt was cold and alone. A few seconds later, I heard a throat clear behind us and looked up to see Betty standing in the doorway of what had become the busiest hotel suite in the city.

"Am I interrupting?" Betty asked in a tone I recognized as sorry, not sorry.

"No," I said before Ann could speak. "Ann was on her way out because we've probably tested the bounds of luck already." I ducked her kiss and shooed her out the door, which I then bolted behind her.

"What was that all about?" Betty asked.

"I think she just wanted to inspect the goods before she finalized her purchase." I sighed. "Help me finish getting ready so we can get this over with?" I picked up a brush and started in on my hair, counting down my freedom with each stroke.

"About that…"

I heard the uncertainty in her voice, and I paused midstroke. "What?"

She pointed at the door. "There are some people here who want to see you. I invited them up to the suite."

"Seriously, Betty? I'm not up for any more visitors." But curiosity compelled me to ask, "Who are they?"

She reached for the bolt on the door and slid it back in her usual dramatic fashion. When she pulled the door open, I stared at the familiar face framed in the doorway and stood frozen in place, barely hearing the hairbrush clatter to the surface of the vanity.

❖

Emma wasn't wearing a custom-made tux, but her navy-blue suit with its tapered jacket took me back in time to the first and only Air Force dine-in we'd attended together, the night she graduated from officer training school. She was even more beautiful now than she had been that day, decked out in mess dress, a newly minted soldier, ready to take on the world.

And now she was standing here with me while I was dressed in a white gown, a scene we once planned, snatched away by my own immaturity. For a moment the rest of the world fell away and I longed to step into her arms, will away the past, and reclaim the years we'd wasted. Could she want that too?

"What are you doing here?" I whispered the words like I was afraid if I spoke too loudly, I would puncture the bubble of us.

"I read your letter."

I searched her face for a clue, but I detected no signs of anger. Her eyes were gentle and kind, wistful even. "It's not enough, but I had to tell you the truth. I never should've doubted you."

She stepped closer. "I should've found you, made you talk to me, tell me what was wrong. Instead I ran as far away as I could." She reached for my hands and held them tight. "We both made mistakes."

I felt the first tear fall, but I didn't let go of her hands to wipe it away. More tears followed and I gave in and allowed myself to indulge the loss I'd never fully processed. How stark it seemed now with Emma less than a foot away while a woman I did not love was headed to the altar to become my wife.

Like a dash of cold water on my face, the memory of Ann in her tux and my carefully crafted plan to save James Drilling rushed in to take the space between us. I stepped back, searching for something to say to close the door on our past. "Thank you for…this, but I have to go."

She shook her head. "No, you don't."

Damn, this was hard. I broke our shared gaze and swiveled my head, looking for Betty. As maid of honor it was her job to keep things on track, and I was dangerously close to going off the rails. As if on cue, Betty walked through the door again, this time with more unexpected visitors in tow.

"Lily, Peyton, you came."

Lily hugged me tightly and whispered in my ear, "I promised I would, but please don't be mad when you hear what I have to say."

She stepped back before I could fully process her words. I glanced between her and Peyton, and then at Emma. "Why do I feel like you all are up to something?" I looked at Betty, who hunched her shoulders, and then I reached for her hand in a show of solidarity since it appeared we were the only ones in the room who weren't in on the secret.

Lily spoke first. "I went to find Emma after you left Circle Six yesterday. I know it's none of my business if you marry a woman you don't love, but before you do, I want you to hear I've been where you are, faced with secrets about who my family is and what they've done. The only way I was able to find happiness was to uncover the truth, shine a light on the darkness. Yes, it was painful and"—she turned to look at Peyton who gave her an encouraging smile—"it almost tore us apart, but in the end, what we endured only strengthened our bond."

She waved a hand at me and Emma. "If you love each other, nothing is impossible."

I wanted to believe her, desperately, but nothing had changed. "You know why I'm doing this."

This time it was Emma who spoke. "We do, but we're here to say you don't have to go through with it. After Lily came to see me yesterday, I did some research and I met with Peyton." She gestured to Peyton who nodded. "Did you know she's the criminal chief for the US Attorney's office? Of course, we could only discuss hypotheticals, but we agreed if a now-deceased CEO had committed fraud, but no other company principals were complicit, then the US Attorney would be inclined to accept a plea on behalf of the corporation without indicting the other owners, provided the company was willing to pay back the illegal gains with interest."

"There would be a sizeable fine," Peyton said. "And there could still be civil lawsuits, but—"

Lily interrupted, "But as your friends, we will be there to help you raise the money whether you decide to go into business with me or not. I promise you, we'll find a way, and once you're free from this secret, you'll feel so much better."

And I wouldn't have to marry Ann. I closed my eyes while my mind played the words Lily hadn't said out loud, over and over as if repetition could make it true.

Could this work? Could I accept Lily's generosity and trust there were no real strings attached? Even if there were, wasn't this a better obligation than the faux marriage waiting downstairs?

When I opened my eyes, Emma was the only other person in the room, and she was standing several feet away. "They left to give you space."

"And you stayed?"

"We've already had too much space between us." She walked over and stood mere inches away. "What do you want to do?"

I couldn't remember the last time what I wanted to do had taken precedence over obligation. I took a deep breath and exhaled slowly. "Is it as easy as doing what I want?"

"It can be. If you let it." She reached out and placed a hand on the side of my face and gazed intently into my eyes. "I want you."

"I want you too." The words were effortless, natural, real, and in that moment I knew I was capable of so much more than settling for a life built on a stack of lies. I reached up and grasped her hand, still resting on my cheek, and tugged her closer until I could feel her breath on mine. The moment our lips touched, memories flashed before me—idealistic, youthful promises of a happy life I'd let others dim. Our kiss started softly, with slow, gentle touches as we reconnected, then grew into the intense, searing heat of a well-tended passion.

When we finally broke for air, Emma held me tightly and whispered, "You *can* have it all. You just have to believe."

Every cell in my body told me she was right. Emma Reed was my one true love, and I had a choice to make. I could walk down the aisle toward a future I knew would make me unhappy, or I could be a runaway bride who was running toward happiness instead of away from it. The answer was simple and clear. I grabbed Emma's hand and flashed the biggest smile I'd ever felt. "Let's go!"

ON THE ROCKS

Ali Vali

CHAPTER ONE

The whip of a fishing line was the only unnatural sound that disturbed the peacefulness of the bayou and the birds in the trees. Preston Cinclair had snuck away from her job early and headed down to her favorite spot with her fly-fishing gear and her waders. The Cinclair Bayou didn't have the steelhead salmon she loved to fish, but it was the perfect place to practice her technique, and not getting the fly caught in the low-hanging branches took skill.

If there was one drawback to the spot it was that it had perfect cell service. She would've ignored her phone, but the song "Crazy" was her mother's ringtone, and Sienna Cinclair was not a woman who liked being ignored. Especially by her only child, the one she was in labor with for fifty-seven agonizing hours.

"Put the rod down and take some notes," Sienna said, not bothering with any niceties.

"I don't have a notepad in my rubber pants, so if it's important you might want to wait." She closed her eyes momentarily, enjoying the breeze through the ancient live oaks that populated the banks. The rustle of the small leaves was better than anything for making the world and all its responsibilities fall away.

"Roger called and said your shipment is in. They had some problems through Customs but it should be here in less than a week."

The relaxed feeling gave way to excitement, and she held her phone against her shoulder to reel in her line. "Thanks, Mom. Anything else?"

"In your dreams, Preston Maxwell Cinclair. What's he talking about?"

"It's a surprise, and don't start with the million questions—there'll be no hints." She walked slowly out of the water, her feet sinking to the ankles in the rich dark mud with every step, bringing back memories of doing this as a child, only barefoot. Life had certainly evolved since then, but not all change was good, or bad. And that, hopefully, was her last philosophical thought of the day. Any more, and she'd get a headache.

"Are you coming back? Or will tonight be the first time I see you today?"

"I need a shower first. Then I'll be a bit, but I'll see you for dinner." She dropped her stuff in the back of the 1953 Jeep that had been a gift from Gramps, her grandfather on her father's side, when she'd graduated from high school. The old green vehicle had seen plenty of good times in its day, and she hoped to pass it down to her own children.

Children—that was a fantasy so far out of her reach she sighed. "You need to get your head out of the booze and get to finding a girl if you're thinking that." She cranked the engine and fought with the old gearshift to get going.

Her grandfather also taught her that talking to yourself was a healthy way of getting out all those cobwebs that tended to slow your brain into obsession. The girl was definately on the list of things she wanted, but had yet to materialize. She was the next in line to run Cinclair Distillers, and the only obsession she was supposed to have was the award-winning whiskey the family had produced for generations. Taking over the business wasn't optional for her, since her mother—according to her mother—had produced one perfect kid, and there was no reason to try and top perfection. The agonizing labor had also been mentioned on occasion.

The main distillery was on River Road right outside New Orleans, but the place a mile from there was the newest addition she'd purchased to experiment, or *play*, as her father reminded her often. Whiskey was their wheelhouse, but there was no reason not to consider new avenues for the future, though whatever came out of her playtime would never grace a bar shelf if it didn't measure up to the Cinclair label.

Roger Savoy was waiting outside tapping on his watch. "Did the trees and turtles make you forget the time?"

"No, but I need to remember to leave my phone in the Jeep from now on."

"What you need is a haircut and new pants." Roger looked her up and down and shook his head in apparent disapproval. His perfect appearance from his hair down to his shoes made it easy to imagine him as the master distiller and not her, or to guess that he was auditioning for a part in *Queer Eye*. Either way, Roger turned heads with his handsome face, fit body, and stylish clothes.

"Don't worry, I'll be ready for the event next month, but for now leave me to my slovenly ways." The khaki pants were starting to fray at the hem, and her hair was starting to bug her, but not enough to do anything about either. "For now let's go pop open some bottles and see what we have."

"Your dad's here."

She stopped and stared at Roger but didn't want to accuse right away. "Did you invite him?"

"You know Dale Cinclair. You think I had to?"

"Let's go face the kraken and get it over with." She walked to the back storage room where a thousand cases of molasses stout were waiting for their debut. "Hey, Dad."

"You didn't scream at Roger, did you? I'm not here to pry."

"It's not prying if you own the building, big dog." She unlocked the door and flipped the lights on in the big room. "Are you thirsty?"

"Beer." Dale put his hands on his hips and smiled at her. "If the devastating good looks didn't give it away, this proves you really are my kid. This was the first thing I tried outside of my job, and your grandfather almost kicked my ass."

"You tried wheat ale, boy," Carter Cinclair said as he tapped in with his cane.

Preston's grandfather was stronger than her and her father combined, but he'd broken his toe getting off his tractor in their cornfields and was grudgingly using a cane.

"Thanks, sir," she said, hugging him. "You guys go sit in the office and I'll be right in."

She grabbed a case and took a deep breath. College and all it had thrown at her while she got a chemistry degree wasn't as tough as her family when it came to final exams. Roger was setting up the beer glasses with the Cinclair logo on them, and he winked at her as she took out a couple of bottles.

"It's a molasses stout with a hint of our blended five-year-old whiskey. I thought the extra punch would give it a smooth finish, and if we decide on a small production run, it'll be cross-marketed with everything else in our lineup. With a taste of our whiskey, it'll fit right in." She popped the top off a bottle and poured a finger into four glasses.

Carter and Dale raised their glasses to check the color before taking a sip and holding it in their mouths. She closed her eyes for a moment and took her own taste, distinguishing every ingredient she'd used. It did have an edge serious beer drinkers would appreciate, and from the smiles she was seeing, maybe the market would agree.

"How much did you make?" Dale asked.

"A thousand cases. Enough to provide our suppliers and a few key publications. Once we create demand, the next batch will be ready."

"What else you got up your sleeve, kid?" Carter asked. "I had to sign my life away to get your shipment cleared, and the feds probably made a file on my ass."

"The stout is made with Louisiana molasses from our fields, but I'm planning on using this facility and the building next door to create Sueños in Gran's honor." Her grandfather had met his wife of fifty-six years at the World Whiskey Competition, and they were married four months later. Her grandmother Rosa had taught her Spanish and to embrace the country of her birth, Cuba.

Gran had died the year before, but her last message to Preston was one she'd treasure always. Gran had stressed that to be happy, it was important to dream. Preston still missed her steady presence in her life, and how she understood her like no one else ever could.

"Sueños," Gramps said as he stood and motioned her over. "Dreams is the perfect name." He hugged her and kissed her cheek. "But for what?"

"Dark rum, Gramps, but I want it to be a true añejo, so you have to hold out for the ten years I'm going to let it mature. The molasses we're getting is from Cuba, and now that it's here, I have everything we'll need to start distilling."

"I might not be around in ten years, kiddo," Carter said.

"You're going to outlive me and everyone, so I'm not worried."

"Nope, all you have to worry about is the office and the meetings your mother set up." Dale poured himself some more stout and pointed his finger at her when she opened her mouth. "We're harvesting, and I need to keep my eye on the new guys we added to our supply chain. The office and new marketing promotions are all you."

"No way. That's all you."

"Remember our deal. You have to learn all the business, and that means office time, buddy." Dale slapped her on the back. "You've got a day to play, but then you have firms to interview."

"All right, but you owe me."

❖

"You'll owe me big," Hayley Wyatt said to her twin brother, Percy. Preparations for his impending nuptials were at a fever pitch, and he wanted to stay in town to be around for the planning, but Hayley figured it was really the bachelor party that had him wanting to oversee the details. Getting called into the office at what seemed like the crack of dawn meant she'd be going alone to the meetings her father had set up.

"He will, and if he cancels one more thing, he'll be working on his honeymoon," Major Wyatt said loud enough to drown both of his children out. "We need to get this account. We do, and it'll open a new avenue that'll help us gain a segment of the market we're unrepresented in. They're unhappy with their advertising group, and they have a few new things coming to market that will need a new vision."

"You mentioned all this in your email, Dad, but what can be new about whiskey?" She wanted to know the answer, but she asked really more to aggravate her father.

"Sweetheart, we don't have time for your jokes, and I'd think you'd want to go if only to see old friends. College wasn't that long ago that you've forgotten the city."

Her father had been unhappy when she decided on Tulane when she'd been accepted to what he thought were more prestigious programs, but there had been no changing her mind. Joining the Wyatt and Simon Firm after graduation wasn't going to be optional, and once her career began, there would be no freedom in any future choices. Her undergraduate degree and the time away had been her own, and the nicest part had been no one had known she was Major Wyatt's daughter.

"It actually feels like a lifetime ago, and I already agreed to attend in Percy's place. Did they give you any idea of what they want or what they're bringing to market? The team came up with something preliminary, but we could be better prepared if I had a hint."

"Dale Cinclair says they want to get a feel for us and the other firms before they make a decision. I think the last time they went with the big firm before figuring out they knew zip about whiskey and what the average drinker wants in their bar."

"They have a good product for the average drinker, and they have the awards to prove it, and they don't have a hundred-dollar price tag for a bottle. They were able to make a hoity-toity product, but at a hoi polloi price."

"After talking to Dale Cinclair, avoid terms like hoity-toity and hoi polloi," Major said, laughing. "These people have a hoity-toity bank account, but a working man's outlook on life."

"Don't worry—I'll keep my fancy vocabulary at home, and I'll be ready to win this." She texted Josie Simon to join her for some last-minute strategy. Josie was the daughter of the minority owner of the firm, and her best friend. Josie had gone to England for college but she'd fallen in line and come home to get her master's before starting her career in advertising.

"Do you want to get the team together?" Percy asked.

"Let's not overwhelm them right off. Josie and I will handle it."

"Good, and I expect regular updates. It should take about a week or so," Major said before he slapped his hands together and left.

"Are you going to look for her while you're there?" Percy asked when the door closed. "And don't give me the death glare. You know who I'm talking about."

"This job threw me for a loop, but Max doesn't have anything to do with these Cinclairs. She was just a bartender who didn't do a lot of partying and was easy to talk to." She stared out the window in an effort to forget just how easy Max was to talk to, and how wonderful it had been to sleep under the stars when Max had surprised her with a fishing trip to Alaska, of all places.

"Give it a rest. You were born twenty minutes before me, which means I know you pretty well, and you've been miserable for a long time. Hell, you skipped your graduation to come see me walk across the stage, and don't lie and say it was because you were dying to see me in a gown." He reached across the desk to touch her hand. "This could be your second chance to find what you haven't in all this time."

"My life isn't a Hallmark movie, Percy, and she made it clear that was her home. She would've never been happy in New York. Besides, I doubt she'll remember me, and if she does, she won't be happy I left without a word, much less without telling her who I really am."

"You won't know anything unless you try, and I didn't blame you for leaving all that out." He sat back and crossed his legs. "God knows I'm in love, but that naggy little voice in my head always questions if it's because of me, or me and all this." He pointed his finger at the room. "Would she feel differently if I was a bartender in New Orleans?"

"You're pretty charming and you have a gorgeous face, so I'm sure it's more than the money." She blew him a kiss and smiled. "The cash is secondary to that."

"I want you to be happy too, buttercup, so that means searching her out while you're in town. Come on, don't chicken out."

She laughed at the idiotic nickname and threw a wadded piece of paper at him. "She's probably working in one of those river plants and has a wife and kids at home." Max and her beautiful blue eyes and black hair was the subject of many of her fantasies. It really was more than that, though. She remembered Max's easygoing personality and how special she could make her feel. They'd had a year of bliss, but then graduation and, more importantly, reality had slapped her across the face. Once the fun was over, she was expected somewhere else.

"Or she could be wondering about the beautiful girl who rocked her world and disappeared without saying good-bye." He pointed at her and shook his head. "That was seriously uncool, by the way."

"Another reason to completely forget it. Now, get out of here and let me study all there is to know about whiskey."

"If they give away free samples, make sure to bring me some home."

"I'll spring for some of those tiny bottles." She threw another paper at him and laughed when he stuck his tongue out at her. "Get out of here."

She pulled up the Cinclair website again once she was alone and was surprised at how good it was. It concentrated on the product and had great content. The only thing she'd change would be to personalize it more. The Cinclairs had made whiskey since before the Civil War and their company had the feel of a family owned business—at least it would if she got her way.

According to this site, the current CEO grew his own corn on thousands of acres of family owned fields, and every bottle of Cinclair's, no matter where you purchased it, was made right on the banks of the Mississippi River from water that came out of a natural spring that eventually became the Cinclair Bayou. They were the average man's choice, and they were proud of their hard work ethic and damned good whiskey.

Her phone rang. Josie.

"I'm waiting for you in the coffee shop downstairs. Can you come down? I want the scoop probably as much as you want to get out of the office," Josie said. "Besides, I need to finish packing."

"Be right down, and remember what I told you. Concentrate on cool clothes."

"All my clothes by definition are cool, sweet cheeks."

She loved Josie's lovable but insulting ways. "Keep it up and I'll stay quiet about any more advice."

Any thoughts of Max and all those good times were put on her mental shelf to collect dust again. Their time together had been idyllic while it lasted, but there wasn't room in her life for a perfect butch with gorgeous eyes. Not that she'd minded Max's appearance, but their lives were worlds apart, and neither of them could jump that far to clear the chasm. Max might've proved that love was possible, but that was all in her past, along with the multitude of memories.

Her life was here. New York was the center of the universe when it came to advertising, and it was also full of eligible women who took the edge off when it was convenient. None of them came close to Max's powerful build and talented fingers, but life had to be more than just great sex and epic love.

"Shouldn't it?"

CHAPTER TWO

"Shouldn't it what?" her mother asked as Preston opened a bottle of wine for dinner. The stout had been a hit with her mother as well, and they'd strategized their plan for the rest of the week.

"Shouldn't it be your job to oversee advertising? I'm pretty sure I saw that on your job description." She pulled the cork and poured the bottle into a decanter. "If I spend all that time in the office, you won't get treats like the one you drank tonight. Paperwork and marketing strategies dull the imagination."

"Honey, if it was up to me, you could play all day, but it's not up to me." Her mother took a roast out of the oven and handed her a carving knife and fork. "Your father did it until you were old enough, and now he's free to do what he really loves."

"Yes, I noticed the fields appeal to him more than the damn office."

"Get married and produce the next Cinclair heir, and we'll release you from your corporate hell when *your* little bunny shows up with a chemistry degree and the imagination to think of new stouts to complement and expand the label." Her mother moved to finish the salad and chuckled. "Lose the pout, baby, and think about what we need in a new ad agency."

"For starters, someone who knows the difference between whiskey and bourbon."

"See, and you say you don't have the business in your blood."

"It's hard to purge when I've had a steady diet of it since birth." She carved the roast into the thin slices she and her father and grandfather liked, doing a few thick slices for her mother.

"Are you upset about that?" The salad seemed forgotten as her mom appeared really curious.

"Get real, Mom. Being the Cinclair heir is like winning the lottery. I love my job, and more importantly, I'm crazy about my board of directors."

"You're a sweet-talker, Preston Maxwell Cinclair, but you still need to meet with the prospective advertising firms." The use of her full name meant the subject was closed.

"If you're not budging, it's obvious I have a limited talent in the sweet-talking arena." She placed the roast on the platter and washed the carving knife like her mother had taught her. Her mom had a certain way of doing things, and if you didn't have time for lectures, you simply followed her rules.

"Think of it this way." Her mom pointed to the table when she picked up the platter. "You only have yourself to blame if there's something to complain about after you choose a new firm."

"If anything, Roger will be happy that I'll have to retire my khakis until this is over." She continued to put dishes at the antique farm table in the kitchen. It wasn't often they used the formal dining room of the estate, and that's the way her grandfather like it.

The house along the banks of the Mississippi had been in their family for almost two hundred years and had as much history and tradition as the liquor they distilled. It was where her grandfather and parents lived now, and she'd moved into the house her parents had used until her grandmother passed away. The home close to the property's ponds was where she'd grown up, but every Sunday was spent around this table.

"Did you get your invitation to the Brinwoods' party?"

"I have a stack of mail I haven't gotten to." The last thing she wanted was to spend a night with a group of boring overly privileged people.

"Preston, is it time for another long talk about your hermit ways? There's more to—"

"Life than work," she finished for her mom. "I know, Mom, but work has been a bear lately, and I don't know if you heard, but we're getting a new ad agency."

"Don't sass your mother, and go get your father and grandfather."

Their dinner conversation revolved around the new stout and

planned rum. What her grandfather and parents didn't know about was the five-year-old whiskey aging in the rickhouse she'd purchased on her own. She'd done what was sacrilege in their family and messed with the tried-and-true formula that defined Cinclair whiskey in the market. If what she had in mind was a failure, it'd only be her money and ass on the line.

There'd been subsequent runs after that first batch, and it'd be the centerpiece of the new advertising campaign if it was as good as she knew it'd be. It was one thing to know your job as a master distiller, but she also understood the market for good whiskey and what would sell. What she'd come up with would be their first foray into the over a hundred dollar bottle realm they'd never considered before.

"Dinner was great, Mom. Thank you." She kissed the entire family good-bye and decided on the Harley-Davidson Street Rod she'd purchased a few months before to replace the one she'd driven since college.

The ride into the French Quarter gave her time to think about the coming months. Their desire for new representation for their advertising was one thing, but she also had the World Whiskey Competition to plan for. They'd been lucky to place every year, but this time she wanted the top prize as a way to prove she deserved a job she'd eventually have simply because of genetic luck.

She parked in the back of the bar On the Rocks and carried her helmet into the small office she kept on the premises. The place was owned by Cinclair Distillers and was where she'd perfected her bartending skills in college. Both her grandfathers as well as her dad believed in a full day's work to pay for any fun she wanted to have, even though any of them could've easily paid for a lifetime of fun if that's what she'd wanted.

Her mother's father, Russell Maxwell, was the president of Maxwell Distributors, the largest liquor distributor in three states. Gramps might have the greatest knowledge of the business of anyone alive, but Granddad Russell wasn't too far behind. It was the businesses that were responsible for her parents meeting and falling in love.

"Maxie," Portia Russell said when she spotted her. "Are you putting in a shift for me?"

Portia was a senior at Tulane, and her night manager as well as bartender. The kid had started on the waitstaff but had quickly proven herself, so Preston had promoted her. The business degree Portia was working toward was important to her, and Preston planned to keep her on the payroll as long as Portia wanted to stay.

"Put me to work, but I have to be out of here by eleven. The office is a must tomorrow, and my mother gets pissed when I doze off in meetings."

"Great, there's some kind of legal convention in town and they love to drink. We've been slammed since five." Portia pointed to the uniform shirt on her coat tree and gave her a stern look. "Don't forget your name tag."

On the Rocks was a fun and relaxed place for customers, but the standard uniform for everyone who worked there was a pressed denim shirt and a bow tie with sharks on it. The sharks had nothing to do with booze, but she did like to fish.

"The girls okay? Sometimes these guys get kind of grabby once the whiskey starts flowing." They poured everything, but On the Rocks was predominantly a whiskey bar.

"Bunny's had a talk with a few of them, but they're well behaved for the most part."

Bunny was their bouncer, a three hundred pound, bald, muscled guy who in no way resembled any kind of rabbit. He was extremely sweet until you put your hands where they didn't belong, and then he turned into an experience you wouldn't soon forget.

"Let's get started, then. Maybe I'll get schooled on some new fruity drink I haven't heard of and will have to clench my teeth while I waste perfectly good liquor."

"That's cold, boss."

"If it's true, it's not that cold."

"It *is* that cold," Josie said.

Hayley pulled her coat closed as much as she could without taking her hands out of her pockets and tried not to laugh. It was never this chilly in New Orleans in fall, but freaky things were the norm for the city. No matter what, the locals complained for about a nanosecond, then went back to the party that seemed to never end here.

"*Pack cool* you said," Josie said in a sarcastic singsong voice. "I'm freezing my ass off."

"You're such a drama queen. It's barely fifty, and you're a northerner. Shouldn't you be made of tougher stuff than this?" They'd had dinner at Le Coquille D'Huître and were trying to walk off their meal as they made their way back to the hotel.

There'd been some changes, but for the most part, the place had remained like she remembered it. New Orleans was timeless—a city full of history, fun, and fabulous people. It was why she'd chosen to go to school here, and it was the last time in her life she'd been that relaxed and carefree. The other thing about New Orleans, when she chose to acknowledge it, was how happy it made her. She'd been happy here, especially that last year of school.

"I *am* tougher than that, but it's this damp cold that'll cut right through you that's killing me." Josie tried to wrap her suit jacket tighter against her body, but it was ridiculously cold. "Hey, isn't that the place you told me about?"

On the Rocks—the sign stopped her from another step as she stared at it. How many nights had she spent in there, staring at Max tending bar, or waiting in the office studying. When Max's shift was over, she'd give her a ride home on the back of her bike and they'd spend the night making love.

That short year had been perfect in a way that had scared her to death. It was the fear that made her run, and she'd never looked back. She couldn't, because remembering and dwelling only proved to her that she couldn't ever replicate those feelings, or find someone like Max who filled everything wanting in her. "That's the place," she said, glancing at Josie, who was staring at her with compassion.

"Seems popular." Josie startled her when she locked arms with her. "Let's go have a drink."

"Why?" She was unreasonably panicked at the thought, and she didn't know what scared her most—that Max wouldn't be there, or that she was still charming customers with that magnetic personality.

"Why not?" Josie came close to knocking her down when she jerked her forward.

The bar was full, and the live band seemed to be having fun as they played. All the guys in khakis and navy blue sweaters were talking at once, making it hard to hear anything Josie was saying. It hadn't changed much, and the familiar surroundings brought back the memories like an avalanche.

"What do you want?" Josie finally screamed in her ear.

She grabbed Josie's hand and gripped harder than she should, but the sight of Max talking to four women at the center of the bar made her want to run out of there as fast as she could manage. "Jesus, we need to go."

It was doubtful Josie heard her, but she did follow her out and jogged to catch up to her. "What's wrong?" Josie grabbed her hand and forced her to slow down.

"She still works there."

"She?" Josie's eyes widened. "You mean *she's* still in there? Who keeps a job as a bartender for eight years after college?"

"You think it's because of me?" She bent over, not able to breathe.

"Try knocking the opinion of yourself down a few pegs, babe. Maybe this is a good wake-up call, and you should stop feeling guilty or bad about leaving."

"What do you mean?" She tried getting air in her lungs and felt the need to find a paper bag to breathe into so she wouldn't hyperventilate.

"If that was Max—"

"That was her. No ifs about it."

"Okay, that was Max chatting up young girls at the bar, meaning she's either got a Peter Pan complex or she's a loser with no goals. Either way, you dodged a bullet."

"I never got that impression in college, which means something went wrong. You don't graduate with honors in chemistry being a loser with no goals." The tightness in her chest and the buzzing in her ear started to subside, and the noise around her came crashing through, making her crave the quiet of her suite.

"Either way, you can move on." Josie raised her hand when she started to argue. "You haven't moved on with your personal life, and don't try to deny it. I've known you since birth."

"I've already settled career-wise, so I refuse to do so in my personal life." Josie's hand was a comfort, but it sometimes saddened her that they'd never had any kind of spark. A romantic union between them would've made perfect sense, and been the most convenient. They understood each other as well as the demands of their jobs, but there'd been zero chemistry there, except as the sister each had never had.

"Then forget all that right now, and think about whiskey. The sooner we kill this presentation, the sooner we get back for the bachelor party." They crossed Bourbon Street and the craziness of the Quarter finally died away. "You know Percy's going to have enough hot women at his farewell to single life that you'll have no problem forgetting your name, much less someone you knew years ago."

"Thanks, Josie." That was in no way true, but it was a nice thought.

"You got it. Let's go relax over a whiskey to get us in the mood for tomorrow, and then we'll go to bed. Our appointment is for nine, and we want to look perky."

"If perky gets us out of here quicker, I'm all for it."

❖

"I said I'm all for it, Mom, I promise," Preston said as she slowed to a walk after running a circuit around the sugar cane fields that took up the back pastures. The corn had been harvested, but the cane needed a few cold snaps before cutting would begin. Winter would bring a bleakness to the land that made her crave spring, but the cooler temperatures were a blessing, and she stopped on her porch to take her last stress-free breaths of the day. "Yes, I'm listening."

"No, you're not, but make sure you at least read the prospectus Roger put together for you. Your father doesn't want to make a rash decision, but we don't want to delay any more than we have to. It's up to you to spend time with these people and get a feel for them and, more importantly, what they know about our business."

"I promise they'll be sick of me and my annoying questions before we're done."

"Dress like you aren't blowing off work to fish later."

"Did Roger tell you to say that?" She stuck her tongue out at the phone.

"I gave birth to you and don't need Roger to know what you're like. You don't just look like your father, and that hardwiring is hard to get around."

"I promise I'll be a responsible grownup."

Time in the office meant she had to ignore the right side of her closet where all the comfortable casual clothes hung and concentrate on the row of suits and pristinely white shirts on the left. She gelled her hair back and opted for her glasses since she'd fallen asleep with her contacts in, and her eyes felt raw. Impressing anyone wasn't on her agenda today. "It should be the other way around for once."

The keys to the BMW X5 M were in the same teak box that held the Patek Philippe watch Granddad Russell had given her when she'd gotten her master's degree. He understood her and what she liked, opting for the alligator skin strap and the sun-and-moon face.

"This will have to do." She spoke to her image in the full-length mirror her mom had placed on the back of the closet door. Time to hit the road.

"Good morning," Roger said when she answered his call over Bluetooth.

Traffic was light so she made it to the interstate in no time, making her wish she'd taken the time to make coffee. "Good morning." That would probably be the end of any friendly conversation, since Roger probably had a long list of stuff for her to do, and she wouldn't be home before midnight. "What time does the inquisition begin?"

"Trust me," Roger said in his usual patient way. "I've already vetted quite a few off the list, because they wouldn't know good whiskey if someone dropped a barrel of it on their head."

"You're the best, and I'll think even better of you if you stop and get me a latte with an extra shot. If not, these meetings might be short."

"I'm already in line. Just don't wander off somewhere once you get to the office. Our first appointment is at eight thirty, followed by one at nine, and two more in thirty-minute intervals."

"I'm all for getting out of the office early, but won't we need more than thirty minutes to make a rational decision? Or did you and my mother set up some sort of bizarre speed dating and disguise it as an advertising firm search?" She merged left to get into the fastest lane of traffic and stepped on the accelerator. "Is that what this is?"

"No on the dating. I'd fear for my safety if I did that to you. Today is more of a meet-and-greet where you tell them what your vision is. It'll give them time in the next week to adjust their presentations if need be." Roger stopped talking to her, and she heard him place their order, which included blueberry scones. "Once the major presentations are done, you can take some time to decide who will be the best fit."

"We can't take too much time. Competitions aren't that far off, and I need someone to have something in place by then, even if it's preliminary." She exited toward the city and headed to the Quarter. Their offices were in four adjoining buildings on Royal Street. "And I mean ready."

"What are you up to?"

"I'm doing what you all keep preaching about and taking responsibility for the business."

"Everyone from here to Dubai knows the Cinclair brand, Preston. Why the urgency?"

She couldn't see him but could imagine him slitting his eyes in suspicion. That was something he'd learned from her mother. "You know what Gramps and Granddad say. The future is best toasted by the bold."

"Stout isn't your future, love bug."

"Remind me to punch you in the throat when I get to the office."

"You love me too much to resort to violence." He made kissing sounds into the phone.

She parked in her designated spot and laughed. "Yeah, keep telling yourself that."

CHAPTER THREE

"Telling myself what?" Hayley asked as she tucked her silk blouse into a skirt that was shorter than the style she usually opted for. The vee on her blouse was a little too low cut, but good Southern boys sometimes appreciated a bit of sexy with business. "Who am I turning into?" She whispered that question as she contemplated changing, not believing she'd resort to behavior she criticized in others.

"That you're not interested in seeing Max, and you might start to believe it." Josie came in from her bedroom in her bare feet and turned her back so she could zip her dress. "I thought about it last night, and I need answers, and so do you."

"Why didn't you say it was all about you?" She faced Josie and pointed at her cleavage. "Too much?"

"Just enough, so stop obsessing over your tits. I doubt people who distill whiskey are in any way prudes. Well, unless the Lord commanded them to make the devil's brew to test our resolve, and we're all failing miserably."

"I doubt the Cinclairs are that crazy religious, but I could be wrong." She put in the diamond studs that had been her grandmother's and stepped into her heels. There wasn't enough money in the world or weather cold enough to get her to wear pantyhose, so she was ready. "You look good."

"Back at you. Let's go slay these people."

They went down for breakfast, and Josie smiled at her while they waited for their order. Hayley sat back and enjoyed the outdoor space of the Piquant and their incredible service. The best thing was there were no memories of Max here. This place had been a bankrupt department store that had closed its doors, last time she'd been in the city, which gave the Piquant a new beautifully clean slate.

"We'll be happy to provide a car, but you might enjoy the walk. The Cinclair offices aren't that far actually." The waiter refreshed their coffee and smiled when she'd asked about the distance. "If you want to skip it in those heels, I'll have one of the guys on standby."

"Let's opt for walking today since it won't be hot," she said. Today's meeting would probably be bullshit, and lunch out might be nice.

"You got it," the waiter said, smiling again before stepping away.

"Do you miss it?" Josie asked. "The city, I mean?"

"Sometimes." She stirred in some sugar and plenty of steamed milk. New Orleans coffee was good, but it was as strong as a gorilla on steroids. "There was never any sense of rush here, and everyone I knew was always so friendly. It's one of the only places I've been where people greet you on the street if you make eye contact. I found it easy to get lost here, especially from myself."

"Did you love her?" Josie tapped her finger on the handle of her cup. "Percy's right—you never really talk about it."

She shook her head, but more from frustration than denial. Lying to herself had saved her the misery of overthinking her decisions, and she wasn't about to start baring her soul now as she curled the hand in her lap into a fist. "It was eight years ago. That's ancient history, and that's where it needs to stay. Nothing good will come from dredging it up."

"Actually, there's only one good option here, sweetie. Talking might allow you to finally let it go. Stop bottling it all up inside, and let it out so you can move on."

"You want me to talk about my college girlfriend right before a big meeting to purge my feelings? Do you really think that's a good idea, Dr. Feelgood?"

"It doesn't matter, so it shouldn't be that hard to do. That's the only thing you've ever told me when I pushed you. That time, Max, and what you shared wasn't a big deal, and it doesn't matter."

"I lied." Maybe conceding one point would get Josie off her ass.

"No shit." Josie took her hand and stared at her compassionately. "I know, and now you have a chance to either put it to rest or rediscover what you let go."

"I'm sure my father would be thrilled if I chucked everything for a life here." She laughed but it couldn't cover up the memories. The damn memories she never tried to think about because they made her drown in a sea of regret, and there was no life preserver except to admit to herself what a mistake she'd made.

Nine Years Ago

"What can I get you?" Hayley stared at the bartender, who was in her economics class. She'd been curious from the first time she'd seen her, and she'd asked the guy who kept hitting on her where their classmate, the butch she was starting to dream about, worked. It wasn't the conversation he'd hoped for, but that's all she'd been interested in getting from him.

"Vodka and cranberry," she said, smiling when she got a head shake and a grimace. "No?"

"No." That smile and those killer blue eyes made Hayley want to cover her chest with her hands when her nipples tightened so hard she could use them to chip away at the ice block the bartender had been cutting away at all night. "Any woman who's acing economics needs to up her drinking game. When you take over the business world, you can't do it with vodka and cranberry."

"Then enlighten me." The bartender's smile got wider when Hayley held her hand out. "Hayley Wyatt."

"I know that, Ms. Wyatt." She stiffened, but tried not to completely withdraw. "You volunteer to answer in class often is what I meant." The bartender squeezed her hand once before letting it go. "Max."

She stared at the woman, letting her imagination run wild now that the worry of being treated differently because of her name and her family's wealth was gone. "Um, I'm sorry. Max?"

"It's my name." Max placed two glasses on the bar and put her finger up. "You don't detest whiskey, do you?"

"I don't believe I've ever drunk whiskey in my life, Ms. Cinclair. You ask as many questions as I do, so I know your last name," she said when Max arched an eyebrow at her. She glanced at the bottle Max held up and smiled. "Do you drink it because you share the name?"

"Nah, it just used to be a popular name way back when, and that's sacrilege."

"Your name, you mean?"

"No, that you've never tried whiskey. My name isn't something I can change, but introducing you to something better than vodka is something I can."

Max poured whiskey into both glasses, added a couple of dashes of something, before finishing with sugar and a little water. "The cherries are cooked down with simple syrup and a dash more Cinclair's, but the drink wouldn't be the same without them."

"And the drink is?" She had to speak louder since the band had started up again.

"I'm going on break, Joe."

"Sure thing, Maxie." The old guy smiled at them as Max grabbed both glasses and pointed to the stairs.

Max led her to two empty club chairs on the second floor, and they joined the other patrons having quiet conversations. She took the glass Max held out and tapped it against the one she still held. "To time well spent, and to learning new things."

"And making new friends," Max added.

"This is delicious." The drink was strong—not a surprise, considering it was predominantly whiskey—but it was smooth with just a dash of sweet. "You've converted me from the evils of vodka."

"Vodka has its place, and there's plenty of it downstairs, but whiskey is all about history and the slowness of doing things right." Max gazed at her like she could see right to the heart of her.

"Are we still talking about drinks?" She took another sip knowing she had to go slow or risk losing control of herself. After all, her nipples were having a fabulous time and hadn't softened since Max started talking to her.

"Of course, but I'd love to change the subject."

There was flirting, and then there was expert flirting. Max was as smooth and intoxicating as the amber liquid in her glass. "Will you go out with me?" She blurted out the question feeling the heat in her ears from her runaway mouth.

"That's exactly the subject I wanted to touch on. I've got to work this Saturday, but how about Friday?" Max put her glass down and placed her hand close to hers. "I've been an idiot for not asking before now, but I've certainly been interested."

"Same, and what's wrong with now?"

"Nothing, but my shift doesn't end until ten." Max stood and offered her a hand. "If you don't mind some interrupted conversation until then, I'll set you up at the bar until I'm done."

"Do I get a reward if I accept that offer?" She followed Max to a large wooden door with medieval-style cast-iron hinges, smiling as she swung it open to reveal the room beyond. There were barrels of whiskey along one wall, and another beautiful wooden bar at the back, but the best thing about the space was it was free of people.

"This is more a reward for me," Max replied.

She lifted her head when Max cupped her cheeks and got lost in those blue eyes that softened at the sight of her.

The anticipation of Max's lips on hers was something new, and she held her breath, wanting to savor the moment it happened. It was early, but she had a premonition this would become one of her favorite memories no matter how many years would pass.

Present Day

"And is it one of your favorites?" Josie asked.

"Max lucked out—she had to finish her shift, or our first time would've been on that beautiful bar." She closed her eyes, remembering how one kiss had completely undone her. "I've never had sex with someone that fast, but Max was the exception."

"Then why did you leave? Did all that hotness fizzle?"

"No, but graduation was the alarm finally waking me up from that great dream, and I didn't want any long-drawn-out good-bye. Leaving without loads of drama was the best thing for both of us."

"You're an idiot—not to mention, you're kind of an asshole." Josie signed for the check and winked to take the sting out of her words. "I do understand what you're talking about, but be honest with yourself."

"I'm not being honest with myself? How do you figure I'm not?"

"You were afraid of becoming one of those Hallmark romance movies they binge play over Christmas."

They started walking so they wouldn't have to rush. "This should be good."

"They're all the same, those movies. It's usually some high-powered businessperson, which would be you." Josie pointed at her as she smiled at the doorman. "Then there's the country hunk who doesn't realize how fucking sexy they are, especially when they're with their dog, Roger."

"Roger? Not Rex or Spot?"

"This is *my* Hallmark moment, babalicious, so, Roger. Anyway, the only way for the business goddess to keep the hunk is to move to Bumfuck USA and learn to can shit she'll be growing in her vegetable garden. She'll be doing that with her new Chihuahua, Tiffany."

She had to laugh at Josie's lunacy. "Do Tiffany and Roger fall in love too? And why Tiffany?"

"To remind you of the big city and all the things you loved before losing your mind and moving to Bumfuck. You won't have time to mourn that engagement ring you'd fantasized about, though, since you're spending all your time learning to cook." Josie put Chanel sunglasses on and put her hand on Hayley's elbow as they crossed the street.

"Why am I learning to cook?" She was laughing now, thankful to Josie for getting her through the process of reminiscing.

"Because there's only a feed-and-seed store in Bumfuck, thus no takeout or fine dining. The rest of your life will revolve around meatloaf and the canned vegetables you and Tiffany put up for the winter."

"If we're talking food, New Orleans wouldn't have been a bad choice to settle on. You'll never starve here." They turned on Royal and window-shopped antiques as they continued their slow pace. "And there's a Tiffany jewelers at the end of Canal Street."

"Ooh, you shouldn't have admitted that." Josie cringed as she stared at her.

"I'm almost afraid to ask, but why?" The Cinclair buildings were in the next block, and they were early. That gave them the chance to appraise their competition.

"It puts you back in that asshole category." Josie air-kissed close to her cheek so as not to leave a lipstick mark. "Listen, do you want the truth? The way I see it anyway."

"Sure, we have time, and anyway, the only way to shut you up is to punch you in the mouth."

"You were, what, twenty-two?" Josie asked and she nodded. "You freaked out at deviating from the script you'd written for yourself. The rebellion against your father's expectations ended here, but that had more to do with what your expectations were."

"You lost me on the last thing."

"I could be wrong, but knowing what the future was going to be was comforting. Giving up everything, plus the life you knew was waiting for you, was too scary to even contemplate, and you ran. There's no shame in admitting it."

"It wasn't that simple." They should've never started this conversation.

"Hey, I love you no matter what, you know that, but ask yourself one thing before you blow me off. If it didn't mean anything, then why not forget about it and move on?" Josie tugged her into moving. "You're also free to tell me to fuck off."

"I'll be happy to later, but for now forget everything except this account."

"Dale Cinclair won't know what hit him."

"I doubt we'll see Mr. Cinclair until his flunkies deem us worthy." She smoothed her hair down before pushing the door open and plastering on a smile. "Showtime."

❖

"Did you honestly just say *showtime*?" Preston asked, staring at Roger. "Seriously? This isn't Vegas, buddy."

"Okay, how about anchors aweigh?"

"Not in any way better. Let's get started, so I'll have time to meet with Pedro this afternoon. I'm ready to start on Sueños, and there's a few other things I need to review with him." Preston stood and put her jacket back on. The big office had been her father's until recently, but now he was happy to share the one next door with her mother whenever he actually came in.

She complained about this place, but she did like this particular space and the large oak desk that had been in her family for generations. She had a sense of belonging whenever she sat behind it, but it was also a reminder that the future of the company was her responsibility. All the awards and history would mean shit if she somehow fucked up.

"You're staying for these, right?" The decision would ultimately be hers, but having Roger to bounce ideas off would be helpful.

"I'll be taking notes so you don't have to." Roger brushed her shoulders off and winked. "The first candidate is Hopper Consultants. Up to now they've concentrated on mostly food products."

"What kind of food?" She'd mostly ignored Hopper after reading Roger's short description. Food and making people want to buy it took talent, she guessed, but it was a market that had nothing to do with alcohol.

"If you've ever eaten cheese from well-adjusted cows, then you're familiar with their work. They've been really successful."

"Everyone will get a fair shot, but cute isn't the way I want to go here."

"I think they all understand that and are willing to dig deep to get you what you want."

The team from Hopper, two guys, listened as she explained their business and what they were looking for going forward. Their current customers were important to them, but she wanted the whole world to know how seriously they took the process and their product. It was the only way to pave the way for something new.

"Thank you for your time this morning, and I'm curious to hear your presentation. I'll see you again for the tour of the distillery, but please let Roger know if you have any questions." She shook hands with them before going back to the desk and reviewing her notes to see if she needed to add anything for the next candidate. "Who's next?"

"The Wyatt and Simon firm," Roger said, but she wasn't looking up from the information Wyatt and Simon had provided. She hadn't heard the name in years, but it did cross her mind every couple of days.

Hayley Wyatt, the one memorable girl in her past who'd rooted herself in her memories like a stubborn unwanted weed.

Why hadn't anyone told her that your first love was the same as a measuring tape? That you spent the rest of your life comparing and measuring everyone who came after against them seemed to be a rule, but maybe that was only her. Her first love had been perfect—before she fucked her in the head and broke her heart as effectively as if the girl had used a ball-peen hammer.

"You okay?" Roger stood there while she dug herself out of the black hole the name *Wyatt* dropped her into. She'd long ago accepted that they'd had that one year and there'd be no more, but no closure still bothered her. That Hayley had walked away meant she really was oblivious as to who she was, or knew and didn't give a good goddamn.

"I'm fine. Let's not keep them waiting. It'll mess up your schedule."

"Let them wait. The Wyatt and Simon firm is more well-rounded than Hopper. No experience with alcohol, but enough serious campaigns to make me think they'd understand the business and do it justice."

She nodded and flipped through their top work. "Did you line up anyone with experience? Not to knock the list you put together, but I'm curious."

"That's not what you asked for, but I can add some if you've changed your mind."

"No, I'd rather start with a firm with no preconceptions about something most people think is a simple drink. Most of the imbibing public think there's no finesse in whiskey, unlike wine, and I'm planning to show them otherwise."

"I love it when you talk fancy," Roger said and shivered. "Ready?"

"I'm guessing my answer should be yes for the rest of the morning, no matter what." She winked at him and let only one side of her mouth lift in a smile. "I'm kidding. I know how important this is."

"For what it's worth, you really look good in that suit, and your hair is to die for. I should come up with projects like this all the time and fantasize about you being a man. It's your one flaw in life."

"You're a riot. Let's get going."

She glanced down at the numbers and ingredients for the new project she was excited to start, knowing it would take a few minutes for Roger to get through introductions and describing the selection process. Then her door opened, and she lifted her head as she started to stand and button her jacket. The sight of the people who entered stopped her cold, and she sucked in a breath and held it as her fingers stayed on the last button.

Hayley Wyatt. The eight years since she'd seen her last seemed like an eternity, but this sexy put-together woman brought her back to her senior year at Tulane in a blink, and she was pissed at herself for giving a shit. It was obvious Hayley'd had no second thoughts about leaving her for better things, which was acceptable. How Hayley had done it was not.

"Max?" Hayley appeared confused as she said her name slowly.

"Ms. Wyatt and Ms. Simon, I'd like to introduce you to Preston Cinclair," Roger said, seeming as confused as Hayley.

"Max, what are you doing here?" Hayley's voice sounded as if it couldn't get any louder than the breathy whisper she was using, and her feet seem nailed to the floor outside the office.

"Making whiskey and looking for a new advertising firm." There was no way in hell she was going to show any kind of emotional response in front of this woman. "Have a seat and we'll get started."

"Thank you for inviting us," the woman with Hayley said. She really hadn't caught her name after seeing Hayley. "I'm Josie Simon, and we look forward to showing you our presentation."

"We'd like to explain our company before you start," she said, dropping into the office chair. It was bizarre, but for the first time in her life she wanted to run and not look back. Hell, Hayley had done it, and it seemed to have worked for her. "Cinclair is a family business, and we're proud of the product we have out on the market. In the coming months, though, we'd like to put something new out that we'll be debuting at the World Whiskey Competition."

"Are we meeting with Dale Cinclair today?" Josie asked, talking over her since Hayley still appeared shell-shocked. "We'd like his input on what we have before we change the trajectory of the campaign we have in mind."

Preston stared at Josie but she couldn't form words.

"Mr. Cinclair won't be available for these initial meetings, but you're free to wait," Roger said when it was obvious she wasn't going to add anything else. "Mr. and Mrs. Cinclair will be hosting a cocktail hour tomorrow night to introduce you to the Cinclair line. If you can't proceed without talking to him, that might be the appropriate time to address any of your concerns."

"We are the best fit for you, Max, and we'll do everything we can to prove that to Mr. Cinclair. Can you pass along that message?" Josie sounded confident, but somewhat condescending. "Please feel free to join us when we talk to Mr. Cinclair and get down to business."

"Ms. Simon." She said the name slowly and with emphasis. "We'll see, and if you don't mind, my name is Preston. Max is a nickname reserved for my friends, and we're not quite there yet. Thank you again for stopping by." She stood and left through the side door that led to the conference room and the stairs. Leaving wasn't an option, but she needed a minute to tighten her armor back up before facing the rest of the day.

"What the fuck was that?"

CHAPTER FOUR

I mean, really, what the fuck was that?" Josie said as Roger led them out without saying too much. "Did your father give you the impression this was going to be a drawn-out affair?"

"He didn't say much, and believe me, I researched before we got here. Cinclair Whiskey *is* a family business, but the only person mentioned in their corporate information is Dale Cinclair."

"Obviously Max—" Josie put her sunglasses on and smirked. "I'm sorry, I mean *Preston*, is related to him, and he trusts her enough to let her start the process."

"She always said she wasn't one of those Cinclairs, but maybe she found a use for her degree, and the last name got her an in." Hayley walked down the street, glancing back every few steps. "We need to call and get another appointment later today. If we wait any longer than that, we'll be out of this."

"You heard Roger. It's going to be at earliest tomorrow."

"She threw me, but we fucked up, Josie, and we need to fix it before we meet with Dale Cinclair. He obviously gave Max the assignment, and dismissing her wasn't the smart play."

"Dismissing the bartender wasn't a smart play?" Josie snorted and stared at her like she was crazy.

She loved Josie like a sister but she could be a snob at times. "Did she look like a bartender to you?" She turned around and headed back. "I'll meet you at the hotel later."

"You want me to come with you? I can do apologies."

"That's okay—go have lunch, and I'll take care of this."

There were a few people sitting in Cinclair Distillers' outer office when Hayley was allowed back upstairs, and she recognized them as more competition. The man and woman from a smaller firm were both wearing jeans with white shirts and jackets. It summed up their firm's appeal to the trendy and more casual approach to the business, and totally not what Cinclair needed.

Roger opened the door fifteen minutes later and raised his eyebrows slightly at the sight of her. "Ms. Wyatt, I'll be with you in a moment."

The door closed again, and she released a long breath, glad he hadn't smirked and kicked her out. Seeing Max behind that big desk had been a total shock. Not that she wouldn't have been happy with her as just a bartender—at least that's what she'd told herself forever. She'd wanted to live up to what her parents wanted of her, expected, really, but she'd had no idea she'd have to sacrifice so much.

From Max's expression and aloofness, there was no going back, but seeing her made her want that not to be true. That had been plain to her when she'd seen Max the night before. The sight of her had fueled her dreams last night, but Max was always right out of reach. The main problem was Max really had set the bar when it came to anyone who'd come after her.

That was something someone should've told her before she'd run like a coward, but in truth, it was something she should've gotten over way before now. Max's ghost had haunted her life from the day she'd packed up and gone home, and this trip had raised that specter from the grave of her past, and nothing short of driving a stake through her heart was erasing Max from her head.

"Thank you all for coming," Roger said as he bid the other team good-bye. He waited until they were gone before he glanced her way. "What can I do for you, Ms. Wyatt?"

"I need five minutes with Max." She knew the way he was staring and the way he drew his shoulders back meant the *no* was on his lips. "Believe me, all I want to do is apologize. My colleague was way out of line."

"Let me check, but she's already running late for a meeting with Mr. Cinclair."

"Dale Cinclair?" She regretted saying the name the second it came out.

Roger shook his head in obvious disapproval. "Actually Carter Cinclair, and the old man doesn't like to be kept waiting."

She nodded and wished there'd been more information about this company available, but it seemed like they wanted the public to concentrate on the product and not the family. She wasn't lying when she'd told Josie the only Cinclair mentioned in the company materials was Dale, so Carter was another mystery.

"I'm sorry, Ms. Wyatt, Preston has left the building."

"Her and Elvis, I guess, and I'm sure she'll be as hard to find." She shook Roger's hand again and smiled. "Thank you for asking, I appreciate your trying, and I hope I didn't put you out."

"Preston isn't someone who puts people out unless it's rightfully deserved." He pressed his hands together as he said it, projecting an uptight and scolding posture, but his face was warm and open. "You'll have a chance tomorrow night, but if you'll excuse me, I have plenty to do before then."

"Thank you again, and I'll see you tomorrow night." She walked back outside but headed to On the Rocks instead of the hotel. It was time to remember and own up to all her mistakes. The expression on Max's face was right there, plain and real. Whatever they'd had was gone and buried so deep there was no resurrecting it. She couldn't go back, and there wasn't a chance of getting back in. "Oh my God, Max, I'm so sorry."

Nine Years Ago

"Sorry, sorry, I'll be right there," Hayley said, hopping on one foot toward the door, trying to get her heel on. This was her fifth date with Max, and Max wanted a change from their usual casual outings.

She opened the door to Max wearing a summer linen suit with a blue bow tie with pink flamingos on it. The white shirt set off her tan and those eyes Hayley often dreamed about. Max Cinclair was the whole sexy package and everything she wanted in a woman, and she couldn't get enough of her.

"Would it be rude to say you look good enough to eat?" Max asked as her eyes slowly roamed her body, and Hayley felt as if Max had caressed everywhere she wanted those strong hands to touch.

"Only if you don't mean it." She grabbed Max by the lapels and dragged her into the apartment. "Do you mean it?"

Max kissed her hard with her hands on her hips holding her close enough that she could feel Max along the length of her. "Every word," Max said before kissing her again.

They hadn't slept together yet—well, that wasn't technically true. Max had invited her over to study, and they'd fallen asleep on the couch, but the lead-up to sex had been a slow and extremely torturous road that was mostly her fault.

It wasn't that she wasn't interested, but her mother's lecture about Wyatt women and how they were supposed to act was hard to overcome. The good thing about the courting process, as Max referred to it, was that Max seemed to have been raised by someone similar to Lily Wyatt. Until tonight, whenever they got too worked up, Max took a stroll around whatever block they were on to calm down, but she was too polite to complain.

"You look beautiful." Max spoke softly right into her ear and it made her shiver. Max was the first person who had that effect on her—not that she had a lot of experience, but she craved Max like addicts craved booze and drugs.

"Too much?" She took a step back so Max could look at her again, but kept hold of Max's hands. This was the first time she'd gotten really dressed up in a while, but it'd been fun shopping for their night out.

"You're perfect." Max always sounded so sincere. "Now put these in some water and let me take you to dinner. We have to celebrate those perfect economics test scores."

They left the apartment, and it took some maneuvering for her to get in the old Jeep without flashing Max before she was ready to do so. The drive to Blanchard's didn't take long, since it was less than two miles from her place. Their destination surprised her. She'd been wanting to go but didn't want Max to be this extravagant.

"Welcome back, Ms. Cinclair," the hostess said before Max gave her name, and the familiarity made Hayley relax. "We have your table ready."

"This is beautiful," she said as they sat in the corner. Of all the tables in the main dining room, theirs was the most secluded.

"You haven't been here before?"

"No, it's my first time."

Max ordered wine and lifted her glass once the waiter was done pouring. "To many more firsts, and the pleasure to enjoy them with you."

They had a wonderful meal, and Max took her to a jazz club after and danced with her, making the night even more perfect. When they got back to her apartment, Max lifted her out of the Jeep and held her hand as they went upstairs.

"Do you mind sitting for a minute?" She turned her back in silent request and held her breath as Max lowered the zipper. "I won't be long." Max kissed her before she walked away, then unbuttoned her cuffs when Hayley helped her off with her jacket.

"Take your time. I'm not in a rush."

Hopefully tonight you will be, Hayley thought as she stepped out of her dress in the bedroom and studied herself in the full-length mirror leaning against the wall. She'd gone shopping earlier in the week not only for the dress, but for the dark green bra and panties. Yes, she thought the color would look good with her hair, but the truth was she wanted Max to chew through the leash of her self-control. There'd be no more strolls to calm down tonight.

She put on a robe and left it hanging open, stopping to enjoy Max's expression when she walked back into the room. Knowing someone wanted you and seeing it so clearly on their face was an overwhelming experience, and she needed to have Max pressed up against her. The hunger in Max's eyes made her nipples so hard the silk of her bra was almost painful against them. She had to have her—there was no more waiting.

"My God," Max said as she walked slowly toward her. "You're so incredibly beautiful."

"You know what I've been thinking about for weeks now?" She shivered when Max pushed the robe off her shoulders and ran her fingertips lightly up her arms. The only way to stay on her feet was to take a breath and close her eyes for a moment to center herself.

"What's that?" Max lowered her head and kissed the side of her neck.

That was the thing about Max that made her wild. She was tall, strong, and solid, but she was incredibly soft and gentle when it came to her. "The first time I saw you walk into that classroom, you made me want you. It's all I've thought about and what made me chase you down."

"Why do you think I sat next to you?" Max lowered the straps of her bra and stopped briefly, as if letting her decide if she could keep going. "Seeing you on that barstool a few days later made me think I'm luckier than I have a right to be."

She let out a whoosh of air when Max placed her hands on her ass and picked her up so she could wrap her legs around her waist. Her center pressed into Max when she sat back down, making her so wet she wanted to rush. The only problem was Max acted like one of those infuriating people who carefully opened presents like they were determined not to tear the paper.

"You're all I've thought about from that first kiss, but I want so much more." Max kept her hands still as she spoke and encouraged Hayley to start unbuttoning her shirt. "You're making me as insane as you have from the second your lips touched mine."

"I want you crazy," Hayley said, aggravated that shirts had so many damn buttons. "That's what you do to me, and I want to know if you're as desperate to be naked as I am." She trapped Max when she pulled her shirt down but didn't leave Max enough room to take it off.

"I need to touch you, baby." Max leaned forward and kissed her until Hayley lifted her hands and threaded her fingers into Max's hair, holding her in place.

She wanted to celebrate the fact that Max sounded so undone and that she was the reason why, but she didn't want to wait anymore. Max gazed up at her, stood, and shrugged her shirt off before accepting Hayley's hand. She wanted to take her time and hoped Max didn't mind.

Her answer came when Max stood next to the bed and let her undress her. She touched Max's naked chest as her other hand went to Max's belt, and she smiled at how hard Max's nipples had gotten. The act of undoing Max's belt was her way of announcing her intentions, and Max stood there as Hayley unzipped her pants, letting them drop to the floor. Max Cinclair was incredibly gorgeous, but her body was enough to make you sweat.

The tight black boxers made Hayley's nostrils flare, and she stared before putting her fingertips into the waistband and drawing them down. It didn't take long for Max to kick her clothes aside, then wait for her to decide where they went next. Hayley wasn't a virgin, but she wasn't as experienced as most, and she didn't want to disappoint Max.

"We don't have to do this," Max said, clearly interpreting her hesitation for reluctance. "Don't think that you have to."

"I'm not reluctant, honey—I'm trying to decide where to start." She smiled at how sexy Max's laugh was. Before now, all this would've been was sex, but Max was fun, and this wouldn't simply be an act to satisfy a basic need.

"Take all the time you want, then. I'm all yours." The words rang true, and she had no doubt because Max was, above all things, honorable.

"Do you have any idea how crazy you make me?" She pushed Max onto her back and straddled her at the waist. "That first night you kissed me, I wanted you to touch me. I've never experienced that kind of overwhelming want in my life."

"I really want to touch you now." Max lifted her hands and started at her hips, sliding them up until Max reached her breasts.

Hayley sucked in a breath as the touch seemed to double the wetness between her legs. She needed Max to touch her, but not yet. She interlocked her fingers with Max's and lifted their hands over her head. The beautiful smile Max gave her lulled her long enough for Max to suck in the nipple closest to her mouth.

"Behave, baby." She said the words, but Max's mouth felt so good she had a hard time pulling away. "There are so many things I've been waiting to do to you."

"I can't help it." Max was six inches taller than her and a lot stronger, but she didn't break her hold. "You've been the subject of all my dreams from that first kiss."

"Such a sweet-talker." She leaned down and kissed Max, making it slow, and it seemed to torture Max as much as it did her. "I want you so much."

"I'm all yours, and the desire is mutual."

She knew that, but it was all she needed to hear to move down and suck Max's nipple until it pebbled against her tongue. The moan Max let out made her move to the other breast and let Max's hands go. Now was the time to tattoo herself on Max's heart and hopefully make herself unforgettable.

"Damn, you feel good." She started to move down, stopping when she straddled Max's leg, and Max flexed her thigh to press against her center. It was enough to make her want to not move from the spot, but she didn't want to get distracted. "Jesus, baby."

"You're so wet. I can feel it. Please let me touch you." Max ran her hands from her knee to her waist, and it spurred her to slide down farther and repeat the move on Max. She started at Max's knees and moved up until her hands landed between Max's legs. "Shit," Max said when Hayley spread her sex and stroked her clit with her thumb.

"Can I touch you?" She heard Max agree, and she lowered her head and flattened her tongue on Max's clit. It was hard and pulsing, and she smiled that it was her Max was this hot for.

Max's hand on her head urged her to stroke with her tongue before she sucked her in, and Max's hand tightened and fisted in her hair. "Fuck, that feels so good." Max sounded winded and desperate, and Hayley wanted to stop to enjoy how turned on Max was. "So fucking good."

She slowed her movements and almost laughed when she heard Max's groan of protest, but she'd waited too long to have it end so quickly. "Do you like this, honey?" She flicked Max's hard clit with the tip of her tongue.

"Are you teasing me?" Max lifted up on her elbows and looked down at her. There was nothing sexier to her than the way Max was staring at her right now. It was like Max's eyes broadcast the message *I know every one of your secrets, but you're safe with me, and your biggest secret is you want me to fuck you.*

That intensity in Max's expression undid her, and she lowered her head. This time she'd give Max what she wanted. "Shit," Max said, dropping back on the bed and putting her hand behind Hayley's head again. "That's good, baby, good."

Max's speech pattern had gotten simplistic, and Hayley figured that was a sign of approval. Max kept her hand on the back of her head and pumped up and into her mouth, only making grunting noises and breathing hard. Max's clit was hard against her tongue, and she tasted so fucking good. There weren't words enough in her vocabulary to describe how utterly exquisite this moment was.

She'd brought Max to the brink, and she hoped the act of loving her seared herself into Max's heart and onto her skin. "Oh fuck," Max said right before the muscles in her legs went rigid, and she bucked her hips two more times.

The moment was over, and she slowly lifted her mouth after kissing Max's sex one more time. It was only then that she became aware of how turned on she was and how she didn't want to wait anymore. She needed Max's hands on her, her fingers inside her, and her mouth where she'd never allowed anyone else.

Present Day

Max had done that and so much more before the night was done, and she'd been the one tattooed by Max's touch. She left a mark on Hayley that had never faded and reminded her often how lacking everyone who followed had been.

There wasn't anyone who'd come close. Granted, she'd had satisfying sex since Max, but no one came close to the connection they'd had. That sense of being claimed had left her wanting, and she'd tried to bury that need in work. She and Percy were equals in the firm, but she'd closed considerably more accounts than he had. It was the best way to stay sane.

"What can I get you?" The bartender dropped a coaster in front of her and waited with a slight smile on her lips.

"An old-fashioned, please."

"Do you have a preference on whiskey?"

"Cinclair's five-year-old single barrel, please." She might've walked away from Max, but not the advice she'd given her about alcohol.

"The lady knows her stuff."

Hayley smiled back and glanced at the woman's name tag. Portia was nice looking and started mixing the ingredients for her drink. She didn't have the flair Max had behind the bar, but only because she seemed young. "I learned from the best a long time ago, and it stuck."

"Where you from?" Portia added two dark cherries Hayley knew had been poached in Cinclair's whiskey.

"New York." She nodded when Portia placed her drink down and pushed it closer with her fingertip. "What's your take on Cinclair?"

Portia gazed at her as she cleaned the cocktail shaker she'd used.

"Overall, or in a you're a reporter and you're dying to know kind of way?"

"In a you're a bartender, and there's quite a few choices back there kind of way." She took a sip of the first old-fashioned she'd had in years. "What do you think people would need to know that would make Cinclair their first and only choice?"

"There are plenty of great choices when it comes to whiskey, ma'am—it's why we carry so many." Portia picked up the bottle she'd used to mix her drink and poured a finger in a glass. She took a moment before picking a different bottle and pouring another finger in a new glass. "See the color of the second one?"

"It's a little lighter." She rested her chin on her palm, really interested in this woman's take. Maybe it would give her a new idea for their presentation because now she was thinking their preliminary stuff was way off the mark.

"They're both aged the same amount of time, but Cinclair's is put in oak barrels that are smoked dry with a mix of woods that only the family knows. The char is what darkens the liquor and smooths out the flavor." Portia handed her the glass with Cinclair's in it and she took a sip. "And before the liquor makes it to that barrel? I can tell you exactly where every ingredient that it takes to make it is grown, and where the water comes out of the ground like it has for as long as the Cinclair family has owned the land."

"So it's the fact that you know where it comes from?" That would be the quickest way to lose a market audience.

"No, it's that I know the cornfields have been farmed by the Cinclair family for generations"—Portia held her index finger up—"that a Cinclair family member is the cooper who makes the barrels"—another finger went up—"and a Cinclair is the master distiller who guarantees it'll always taste like this."

"So it's the family?"

"It's a mixture of both. You can't have a glass of Cinclair's without all those ingredients plus the care that drives the process."

Hayley stared at Portia and finished the Cinclair glass, leaving the other one for Portia. "Cheers to your excellent salesmanship."

"My boss always says that to know where you're going, you have to remember where you've been." Portia put her glass in with the rest of her dirty dishes before reaching for the one Hayley had used. "I'm sure it's a famous quote, but in this business it makes sense."

"It's a good philosophy." She swallowed another sip of her drink and closed her eyes as the warmth spread across her chest. "Do you know the Cinclair family? You must, to have all this information on them."

The question made Portia's eyes narrow, and she lost her friendly open expression. "Everyone in town knows the Cinclairs if you're in the bar business. The whiskey's a local favorite, and the family comes by every so often."

"Sorry, I promise I'm not a reporter out to ruin their good name." She twirled the glass with her drink in it and liked the coldness against her fingers. "I was just curious."

"What are you after, then?" Portia sounded like a suspicious cop all of a sudden.

"I'm working on a project and wanted some insight. You have my word it's nothing bad." Great, with any luck Portia would give Max a call right after she left. Or was it Preston now?

"Let me know if you need anything else." Portia nodded to the other bartender before disappearing into the back.

At least Portia didn't know who she was.

CHAPTER FIVE

"Who is she?" Preston asked. Portia's call had come just as she was packing to head out, but she stopped as Portia described Hayley, down to the tapered fingers. "And what kinds of questions?"

Portia gave her the rundown, and it sure sounded like research. "She's still out there drinking her old-fashioned if you want me to tell her anything like go to hell."

"Calm down, slugger, she's only an advertising rep trying to get into my head, or really, Dale's head. Put her drinks on my tab, and tell her to use Google like everyone else."

"You sure? She's hot."

"Hot things often burn, pumpkin." She closed her bag and got her keys out. "You need anything?"

"A raise and a new car."

"How about your allowance and a new bike?"

"I'd tell you kiss my ass, but you'd probably enjoy it."

She laughed before hanging up, anxious to get going. There was no fighting the urge to turn on the cross street that led to Bourbon Street and would take her right by the bar. Sure enough, there was Hayley. She'd picked the same drink, and sat on the same stool. The only difference was the stylish business suit and heels, and the massive amount of bad history between them.

Glancing up and seeing her in the office earlier had shocked her. Eight years was a long time to wait, and she'd planned her speech all that time, but the sight of Hayley had closed her throat and made the pain acutely real again. How love could make you hurt to the point you wanted to break made no sense to her. It was supposed to be love, for God's sake.

"I'm such an asshole." She turned toward Canal and headed for the road home. "That woman never gave you a second thought unless it was to laugh at your pathetic self with people like that condescending bitch Josie Simon." Her palm hurt from slamming it against the steering wheel, but she was aggravated with herself for giving Hayley the power to still upset her.

"Get over it—she sure as hell did."

She stopped at the second distillery and met with Pedro for their last preproduction meeting. He'd worked for Cinclair since he'd immigrated in the early sixties and spoke often of his job making Havana Club in Cuba. When she'd told him what she had in mind, his eyes had gotten teary.

"Are we ready?" she asked as she jotted a few notes.

"Taste this," Pedro said handing over a small glass.

The molasses she'd imported was excellent, and the dark amber color was what Pedro said held the secret of sugarcane. "It's better than you said, and hopefully our rum will be better than this." She handed over a bottle of Havana Club Añejo and kissed his cheek. "See you tomorrow, amigo."

She drove to their main facility next and started setting up for her grandfather and her parents in the tasting room. It was time to unveil the first addition to the Cinclair line in sixty years, and with any luck, her parents and Gramps would give her the go-ahead to enter it in competition.

"It can't be that bad that we have to drink to hear it," her mother said as she entered with her grandfather. "You okay, darling?"

"Despite what everyone says, I'm fine." She smiled as she arranged the glasses and placed four bottles next to them. "Dad's coming, right?"

"He's five minutes behind us," her grandfather said. "He said he needed a shower, but I didn't want to be late."

She shared a smile with her mother, knowing her grandfather was never going to change. Carter Cinclair was prompt and he expected it in others. "We need to narrow down the selection for next month from these three. Once we're all in agreement, I'll have the bottles prepared from the particular barrels. The blend is a no-brainer."

"How'd it go today?" Her father asked, kissing her mother on the lips, then kissing her and Gramps on the cheek.

"It was okay except for one team who can't work until they get an audience with you and kiss the ring." She shook her head in her mother's directions when she gave her a look. "Roger told them they'd get the chance tomorrow night."

"Did Roger not introduce you?" her grandfather asked, both his bushy white eyebrows raised. "The last name should've been a dead giveaway you might have something to do with the process and weren't some vagrant who'd wandered in off the street."

"It was the first name that was the problem, Gramps. It's not Dale."

Her dad chuckled. "Your mother wanted to do that to you." He pointed at her mother and smiled. "She tried to convince me Dale Preston Cinclair, Jr., had a nice ring to it."

"Thanks for holding firm, Pop. School would've been murder." She pulled a chair out for her mother, glad to end her day with her family. Her parents and grandparents had helped her heal her broken heart and find her stride again when her confidence had been rocked. "This tasting, though, will hopefully not be."

"Let's start with the single barrels first before you tell me what's in that pretty box." Gramps sat and placed his cane on the end of the table.

"It's a surprise, so patience." She was about to tease some more but glanced at the door when it opened.

"Sorry, I know you didn't want to be disturbed, but you have a visitor and she's pretty persistent." The receptionist appeared apologetic, so whoever she was announcing must've been fairly persuasive.

"Who is it?" her mother asked.

"Hayley Wyatt, and she needs five minutes with Preston."

"Preston doesn't have five minutes to give her," Preston said. "Have her go through Roger."

"Actually"—her mother said with her hand up—"have her join us. We might need a tiebreaker."

"Mom," she said with a warning tone. Her father and grandfather didn't know the whole story, but her mother did. "That's not a good idea."

"You never know. Anything that might lead to answers is never a bad idea."

Hayley came into the room and stopped as if not expecting three other people. She'd changed out of the business suit into jeans and a V-neck sweater, sending Preston's brain back to Tulane's campus. If there was one thing Hayley Wyatt did well, it was fill out a pair of jeans. The thought was probably sexist, but it didn't make it any less true, and the horndog in her sat up, panted, and took note.

"I'm sorry," Hayley said holding her hands pressed together. "I don't want to interrupt, and I don't mind waiting."

"Nonsense, Ms. Wyatt," her mother said, waving Hayley closer. "You're someone I've been wanting to meet."

"Mom," Preston said in a low voice.

"I'm Hayley Wyatt." Hayley held a hand out and smiled. "Pleased to meet you."

"Sienna Cinclair," her mother said cordially. "This is my husband Dale, and his father Carter. I believe you already know Preston."

Hayley repeated her handshake with Preston's father and grandfather, then said to Preston, "I really don't mind waiting until you're done." Hayley dropped her hand when Preston didn't take it.

"Have a seat, Ms. Wyatt." The last thing she needed was a scene or a lecture from her mother if she physically flung Hayley out the door. "It's not every day you get to do a tasting with the guys who actually make the samples."

She set out another set of glasses along with the club soda they sipped between tastings. The first sample was the only one moved from the middle of their oldest rickhouse, while the other two had spent their entire five years undisturbed on the main floor of the fifteen-floor warehouse.

"The first one started on seven for three years, then was moved to fifteen for the last two years," she said, pouring an inch into each glass. She and her family each lifted a crystal glass, and they held them to light.

"What does that mean?" Hayley asked, holding her glass up too, even though she probably had no idea why she had to or what she was looking for.

"We store our products in insulated warehouses called rickhouses where the inside temperature stays a fairly consistent sixty-five degrees without air-conditioning. Even with those cool temps, heat rises, and the barrels at the top mature faster." She held her glass up and smiled at the perfect amber color. "The char on the barrels accounts for the color, as well as acting as a natural filter that finishes the process of making good whiskey."

"Okay, thank you. I researched the steps, but this makes it clear."

She poured the next one, and to her experienced eye it was slightly darker. "This matured more slowly, never leaving the first floor." They each took a sip and held it for a note before swallowing. To a Cinclair, spitting out whiskey, even during a tasting, was considered a sin. "One more, then we vote."

"What are you looking for exactly?" Hayley seemed genuinely interested, but Preston didn't want her here, much less have to answer questions.

"Overall, a good whiskey is first pleasing to the eye." She held her glass up and studied the amber color. "Darker colors come from age and the quality of the barrel and the char." She lowered the glass to her nose. "Like wine, every whiskey has an aroma. For the sake of time and so as not to bore you, the aroma should be nice." She took a sip of the last one she'd poured before going back to the second one. "Lastly it should not only taste good, but consistently good."

"What's that mean?" Hayley was full of questions, and Preston noticed her family's silence and curious stares.

She poured water in a glass with the blended whiskey and poured another glass straight. "The flavor has to please straight out of the bottle and stand up to a mix, as well. Its uniqueness has to shine through no matter how you enjoy it."

"Thank you," Hayley said, trying the glass with water last.

"What's in the fancy box, kiddo?" Her grandfather was patient but only to a point.

"I know what our market is, and the Cinclair label will always be the leader as a gentleman's whiskey in a common man's price range." She placed her hands on the box, trying to ignore that Hayley was hanging on her words as intently as her family was.

"If you messed with the tried and true, you better have knocked it out of the park," Gramps said, and her father nodded. The tried and true was sacrosanct, and from her father's and grandfather's expressions, messing with it was akin to changing her name and becoming a teetotaler.

"I messed with the formula a little, filtered it ten times with four different charcoals, and had Herman add pecan to the char as well as four slats to the barrels." Her grandfather shook his head, and she could guess it was from his frustration with the change. Gramps wasn't rigid about anything except when it came to the Cinclair formula.

"Pecans are for waffles and cakes, kiddo," her grandfather said, proving her right about her guess.

"Too much and I agree. Sweet isn't my thing either, but a little is transformative." She opened the box and remove the bottle that was distinctly different from Cinclair's iconic look.

"Transformative how?" her father asked.

"For one, it puts us in the hundred fifty range, and it opens new markets." She glanced at Hayley, not wanting to admit this in front of her. "Especially with the right marketing campaign."

"What's the transformative drink called?" her mother asked.

She unlocked the cabinet against the wall and removed the glasses with the *C* etched in them. They were over two hundred years old and had been present at a lot of firsts. It wasn't necessary to use them, but she wanted to emphasize the name she'd chosen for the new whiskey.

"The Cinclair success comes from consistency—that's the driving force behind what every generation believes and follows without question."

"What's that, kid?" her grandfather asked.

"Tradition, sir—tradition." She poured everyone a drink and held up her own. "I give you Traditions by Cinclair."

None of them bothered with color or aroma and immediately tasted it. It was everything she'd hope it'd be, and she wondered if the subsequent batches would be as good without the pain that had driven her to make it. Hanging on to the hurt now would make her feel foolish, considering Hayley appeared unscathed. It was time to let go.

"Goddamn." Her grandfather took another sip. "You're a damn fine addition to the Cinclairs, kid, but tell me now if you have any more surprises for me. I'm an old man, and all this hoopla can be deadly."

"You're still going to be giving me shit when I'm your age, Gramps, so cut the bull and tell me if you like it."

"I don't like it, I love it, and if it meets the criteria, you should enter it. At least, I'm thinking that's what you want to do by unveiling it today." He poured himself a little more after giving her a bear hug.

"I do want to enter it, but only with your blessing."

Her grandfather hugged her again. "That you have."

"Aside from the blend, which we enter every year"—she placed her hands on the second and third bottles—"which one?"

"What's your preference?" her mother asked.

"The blend, the second bottle, and Traditions."

"It's unanimous then," her father said. "I'm damn proud of you, Preston. This is excellent, but don't rest on your laurels. We expect more good things from you."

"Thanks, and you know me, I'll never stop experimenting." She capped the bottle of Traditions, placed it in the box she'd made herself, and handed it to her father. He had overseen Cinclair's massive expansion overseas, so his experimentation in the distillery had been minor compared to hers. "I'll see you guys later, but I've got some work tonight."

"You sure you're okay, buddy?" her father asked.

"A few more minutes, then I'll head back to the office. I might stay downtown, so you guys don't worry." She kissed her mom and dad, liking the longer hugs they gave.

"You're a good kid and an even better distiller. Hell, you passed me up a long time ago. This really was spectacular," her father said, holding the box like a treasure he wasn't willing to part with.

"Thanks, Pop, and let one of the guys drop you at home."

She saw them out before going back, washing the Cinclair glasses herself, and putting them away. Those she didn't trust to anyone, and Hayley sat quietly until she was done.

"Did you need something?" She turned and finished drying her hands. "You've met Dale, so you should be good to go. Though you should've asked him more questions if meeting him was the holdup to working on this project."

"Dale's your father, right?" Hayley cocked her head slightly.

"Yes, he is." If Preston had to guess, the inference of Hayley's question would be the first step in accusing her of lying when they'd met.

"I thought you weren't one of those Cinclairs?" Hayley asked.

Preston sighed. Guessed it in one. "My omission," she said, pointing at Hayley, "was probably for the same reason you didn't mention Major Wyatt is your father. I wanted to be judged on my own merits, not what my future held."

"You're right. Accusing you of anything would be hypocritical of me, and I'm sorry about Josie today." Hayley pressed her hands together as if in prayer and held them close to her chest. She was acting like she didn't know what to do with herself, and that was a real change from when they'd met. "She was way out of line."

"I'm sure she had her reasons, and if that's the only reason you're here, apology accepted. You didn't need to drive out here to tell me that." She turned and locked the cabinet with the glasses and wanted nothing more than to get out of there.

"Do you think we can talk?" The hopeful expression on Hayley's face was hard to ignore, but that's exactly what she was planning to do. "Look, I realize you hate me because of what I did, and I'm eight years too late, but—"

"I don't hate you," she said, needing to stop this before it devolved into the kind of scene she avoided like the plague. "Hate is as strong an emotion as love, and both require that you care."

"Ah, I see." Hayley closed her eyes and sighed. "I'm sorry I bothered you, but thank you for letting me stay for the tasting. Your new product was wonderful."

Hayley walked out after her emotion-fueled apology and Preston was aggravated that she couldn't dredge up the ability to shake it off as bullshit. There'd be no way to predict how much Hayley would affect her until she'd laid eyes on her again, and affect her she had. "Goddammit."

She finished her notes and locked the doors, using work like she always did, to forget all the stuff she wanted to wipe from her memory. It was dark outside, and her car was the only one left in the dimly lit lot, but she stopped and sighed when she heard something. The sound of crying stopped her, and she let her head drop.

"Goddammit."

"Goddammit to hell." Hayley wiped her face, knowing this wasn't the time and certainly not the place to render out eight years of suppressed emotions. If Percy and her father had somehow known what she'd be walking into, there'd be hell to pay.

"Where's your car?" Max asked, stopping fifteen feet from her as if she had the flu and was contagious.

"I Ubered." She grimaced at the smeared mascara and makeup on her fingertips. Her face must be a wreck. "It's okay, I'll be fine, and hopefully it's okay to sit and wait."

"Have you called for a ride?"

She stared at Max and wished there was more light. The years had been kind, and even though it seemed impossible, Max was even better looking than before. She had more muscle and her hair was shorter, giving her a more mature appearance. What would it be like to be held in Max's arms now?

"I will," she said and wished Max would come closer. "I was enjoying the quiet and your beautiful landscaping. Please, I don't want to hold you up."

"I'm headed back into the city if you'd like a ride." The offer was made and Max didn't wait for an answer, walking away and standing by her car.

"You've upgraded from the Jeep, I see." She was a tad out of breath from the jog to catch up. It would be at least twenty minutes into the city, and her only opportunity to get Max alone.

"Where are you staying?"

"The Piquant, and thank you." There would be no small talk in her future, but that wasn't much different than the Max she knew.

They rode in silence along River Road, and from the direction they were headed, it seemed Max was going to take the winding route all the way into town. Twenty minutes just became forty. Maybe Max's *head* was pissed at her, but her heart still remembered how good they were together. Like those times they'd ridden out here and picnicked along a secluded bayou.

"You have to know how sorry I am."

"How exactly would I know that?" Max tightened her hands on the steering wheel but kept her eyes on the road. "I left your place one morning for an early shift at the bar, and that was it. You kissed me, said you loved me, and dropped off the planet."

"I was wrong, Max, but I thought leaving would be the easiest way for us to get on with our lives." She wiped her face impatiently, not wanting Max to see how upset she was. "You never seemed like you could make a life anywhere but here, and my life was in New York. Maybe I couldn't stand the thought of you choosing this over me."

"That's the biggest load of bullshit I've ever heard," Max yelled, loud enough to make her lean away from her. "Stop lying to me, and more importantly, to yourself."

"What do you mean?"

"You left because I didn't fit into your world, Hayley. There was nothing in this world that would've prompted you to bring a bartender home to Daddy." Max wasn't yelling any longer, but the disgust in her voice was the kiss of death. "I was fun during college, but once it was over, you were done slumming."

"That wasn't it and you know it." Shit, Percy and Josie were right. She should've dealt with this way before now. "You better than anyone know what family expectations are about. To turn away from everything expected of you isn't in your nature any more than it was mine."

Max stayed quiet for a long while before she sighed loudly. "You're right about that, and nothing will be gained by dredging up all of this, so forget it. Concentrate on your job, and that's all we both need to do."

"Do you want me to go? We can drop out of the process, or I can have my brother Percy take my place if you don't want to work with me."

"We're adults, Hayley." Max quickly glanced at her, then back to the road. "Adults who knew each other once upon a time, but who can probably set all that aside and work together."

"I always wondered why you never took me home." She spoke softly and Max laughed.

"Probably for the same reason you never invited me along when your family came to visit." They'd reached the city limits, and Max turned into Uptown. There was time but not much. "Let it go, Hayley. We're different people now, and there's no going back."

"How can you be so sure?"

The stoplight allowed Max to really look at her. "Because your friend Josie had no problem dismissing me. Dealing with the bartender was beneath her. You two probably had a good laugh over the mutt you lavished a little attention on, then tossed aside like old shoes when you were done."

"It's been eight years, Max, but you can't have forgotten exactly who I am. I'm an idiot, but I'm not cruel."

The leather of the steering wheel creaked from the pressure of Max's grip. "Just because you say something over and over doesn't make it true even if you've convinced yourself otherwise."

"But—"

Max held up a finger. "Concentrate on work, and do what you do best."

"What?" she asked as Max made the light to turn onto Canal Street downtown.

"Disappear, only this time I won't waste my time wondering what I did wrong, or worrying something happened to you." Max stopped in front of the Piquant and took a deep breath. "I understand now why you left, but how you did it was really shitty."

"I'm sorry."

"Sure," Max said as if placating her. "If you don't mind, I have to get going."

The car sped away as soon as she closed the passenger-side door, and the pain in her chest made her breathe faster. How in the world had she fooled herself all this time that this didn't matter? Max wasn't at all a crush she'd had in college who could be tossed aside like obsolete textbooks.

She turned when someone put their arm around her shoulder, and she went from frightened to total wreck when she saw it was Josie. The tears she'd thought long over came out in sobs that she couldn't hold in any longer. Why the hell had she not been smarter than this?

Josie didn't let her go but led her inside to the elevators, and she followed, not wanting to cause a scene on top of everything else. They sat on the sofa in the living area of their suite, and Josie waited until her emotional outburst calmed to hiccups and residual tears.

"Drink this." Josie handed her a glass of something and helped wipe her face with a tissue.

The slow burn of the whiskey made her take a breath and release it slowly. "Thanks." She finished the drink and fell back against the cushions. "It's been a hell of a day."

"Can you tell me where you've been? I was about to organize a search party." Josie handed her a few more tissues and waited. Hayley had enough experience with Josie's expressions to know she wasn't happy with her at the moment.

"I went back to try to apologize, but Roger ran interference until Max left the building."

"Of course he did." Josie rolled her eyes and frowned. "Asshole."

"We've all been there, and our assistants have done the same." She had a need to defend Roger, considering none of this was his fault. "After that, I went back to the bar and had a drink and some conversation with the bartender."

"Not *the* bartender, right?"

"Her name was Portia and she was *the* bartender." Despite her funk, Josie had a way of making her smile. "I asked enough questions about the Cinclair line that I'm sure she called Max and ratted me out."

"There's a lot of assholes in Max's orbit."

"I'm sure she sees it as loyalty." She blew her nose, and the action made her headache worse. "The girl who took her place told me I should take the distillery tour if I was so interested, and that gave me an idea."

"What's that? To run away from home and not tell anyone?"

"No, and I'm sorry, I should've called, but I did find the whole Cinclair family."

"Including Dale?"

She nodded. "Dale, his wife Sienna, father Carter, and his daughter."

"No shit. Were they nice? Did he give you any insight on this pitch? Wait, who's the daughter?"

"No shit, they were, they have a new high-end whiskey they want to debut, and Dale's daughter is Preston Cinclair." She almost laughed as Josie nodded along until the last bit, and then her eyes got comically wide.

"Should we pack now, so Major and my father can fire me in person?"

"It wasn't like that, and they let me stay for the unveiling of Traditions. That's the new whiskey Max came up with. After that, she gave me a ride home."

"Really? Honey, that's great. Did you get a chance to talk?"

She shook her head and started crying again. It was ridiculous to lose control like this, but the reality of the situation hit her like a brick to the face. It'd been obvious, and it hurt like shit.

"She's…she's…" She took a deep breath and forced the words out. "She's the love of my life."

"I know, honey, and admitting it is the first step to recovery."

"What do you mean?" The damn hiccups were back.

"The more you try and run from the truth, the more miserable you make yourself."

❖

"That's where you're wrong. I'm not miserable," Preston said with as much indignation as she could get away with and not be accused of being bitchy.

"Repeating that line over and over isn't going to convince me," Roger said as the waiter came out with their salads. "It's the fourth time you said it, and I still don't believe you."

"I don't care if you believe me, and if you told her where I was, I'm firing you." She stabbed the romaine lettuce like it'd come alive and attempted to kill her. "Hayley Wyatt can go to hell and take that superior-acting bitch with her. As a matter of fact, you can call them right now and tell them the only way they're getting this contract is if I'm in a coma or dead."

"You need to calm down and eat your salad—believe me, you need the roughage. If you want them gone, I'll give you the number, and you can call yourself. I'm not doing it." Roger ate like he was dining with the queen and would be judged on his table manners. "You also need to grow up and take a few deep breaths."

"Are you kidding me?" She stared at him with her fork in the stabbing position. The only thing that kept her from jabbing holes in him was he was so damn dainty.

"I'm not kidding. Learn to practice a little patience."

"Uh…" She sputtered, not able to articulate the rest of any kind of objection.

"Preston, don't deny you're acting like a two-year-old who hasn't learned the concept of forgiveness." Roger wiped one side of his mouth gently before he moved to the other side, then lifted his hand. "I realize what happened was in no way cool, but it's time to gear up and cut bait."

"Gear up and cut bait? What the hell you talking about? That makes absolutely no sense." She put her fork down as a way of fighting the urge to scar Roger with it. The plan to work late was sounding better and better.

"Whatever the expression, it doesn't matter," Roger said, pushing his plate aside. "You need to make a decision here, and there's only two viable options."

She sat back with her glass of wine and waved her hand at him. "Go ahead, I'm sure you're dying to tell me."

"Either hear her out and kiss her, then tell her you still love her, or hear her out and keep lying to yourself. If you go with option two, I want a raise for having to put up with crabby Preston for the rest of my life."

"Are you forgetting I'm not the one who skulked out of town? And I'm not the idiot who's going to allow someone to shred me one more time." She remembered Hayley's tears earlier and tried to drive those thoughts off a steep cliff where they'd die a fiery death, hopefully wiping them from her head. "Drop it," she said when he started to say something else.

"You do you, my friend." Roger took a small sip of his drink and sighed. "I'm going to love you no matter what, but if you're cruel, I might be a tad bit pissed."

"I have no intention of being cruel but also don't want to revisit things that are dead subjects."

"Okay," Roger said, rolling his eyes. "I'm beginning to question all the stories about the gigantic fish you've caught in the past."

"Have you lost touch with reality?" She wasn't happy with the conversation, but she'd been able to keep up until that last part. "What does fishing have to do with anything?"

"Well…" He tapped his index finger against the cleft in his chin. "If you're able to lie about dead subjects that are in no way dead, then you must be lying about the fish."

"You're a riot and why we're friends is the real mystery." The waiter cleared the table, and it took a few minutes for their steaks to come out. "I admit I sound immature, but she hurt me enough that it left a scar."

"I know that, but sometimes the only way to heal is to allow yourself the one thing that'll make your heart truly happy even if it goes against your nature." Roger placed a hand on his chest and gazed at her with an unreadable expression. "It's taking a big chance, but that's who you are."

"I can't, but I'll think about it. That's the best I got." She started her meal, and thankfully Roger dropped the subject and talked about the new whiskey instead.

She'd walked to the restaurant and declined Rogers's offer of a ride when they finished, and headed back on foot. The night was another frosty one, and she surprised herself by passing Royal and ending up at the Piquant. She followed some guests through the back entrance and headed through the bar to the house phone at the front desk.

"Hayley Wyatt, please," she requested of the operator. This was a horrible idea, but all the crap Roger had laid on her would be mild compared to what she anticipated from her mother, so it was time to act like she was the reasonable one.

"Hello."

"May I speak to Hayley?"

"Sure, who's calling?" Josie sounded like a great geek gatekeeper. "Hello?" Josie said when she hesitated too long.

"Preston Cinclair."

"Haven't you done enough damage for one night? Only an asshole would pile on now."

"I'd like Hayley to decide that, so put her on the damn phone."

"No, I think I'm going to decide this time. You already hurt her today, and if me calling you an asshole costs us your business, tough shit."

The line went dead, and all she could do was stare at the receiver in disbelief. "I'm the immature one, Roger? Seriously?"

"Did you need anything, Ms. Cinclair?" one of the front desk personnel asked.

"No, thank you." She placed the receiver down slowly and turned to leave.

The band was playing, and there were a few couples on the dance floor, so she sat at the bar and ordered a drink. How her life that had been on solid ground two days ago had been completely upended was something she'd have to weather, but not until Hayley was gone.

"Hey, I took the chance you were still down here," Hayley said, startling her into turning around. "I'm sorry about Josie, but she doesn't speak for me."

"I doubt she knows that." She put a twenty on the bar and pointed to the back entrance. "Would you like to take a walk?" Hayley's swollen and red eyes were hard to miss and made her realize she'd never before seen Hayley cry. In their year together there'd never been anything that had caused tears.

"I'd like that."

They walked in silence, and the most private place she could think to go was Cinclair's. Hayley didn't object. She opened the door to her office and allowed Hayley to take a seat in one of the club chairs she usually used to read.

"Would you like something to drink?"

Hayley shook her head, and she sat on the edge of her seat. "No, but thank you for calling me. Seeing you in here today sort of short-circuited my brain, but I'm not upset. It's given me the chance to really apologize."

"You know, it shouldn't matter. It was a long time ago, but it wasn't until I saw you that I realized I'm still mad at you." She rubbed her face with both hands before combing her hair back. "All I need is the why."

"I've been groomed all my life, along with my twin brother Percy, to take over for my father eventually." Hayley spoke softly and appeared ready to cry again. "You weren't planned, but it didn't take you long to completely overwhelm me."

"Obviously not that much." It was beneath her to be petty, but what the hell.

"You don't have to believe me, but it's true. It didn't really hit me until a month before graduation."

She put her hand up to stop Hayley. "Believe me, I understand that. My upbringing wasn't any different, when it came to my future. That doesn't explain why you left without a word. I've spun some scenarios over the years, but none of them make sense."

"I regret that. If I didn't, I'd be married with a couple of kids by now. You scared the hell out of me, Max, and I didn't know how else to handle you except to bury everything I felt for you and leave because I wasn't strong enough to stay." Hayley's tears finally fell, and she appeared completely miserable. "I wasn't brave enough to admit my feelings for you and what I wanted for my future, but it wasn't because I didn't love you." She shook her head in disbelief, and Hayley seemed to panic. "I loved you, Max, never doubt that, even if I was a total asshole."

"There's nothing we can do about it now, but I appreciate you telling me." Cowardice wasn't the best answer, but it beat *I don't give a damn.* "Let me walk you back and I'll see you tomorrow."

"Are you sure you still want us to present something?"

"Your friend is obnoxious, but I understand where she's coming from. It's good to have someone who's so loyal." She stood up and waited for Hayley to join her. "Roger's sending a car, so don't worry about tomorrow night."

Hayley wiped her face before she stood and her sadness seem to radiate off her like a blistering sun. It was hard to ignore and why she couldn't move when Hayley stepped closer and placed her hands on her chest and gazed up at her. This her heart remembered, and she ached from keeping her arms at her sides. Her natural urge to lift her hands and rest them on Hayley's hips was hard to fight.

"Please tell me you don't hate me."

"I don't, and I don't need your apology. Somewhere along the way I could've looked you up and gotten my answers, but I didn't." She gently wrapped her fingers around Hayley's wrists and lowered her hands. "Maybe you were right, and this is the ending we need before heading in very different directions."

"So don't dwell on the what-ifs?" Hayley's smile in no way projected joy.

"I'm sure your what-ifs revolve around a simple life with me if you'd stayed. Bartenders seldom grow up to be successful, do they?"

"Max, if all you'd ever been was a bartender, I would've been happy, don't doubt that. My leaving had nothing to do with finding you lacking, and everything to do with my fear of disappointing my family."

She watched Hayley walk out and close the door behind her, as a hint that Hayley didn't need her to follow. Whatever anger she had left disappeared when the door clicked closed, and she cocked her head back and stared at the ceiling. Why in the world was this happening to her now?

"I'm a good person, aren't I?" She spoke out loud to the empty room and figured if karma was a woman, she was laughing her ass off right now.

CHAPTER SIX

Of course you are, but bad shit happens to good people all the time. It's the universe's way of getting its kicks," Josie said as she slipped her feet into some boots. "My theory is the universe is a fastidious little dweeb who has to be celibate for some reason and, because of the unfairness of it, rains misery down upon us by the bucketful."

"Is there a moral to this story?" Hayley decided on jeans and boots, knowing the distillery facility was no place for a business suit. "Because your theory is depressing as hell."

"My thoughts are you get screwed whether you're good or bad, and if that's true, you might as well have a good time. That usually revolves around being bad." Josie threw on a sweater and a lightweight coat and faced her. "Food for thought—that's all."

"The inside of your brain must be a fascinating place." She grabbed her bag and a leather journal before ushering them out.

"You have no idea." Josie put her hand on Hayley's elbow and kissed the side of her head. "Now tell me what happened last night."

"We cleared the air and she *somewhat* accepted my apology. She also thinks you're a good friend." She was trying to best project happiness when she felt anything but, and was probably failing miserably, but there was no time for the breakdown she was owed.

"Really?" Josie bumped hips with her. "I would've guessed obnoxious, but Max doesn't strike me as the overly intelligent type."

"Why do you say that?"

"She hasn't figured out you're in love with her, so dense, really."

"She's right about the friend part." They stepped outside and

Hayley was surprised to find Roger. "Mr. Savoy, it's nice to see you again."

"Please, Ms. Wyatt, call me Roger." He opened the back door of the black SUV with the Cinclair name on the door. "Are you ready?"

"Thank you, but we were expecting your boss," Josie said, then hissed when Hayley pinched her side.

"We appreciate your coming for us." She spoke quickly to prevent Roger from thinking of a comeback.

The driver merged into traffic and they all stayed quiet until they hit the interstate. "Do you have any questions that Portia didn't answer?" Roger asked.

She laughed. Of course Portia ratted her out. "It wasn't personal, and she answered everything I needed about the product. Selling something is best done by telling a story. Cinclair needs to tell the family's story. It's a fascinating legacy, I'm sure."

Roger nodded and glanced back at her. "The Cinclairs are private people. Their inner circle is small, but the two of you should understand that."

"Why would you think that?" Josie asked.

"Money, vast amounts of it, makes it hard to trust." Roger didn't scream butch, but he was tough. "You, though, Ms. Wyatt, I've been curious about for a long time."

She locked eyes with him, trying to sense if this was a test or not. "Why's that?" If it was a test, she didn't care. No matter what happened, she was going to lose big even if Max dropped the account in their laps.

"It's nothing important." He turned back to the front, and from his profile, she could see he'd closed his eyes.

"No hints?" Max had to have said something about her, and the three-year-old still alive in her brain wanted to know what Roger meant.

"I'm sure you remember your college days better than anyone." He didn't open his eyes, and if he was goading her, it was working. "Preston wasn't expecting you, but I'm glad to finally put a face to the woman she's mentioned a few times."

"I'm not leaving if that's what you're hinting about."

"Good. Try to stick it out this time. If not, what's the point of all this?"

She glanced at Josie and she only shrugged. They were all quiet after that, and she stared out the window, trying to see if she recognized anything. It'd been dark the night before, so she'd concentrated more on what she was going to say than staring at the landscape. The wooded areas they were driving through made it easy to imagine how much Max must've loved growing up here. She'd never been an outdoorsy person, but back then, Max had changed her mind about that just by holding up two airline tickets.

"I should've figured it out then," she whispered as she remembered.

"You should've figured what?" Josie asked in a whisper when she moved closer to her.

"This is as far out of the city as you can get, and she must love it here." She smiled at all the sex they'd had outdoors around here and on that trip. "She used to call me a city girl, and I'm sure she still sees me that way. I might've been an asshole, but maybe it was a good thing I set her free. She'd have been miserable in the city."

"It doesn't matter what Max thinks, honey," Josie said, taking her hand. "All you need to ask yourself is if you'd be happy here. You are a city girl, but you're also in love. Is that enough to consider that Hallmark movie scenario we talked about?"

"I'll have you know that I went fishing in Alaska and cooked over a campfire." She wiggled her eyebrows at Josie and smiled. "And believe me, I cooked up more than fish."

"You never told me that." Josie laughed and so did Roger. Obviously their whispers weren't all that low. "You got naked outside?"

"That's none of your business, but yes." That sense of freedom and fun had been missing for way too long. Everything about her year with Max had been new and exciting. It was all so different than what she'd grown up with, and she missed that version of herself.

Yes, sir, Max taught her a lot of things in that year, but one of the most important was that it was her right to ask for what she wanted. That was one of the best memories of that long weekend, but the amount of great sex they'd had still made her shiver.

"You okay?" Josie asked as the car stopped. "I'm sure Roger will let us hide in here if you need to talk about something."

"I'm okay, just thinking." She stepped out when Roger opened the door, and she stared at a smiling Max standing at the entrance of the main building. Her jeans, navy sweater, and hiking boots reminded her of the younger Max who carried her books to class.

"Stop whatever it is you're thinking, because you're blushing," Josie whispered as they started walking. "Though, now that I've seen her, I'll have a hard time not picturing her standing in the wild, naked."

"Let's not make this harder than it has to be." She pressed her hands to her cheeks, and she couldn't be sure, but she thought Max's smile had gotten wider. "So behave."

❖

"When have I ever misbehaved?" Max asked through gritted teeth when her mother issued the warning.

"We don't have the kind of time for me to go through my list. Maybe later." Her mother smiled and stepped forward. "Welcome, everyone. I'll be leading one group on the tour, and Preston will take the rest of you," she said after introducing herself.

When the first group followed her mother, her group consisted of Hayley and Josie. "Are you ready?" She and her mother would have to have a long talk later about ambushes and inappropriate behavior.

"Roger," Josie said, and Max dropped her head until her chin rested on her chest, "I have a bunch of questions that'll slow us down, so would you mind giving me the tour?"

"I'd be delighted." Roger offered his arm and they speed-walked down the path.

"That was subtle, wasn't it?"

Hayley laughed and nodded. "Brick walls and Mack Trucks have nothing on them. Sorry, and if you point me in the right direction, I'll catch up with your mom."

"I give a pretty good tour," she said, obviously having an out-of-body experience. It was the only way to explain the response. "Are you interested?"

"Yes, but I'd like to start somewhere else."

"Okay, where?" *Fuck me*, she thought as she stared at Hayley's mouth. She'd burned all the pictures of them, so she'd forgotten how beautiful Hayley was—and of course *that* was a total lie. Amnesia would be the only way to forget that.

"The spring, where the process starts."

"Sure, but that's not as interesting as the tour." She led Hayley to the parking lot and smiled at Hayley's delighted laughter when she saw the Jeep.

"You still own it," Hayley said, taking her arm like Josie had with Roger. "I was disappointed last night when I saw the BMW."

"The fancy car is for when I have to play the executive, this is more—"

"You," Hayley finished. "This is more you, no matter how much more responsibility you've taken on." Hayley held her hand as she helped her in, then put her hair in a ponytail while Max started the engine.

The drive down the private dirt road took twenty minutes, and she played tour guide as they went. Hayley placed her hand on her forearm when she saw the ancient oak that grew in the middle of the Y in the road they'd come to. To the right was a spring, and to the left was Cinclair Bayou.

"I remember this place," Hayley said when she stopped. "We came here a few times."

"Cinclair Bayou's that way."

"Do you have to rush back?"

This was not a good idea. Not at all, but she turned and headed for the spot Hayley would remember, the place she now avoided. The ring of cypress trees made the perfect private nook, and they'd taken advantage of it more than once.

Hayley waited while she took a blanket out of the back and spread it out. "There's so much history here," Hayley said as she gazed out at the water. "I could sense that even then."

"My family loves the land—always has." She stretched her legs out and tried to relax. It was like being stress free with an agitated cobra in your lap.

"Can you tell me something about you?"

"I started at the distillery full-time when I graduated and took over for my father as the master distiller five years later." If the questions were all this easy, the afternoon would be a breeze. "He's more interested in farming and traveling with my mother, so I've been pushed to the front of the line of responsibilities sooner than I would've liked."

"I understand that, and that's different than my family. My father will retire when we plan his funeral and not a day sooner." Hayley turned and stared at her longer than she was comfortable with. "How about in your personal life? Who's the lucky woman you married?"

"I'm not married, and there's no lucky woman. Not yet," she added, hoping it'd close the subject.

"We have that in common." Hayley said it and smiled, which meant no such luck to closing the subject. "Why aren't you with someone?"

"Really, Hayley, we shouldn't do this."

Hayley shook her head and bit her lip as if to keep her tears from falling. "Jesus, I don't know what's wrong with me lately, but I doubt you'll want to see me again once this is over." The words rushed out of Hayley like an avalanche, and her tears started down her face and fell on her coat. "I hate myself for what I did, and I deserve your contempt."

"Hey." She reached out and Hayley was in her arms before she could stop her. The promise not to be cruel kept her from pushing Hayley away. "Stop putting yourself down or thinking I hate you. I don't, but our realities aren't much different than they were then." Logic got her more tears, and Hayley held on tighter.

Hell, this wasn't what she had planned for the day, so she decided to do something to make herself feel better. She lay back and enjoyed the feel of Hayley's head on her shoulder and the press of her body against hers. This really brought back memories, and she waited for Hayley to stop crying—her tears made Max want to cry as well, so she did her best to be comforting until Hayley pulled away.

"So, there's no one special waiting for you?" If she didn't know better, she'd guess her mother had gained control of her mouth because that was not at all what she meant to say.

"I've dated some, but not that much. There's no one, and I think you know why."

"Yeah," she said because nothing better or more intelligent sounding came to mind. The best thing to do was to shut up and wait Hayley out. But five minutes later she was about to crawl out of her skin from the pressure of not pulling Hayley closer and kissing her. "Would you have dinner with me?" For the love of absolutely no fucking control, why had she said that?

"I'd love to." Hayley rushed her answer as if sensing Max's internal struggle to change her mind. "We could go to your place and I can cook for you. That'll give us a chance to catch up with no interruptions."

Or get naked and reminisce, her brain supplied, dropping her into a pit of hell of her own making. Why torture herself and uphold that whole I'm-pissed stance, she thought. "Sure," she answered, deciding on the condo in town instead of her house. "Do you still want to see the spring?"

"Yes." Hayley sat up and gazed down at her. "It's doubtful we'll get your business, but that spot is important to our pitch."

"You don't have much faith in me, and I might prove you wrong." She missed Hayley's warmth when they stood, which only proved she'd gone completely insane. There had never been a reason to think crazy ran in her family, but here it was.

They rode for another half hour to the top of the small hill that was almost at the center of the property where the original distillery and the Cinclair House were. "Gramps's family installed the necessary piping to divert the water, but not all of it. This still feeds Cinclair Bayou, which eventually ends at the lake toward the back of the property."

"It's a beautiful spot." Hayley took pictures from every angle, and Max smiled when she aimed her phone at her. "It looks completely untouched."

"The intake is downhill and underground." She pointed to a spot to the right. "The water is pure enough not to need filtering, but of course we do, and it's what starts every bottle."

"Who knew all the bottles of Cinclair's I've purchased through the years had this place to thank for it."

She chuckled. "No need to butter me up."

"You can't think that I forgot your whiskey advice as well as your lessons from all those nights at the bar." Hayley moved her closer to the rocks that marked the spring's opening and posed her. "No way, so I'm not blowing smoke."

The silence on the way back was thankfully not awkward, and she smiled whenever Hayley made eye contact. She needed to hang in for a week, that was all, and then she'd be safe again. At least her heart would be safe, and she could go back to her miserable dating prospects.

They walked through the distillery together next, with Hayley only nodding as Max explained the process from cornfield to the clear liquid that went into the barrels. Then she took Hayley to the building where she was distilling Traditions.

"The building is new, but the equipment is some of the stuff my great-grandfather put online." She stopped them at the top of the filtering silos and placed her hand on the large wooden cover. "It took my team and me a few years to get it all repaired and back in working order."

"The result was certainly delicious. Congratulations, Max." Hayley closed her eyes momentarily and touched her hand. "I'm sorry, do you prefer Preston?"

"You and the guys at the bar are the only ones who call me Max, and it's okay." She lifted the cover and the aroma of whiskey wafted out. "This is the last stop before it goes in the barrel," she said, wanting to change the subject.

Hayley nodded and seemed to unconsciously take her arm when they headed down the stairs. The distilled liquid dripped out like a gentle rain, and the sight always made her smile. That slow trickle was proof of a job done right and done better than anyone else could do it.

"It's amazing that it ends so slowly," Hayley said as if reading her mind.

"My father loves to say the best things in life come from taking it nice and slow, and he's right." They walked to the next room where the barrels were being filled.

One of the workers let Hayley hammer in the plug to the barrel that had just been topped. "If that was his philosophy when it came to parenting, it worked out for him."

"Thanks, and we have one stop left."

She drove them to a set of buildings surrounded by a tall fence topped with razor wire. There were security cameras, but no guard on duty, and the gates opened slowly when she hit the remote. Their rickhouses were generic in appearance and most were scattered along the riverside.

"Leave your phone." She left hers back as well, fishing the key to the door out of the console.

"Are you hiding another secret in there?" Hayley waited while Max unlocked the only door on the windowless structure.

"Static would not do good things in here, and if I burn the place down, my father would kill me right after he fired me." The low lighting was enough to see the rows of barrels that filled the space in neat lines. "Each rickhouse has about thirty million in whiskey each. That's roughly three thousand barrels spread over fifteen floors."

Hayley walked to the center of the nearest row. "You simply let them sit for five years?"

"We shuffle some around, but it's a constant game of roulette to meet demand." She joined her with a glass pipette and pulled the plug on their test barrel. "These are three years old." She held her thumb at the top of the pipette and trapped some of the whiskey inside. It didn't yet have the color associated with their brand. She offered Hayley a taste.

"It's not as mellow as the Cinclair brand I'm used to."

"It's like us," she said, taking her own taste before placing the wood plug back. "It needs to mature." Thankfully Hayley laughed at her joke. "And that, from start to finish, is how we make whiskey."

"Thank you." It was starting to get dark when they went back outside, and Hayley finally seemed relaxed. "Should we go grocery shopping, or do you have everything we need?"

"My parents are having a cocktail hour, so let's decide after that."

"Oh, right, I forgot. Should I change?" Hayley looked at her, her head resting on the back of her seat. "If I had a choice I'd skip it and just have dinner with you."

"My grandfather will like you more dressed like this than in the power suit, and we don't have to stay long. I do need to show up and answer questions, but if you're tired afterward, we can wait on dinner." She started the engine before Hayley's gaze bored right into her heart.

"I want to, and I'd love to talk to your grandfather."

"He's a character, but he's one of my favorite people in the world." She stopped to make sure the gate closed before heading to the big house. "Just don't believe everything he says."

"I'm telling you, if I'm lying I'm dying," Carter said, holding his right hand up like he was being sworn in. "Totally naked."

Hayley laughed at the image of Max that popped into her head and tried to stifle it when Max walked into the kitchen. "Did I hear the word 'naked' come out of your mouth, old man?" Max's question made her laugh harder.

"I hear your mother calling me," Carter said with an exaggerated wink as he left.

"He's wonderful, and he certainly loves you." Hayley stood and handed Max her empty glass. She'd been in the kitchen for most of the night, and she'd enjoyed her time with Carter and his endless stories. "Thank you for not making me mingle."

"My parents and Roger can take it from here if you're ready."

Max's Jeep was out back, and she put it in gear and turned to head farther into the Cinclair property.

"That's one beautiful home." Hayley glanced in the side mirror as they drove away. She and Josie had spoken with Max's parents briefly, to answer questions about their firm, but she had been glad to join Carter away from everyone. "Carter told me a lot about it, but you can tell he really misses your grandmother, and it seems like she's closest to him around that table."

"Gramps is great, but he hasn't been the same since Gran died."

"How long were they married?" She figured the Cinclair history probably had quite a few love stories that spanned decades.

"Fifty-seven years," Max said softly.

"You don't hear about those kinds of relationships much anymore." She stared out at the beautiful home they were getting closer to with the wide porch that seemed to wrap around the entire first floor. The rocking chairs and the bench swing at the left corner defined what she imagined tranquil country living to be.

"Both sets of grandparents and my parents are good role models when it comes to happily ever afters, but maybe you're right." Max got out and waited for her.

"Don't color your world by my failures, especially my shortcomings." She took Max's arm and followed her inside. The house was full of exquisite antiques, but it was in no way stuffy. "I like this place even more."

"I grew up here and inherited it when my parents moved in with Gramps." Max went ahead and flipped on lights on the way to the back of the house. Hayley ran her hands over the stone countertops when they ended up in the kitchen. "Would steak be okay?"

"Why don't you sit and let me cook for you?" She took a chance and opened the refrigerator. There were two steaks sitting on a plate, but the fridge was stocked with provisions that would make for a better option than a quick grill job.

"They'll take ten minutes once the grill heats up."

"Or you can leave me in here, and I can pay you back for my great tour today." She took the meat out and waited for Max's decision. When Max took a seat on one of the stools that butted up to the counter at the end of the island, she let out a breath. Her apartment wasn't tiny, but the kitchen was like a shoebox. "Using your kitchen will be a treat, I promise."

"Thank you." Max guided her around the cabinets. "I only get a home-cooked meal once a week when my mother cooks."

You need to get married was on the verge of rushing out of her mouth, but she was too emotionally unstable to even contemplate that. Max with someone else was easier to accept when they had numerous states between them. She sliced steak and set the thin pieces aside in the marinade she'd made.

"Then I'm glad I'm here." She started on the vegetables and smiled when Max started clapping.

"I didn't think you could get any faster than college, but you've improved your technique. Impressive."

"Cooking helps me de-stress from my job. Not every account is like this."

"Like I said, no need to butter me up, Ms. Wyatt." Max sounded so flippant that it made her squeeze her eyes closed, not wanting to embarrass herself any more than she had.

She tightened her hands into fists and turned away from Max, and if they weren't so far out of town, she would've walked out, not caring how it looked. The pain of leaving eight years ago was bad, but this was worse because it was like being shredded by a wounded animal set to inflict harm. The tears didn't come until Max put her arms around her and held her as if she couldn't get close enough.

"Hey." Max turned her around and ran her hands soothingly up and down her back. "It was a piss-poor joke, but it was a joke. Please don't cry."

"I'm…I'm sorry." This was getting ridiculous. No matter what life had thrown at her in her pressure-cooker job, she'd handled it. Weepy mess drama queen wasn't in her wheelhouse of mood choices.

Max let her go momentarily, turned off the oiled wok she was heating up, and took her hand and led her outside. It didn't take long to get the fire pit going and for Max to sit next to her and put her arm around her. There was enough moonlight to see the cane waving in the slight breeze, but there was no other sound except the crackle of the burning logs.

How different would the last eight years of her life have been with this waiting at the end of every day? "You must think I'm a total nutjob."

"Not really," Max said softly. "You must think I've been a total asshole since you got here."

They faced each other and their closeness, and not being able to touch Max the way she wanted to, made her ache. "Why do you think that?"

"Everyone that's come in contact with me lately has pointed it out." Max closed her eyes and inhaled deeply. "I've spent a long time wondering what I did wrong, what did I do that made you leave, and eventually I handled that by getting really mad at you."

"Totally understandable, and in no way asshole behavior." She lifted her hand and pressed it to Max's cheek.

"Probably, but my problem from the second I saw you is my inability to *stay* mad at you." Max claimed her hand and kissed her palm. It was so innocent, but it woke up every cell in her body. "Stop feeling bad about everything and accept that we both screwed up."

"You're a generous grader."

"Are you seriously arguing with me?" Max scowled at her, and the thought that she really might be forgiven made her cry again. "Stop before Roger and my mother beat me up for being mean to you." Max wiped away her tears and didn't say anything else when she laid her head on her shoulder and sighed.

They stayed there until Max's stomach rumbled, prompting them to finish dinner. The best gift of the night was when Max agreed to sit back outside until the fire died away. Having Max up against her was so right, and it made her question everything she'd done from the second she left this town. Granted, she was successful, but at what cost?

"You ready to head back?" Max ran her hand up and down her back but stopped well short of her butt.

"Not really, but I'm sure Josie would appreciate my input for tomorrow." She sat up and glanced back at Max with a smile. "Thank you for tonight. You can't know how much I appreciate it."

"Tonight was about me too," Max said in a way that made her believe her. "I'd much rather be your friend than carry all those negative emotions a second more."

"For a master distiller, you're quite the poet, Preston Cinclair." She said the name, but it didn't feel right.

"My friends call me Max."

"Am I that?" She took Max's hand.

"I'd like it if you were."

They went inside and when Max picked up the keys to the BMW, Hayley shook her head. "Tonight I'd rather the Jeep, if you don't mind."

"Are you sure you won't be cold?" Max grabbed a canvas jacket as well as a blanket.

"No, I'll be anything but." She hugged Max and thrilled when it was returned.

"You know best." Max held her hand and helped her in before wrapping the blanket around her. How hard would it be to walk away again?

Chapter Seven

"But do you?" Roger asked after the third presentation of the day concluded, with no questions or comments from Preston. "How can you know best if you haven't paid attention to anyone at all? Don't deny it—I know your distracted face better than anyone alive."

"Roger, how many new customers do you think we're going to get by advertising our product is gluten-free?" That she couldn't tune out the last candidate irked her more than being accused of not paying attention. "I fucking love gluten. It makes stuff taste good, and advertising our product doesn't have any will happen right after I adopt naked Fridays around the office."

"That wasn't the direction I was hoping for, no."

"And the dissertation on the occasional worm in the corn adding protein is the way we should go?" It was like she'd gone on a bender last night and woken up in some alternate universe of bad marketing ideas. "What exactly did you and my mother say on your tour yesterday?"

"We covered Whiskey 101. Worms never came up in the conversation since we don't make tequila."

"Tequila doesn't have worms in it either—it's tequila's low-class cousin mescal that has that going for it." She couldn't believe they were even having this discussion. "I'm not doing another round of interviews. If Hayley and Josie push some other bizarre concept these morons haven't thought of, good luck to you and my parents finding a new advertising firm. When I said I wanted something different, I should've been more specific." She leaned back in her chair already peeved with what she'd realized early this morning was sexual frustration. Obviously her body had totally misread last night as badly as the advertising firms had Cinclair Distillers.

"Take a breath and let me go get them."

Five minutes later, the last presentation began. "Good morning, Max," Josie said in a tone that she was sure was supposed to annoy her. It totally did.

"Good morning, Ms. Simon. Are you two ready?"

"We are, and I'd like to begin by giving you an overview before we show you the preliminary layouts." Hayley wove a story that started at the spring and ended with Gramps pouring her and her father a drink. Throughout, the pride she had in her family and the whiskey they'd made for generations had her wanting to fork over money for a bottle she owned a lifetime supply of. "This campaign will go one step further and introduce Traditions with the same concept."

"Once the professional pictures are taken," Josie said, putting up boards with the photos Hayley had taken on her phone, "we can start with the overhaul of your website. The best thing about all this is the camera's in love with the Cinclair family, especially you."

"Shouldn't we concentrate on the product?" The center of attention wasn't a place she wanted to be.

"Is it true you made a fabulous new whiskey?" Josie asked in a sweet voice.

"Yes." This had to be a setup for something.

"That means you're really good at your job, which I believe is master distiller. You keep doing that, and allow us to do the job we're really good at." The thick sarcasm Josie was dishing her way was probably not the norm with potential clients. "Somewhere in the middle, those two jobs will meet, and you'll be happy about it."

"I guess I will." She stood and buttoned her jacket.

"You guess you will what?" Hayley asked, appearing as surprised as Josie.

"Be happy about what you come up with. Have a contract drawn up, send it to Roger, and we'll get started." She had to leave the room or kiss Hayley, so she started walking. "Roger will give you whatever you need."

It was a chickenshit move, but she kept going until she reached her car. An hour later she was standing in the water practicing her casting, but mostly getting her flies caught in the branches. Her concentration was shot—well, when it came to fishing. Thinking obsessively about Hayley leaving, now that she'd given her what she most wanted, was stomping out everything else in her head.

"You catch a lot of fish by throwing the rod at them, followed by screaming?" her grandfather asked when he sat on the bank. "I've never seen that particular technique."

She walked to the bright yellow line hanging from the high branches where her fly was stuck and used it to retrieve her rod, having thrown it in frustration. "Gramps, I'm not in a talkative mood."

"That's okay. All you need to do is listen, and considering I'm meeting Roger in a half hour, this won't take long. You know I don't like being late." He waved her over and pointed to the spot next to him. "First, stop feeling sorry for yourself and take some action."

"Exactly what kind of action?" Her grandfather liked talking about whiskey and growing corn. Feelings were not his forte.

"You been pining over that girl long enough, so quit it and do something about it. That brings me to my next point. You're a Cinclair, Preston, which means you make damn good whiskey and you don't let life scare you. Nothing on that list hints that you come from a long line of dumbasses, so don't disappoint me by being the first."

"I'm not scared, Gramps. I'm a realist."

"Okay, one last thing and I'll leave you to whatever the hell you're doing out here." He slapped her on the back hard enough to make her cough. "Don't make a liar out of your sainted grandmother, or I really will kick your ass."

"What are you talking about?" The one way to get over rejection was confusing conversations, it seemed.

"She knew about this great love of yours, and she told me eventually you'd get it right if you wanted it bad enough. Question is, do you?"

"My life is here, Gramps, and hers is in New York. It has nothing to do with how much I want it."

"And you know this after telling her how you feel and she turned you down?"

She shook her head. "Think about who she is. And I don't need to talk to her about anything. We had a year in college, and that's all it's going to be. Don't worry, I'll find someone eventually."

"You really don't get it, do you?" He leaned over and kissed her cheek. "You might find someone, but it'll be settling. The other thing about us Cinclairs is we know the one when we see her, kiddo. No one else will ever do. If you don't believe me, ask your mother."

"It's not that simple, but thank you." She took her waders off and helped him up.

"You sure about that?"

"Positive."

❖

"How can you be positive?" Major Wyatt screamed so loud it made Hayley cringe. "Did you hit your head when you were in New Orleans?"

Hayley took a deep breath. She wasn't having a hard time ignoring her father's irrational behavior because she wasn't changing her mind. "Daddy, I'm moving, and if you let me work remotely, I won't have to quit outright." Hayley had left New Orleans five hours after Max had walked out and disappeared. Roger, God bless him, had tried repeatedly to reach Max, but apparently she hadn't wanted to be found. Watching Max walk out was the last time she'd been able to breathe normally.

"It's a family business, or has that slipped your mind?"

"Percy's not moving—I am." She was glad for Percy's company as he stood next to her. "And for the fifth time, I'm not quitting my job or my family." It was time to get out of here. Her heart and lungs felt like they'd shrunk five sizes, and there was only one thing that would right her world. To be more accurate, there was only one *person* who could do that.

"Dad," Percy interjected, "take a deep breath and namaste your way into finding acceptance. I want Hayley to be happy, and this is her chance. She's moving to New Orleans, not the middle of the Amazon jungle or changing her name." Percy's humor only made their father's face turn redder. "Hayley's also a grownup who hasn't sold her soul to the advertising gods."

"I need a few days out there to work on some things, then I'll come back, and we'll iron out how the transition will go. I'll even get my team started on the Cinclair account before I leave." She walked around her father's desk and kissed his cheek. "With any luck the bar tab at my wedding will be really cheap—I know people." She wanted to run out of the office, not to get away from her family, but because for the first time in forever she was running *to* something. Something she wanted and needed for the rest of her life.

"Do you want me to go with you?" Percy asked when she walked to her office.

"I'll be okay, but thank you." All she'd been able to think about was sitting in Max's arms and watching the cane blow in the breeze. Eight years was a long time to be without the one person who was the key to life making sense. She was going to get that back, and nothing or no one was going to stop her, not even Max. If it took a year of begging...well, she was packing knee pads, so that wouldn't be a problem.

"Then I'm a phone call away if you need me to make her see the light." Percy hugged her and kissed her forehead. "I'm happy for you, so don't worry about anything here. Josie and I will take care of everything."

"You're a good friend, and I know you probably think this is all crazy." She laughed, wanting to leave now and beg the airline to let her flight take off hours early.

"Would it matter?" Percy asked, smiling.

"No," she said, kissing his cheek. "I love her, and I need her. She's the one."

"It's good to know you can reform your asshole ways, and she's one lucky bastard."

Percy drove her to the airport a few hours later and promised to calm their parents down until they heard from her. "Remember," he said kissing her forehead again, "no isn't an option."

"Even if I have to tie her to a chair to get her to agree." She took her small bag and squared her shoulders. There was no way this could be a mistake. None at all.

❖

"I'm sorry, but that has to be a mistake. Ms. Simon said—" Preston stopped at how absurd that sounded. It was like she was playing a child's game of Simon Says. "Ms. Simon said they flew home this afternoon, so she has to be there."

The receptionist at Hayley's firm talked to her like she was dealing with someone dull-witted. "I'm sorry, I don't know how else to say it, but Ms. Wyatt is out of town. Can someone else help you?"

Why would Josie have lied to Roger? "Is Ms. Simon available?"

"Hold, please."

"Can I help you?" a woman she hoped was Josie asked.

"Ms. Simon?"

"Max?" Josie laughed. "It has to be you because you always say my name like you're telling me to fuck off."

"Where's Hayley?" She didn't have time for this.

"You expect to be rewarded for running out like a scared asshole today?"

She clenched her fist at being called an asshole yet again. "I'm sorry about that, but I need to find Hayley."

There was a pause, as if Josie was digesting what she'd said. "Where are *you* exactly?"

"Pulling away from JFK, and I need to tell the driver where to go." The guy Roger hired drove like he had someplace to be and knew exactly where that was with no directions from her. "Where is she?"

"You're not kidding, are you? Can you hold on a second?"

The traffic was murder and her fingers hurt from holding the phone so tightly, as if clutching the phone would stabilize the lane changing they were doing for no apparent reason. "Josie?" she said when the on-hold music stopped.

"Tell the driver to pull over and hand him the phone." Josie sounded totally serious. "Stop overthinking and get with it."

"Can you pull over, or just talk to this lady since we're not moving?" She handed the driver her phone, and he had a short conversation while he changed across four lanes of traffic with plenty of horn blowing and cursing. Once he put the car in park, he handed her the phone back. She asked Josie, "What now?"

"Give your new ride about five minutes, and he'll pick you up and fill you in. Tell me you aren't going to fuck this up before I give you the benefit of doubt."

"Could you give me a hint, or is this payback for everything you think I did wrong?"

"I know Hayley screwed up, but she took a huge chance today, so don't you make it worse by being a jerk."

She opened her mouth to protest but the knocking on her window scared her into dropping the phone. She powered down the window.

"Grab your stuff and let's go. You don't have a lot of time," the guy said.

"I know you don't like me, but is kidnapping me the answer?" she said to Josie.

"Percy is many things, but he's in no way a felon of any kind. He'd never survive prison without an afternoon martini. Shake his hand and get in his car." In typical Josie fashion, she hung up.

"Preston Cinclair," she said, holding her hand out to the guy as she climbed out of the back seat.

"Percy Wyatt." Percy had a firm shake and really resembled Hayley. "Do you have a bag or something?"

"I didn't have time to pack." She followed him to his car after tipping her driver for the ten minutes of hell. "Where exactly is Hayley?"

"She's gone and she's not coming back." Percy started down the side streets and she guessed he was dumping her at the airport. "So, tell me something before we talk about anything else. Do you love my sister?"

"Yes, I do. Eight years is a long time to be pigheaded according to my grandfather, and I came to fix that." She wanted to cry, but she'd have plenty of time for that later. "Looks like I'm too late again."

"Don't be so pessimistic." How they were back at the airport already was surprising, but Percy knew his way around traffic. "She's gone, but *where* is what you should be asking, not drowning your sorrows in self-pity. You make booze for a living—try that if you're going down that road."

"I try never to drink to excess, and what exactly should I be asking you?"

"No time for that now. Your boarding pass is on your phone, and if you run, you'll make it. Good luck and try not to fuck up." Percy shook her hand, sounding a lot like Josie, and pointed to the entrance where he'd stopped. "Don't forget to run."

"The things we do for love."

❖

"It's the best reason, Hayley." Carter handed her a glass and smiled at her. "Love makes you crazy, but in a good way."

Hayley could see Max in his features. "Where exactly is she?" She'd knocked on the door of the big house because she didn't think she could get all the way to Max's place in a cab. Carter had listened to why she'd come. She'd wanted to run when Carter told her Max was gone.

"New York," Carter said, and she gaped at the answer. "My kiddo finally got it right and went looking for what she wanted most. If you're wondering, that isn't an award-winning whiskey even if she's good at producing them."

"Why is she in New York?" Man, they had the worst luck.

"I'm sure for the same reason you're here. Big romantic gestures only work when you're in the same state. Make a note for the future."

"Thanks, Carter, you're a huge help."

"Call me Gramps, and I'm going to help you, so don't get sassy, young lady. Get your bag and let's go."

Carter drove her to Max's and handed her the key. "Thanks, Gramps."

"Thank you for loving Preston. You do know all this comes as part of the package, right?"

"I'm here to stay, don't worry." She kissed his cheek and thought it sweet he waited until she was inside.

"Hopefully we're on the same page on what has to happen for me to keep my sanity." She left her bag by the door and looked around the living room. The place was neat but unlived in, aside from the comfortable chair with a floor lamp next to it. There were a few books stacked on a side table, but she didn't want to pry to see what they were.

She sat on the sofa, texted Percy to let him know she'd arrived safely, and prayed Max believed her. It was nuts to walk away from everything familiar, and if she was totally honest, she was terrified. Her fear, though, came from how Max was going to react and not from upending her life.

If Max didn't even want to try, she'd have to think long and hard about what her next stage of life would look like. Whatever it was, she was tired of being alone, so it was time to start taking chances. Not that *this* wasn't a big gamble she hadn't necessarily thought through, but there wasn't any other place she wanted to be.

One day with Max, and her world had righted itself, but she wanted the whole package every day for the rest of her days. "I know you feel the same way, so please don't be stubborn." She lay down and stared at the ceiling, hoping the universe would come through on her wish. That's all she thought as the exhaustion of the day gave her no choice but to close her eyes.

A loud creak made Hayley gasp and open her eyes two hours later, now terrified she'd forgotten to lock the door. She was in the middle of a cane field, for God's sake. She was as sure there was some horror movie based on that premise, as she was there was some guy in a scary white mask now loose in the house. "That's the last time I eat airport food," she said softly with her hands over her face.

"You didn't throw up on my couch, did you?"

The sound of another voice scared her into rolling off the sofa and hitting the floor with enough force to knock the air out of her. "Max?"

"Were you expecting someone else?" Max sat across from her in a greatcoat and tousled hair. "I flew to New York. You weren't there."

"Gramps told me, and I wanted to say—"

"Uh-uh," Max said with her hand up. "I flew to New York to tell you something, but instead I got a lecture from Josie, followed by one from Percy."

"I'm so sorry." She stopped talking again when Max raised her hand higher. That gorgeous face did not look happy, so she knelt and sat back on the sofa.

"For some strange reason, everyone I meet, including my family, thinks I'm an asshole when it comes to you." Max pointed at her, still not cracking a smile.

"I don't—"

"Zip it." It was rude but effective. "Let's get a few things straight. You left me, then you came back with the delightful Ms. Simon, left again, and now you're back."

She nodded as Max ticked off her list, not really knowing where this was going, but it wasn't anywhere good from Max's tone. "Um, yes."

"Tell me one thing before I kiss you."

"Anything," she said as she choked up.

"Are you back for good, or just to apologize again?" The tears in Max's eyes and the obvious vulnerability in her voice broke her heart.

"I heard you might need someone in your life who's marginally experienced in advertising and loves you more than you'll ever know." She stood when Max did and moved slowly to her. "You might not believe the love part yet, but if you give me years and years, I'll prove it to you."

Max wrapped her arms around her and lifted her off the floor, filling her with everything she'd been missing since their last night together eight years ago. She pressed her face into Max's neck and tried convincing herself she was not only awake, but this was indeed happening. How in the world had she survived this long without Max?

"You don't have to prove anything," Max whispered.

She kissed Max's neck and lifted her head. "I want to as much as I want you." It was like a miracle, but the sight of blatant want in Max's eyes was a last-minute reprieve before something essential in her died.

"The only thing for you to do is kiss me and show me I'm not dreaming." Max still held her, and Hayley tightened her hold around her neck.

"That's all?"

"There might be some other things on my list, but starting there would be a way to forget a sucky day."

"Put me down and sit." She sat in Max's lap and placed her hands on Max's cheeks. "What about today didn't you like? Are you sorry you hired us?"

"No," Max said hesitantly.

"Tell me."

"You're the only one who gets me." Max's eyes met hers, and then she glanced away. "Josie had nothing to do with that campaign, did she."

"Not really, because she didn't understand something important. I might not have known who your family was, but the way you treated me made it impossible to let anyone else in after I left. Now that I know your family, it's easy to understand how impossible it was not to fall in love with you." She caressed Max's cheeks, moving her hands down to her neck. "Why it was impossible to fall out of love with you and forget you."

"The same exact thing happened to me, and today I saw what it takes to make me happy."

"And that made you feel sucky?" If Max was about to ask her to leave, that would be a total letdown.

"That worry line in the middle of your forehead hasn't changed." Max ran her thumb over the spot and smiled. "I looked at you, and I knew with absolute certainty that no one else would ever get me like that. I knew that, and once I hired you, I also knew I'd watch you leave this time and I'd lose my chance." Max shrugged. "That made for a sucky day."

"You could've asked me to stay."

"If I wasn't a total weenie, I probably could have." Max shrugged again and that did it.

Hayley took a deep breath and leaned forward. Once Max's lips were pressed to hers, she lost all the fear that had choked her from the moment she talked to her family. Max held her and kissed her like she had a thousand times before, but the feeling of being cherished was warring with the truth that the kiss was turning her on. She pulled Max's hair when she opened her mouth slightly to Max's tongue, and it made Max break the kiss and gaze at her.

"Problem?" Max asked glancing down briefly when Hayley started unbuttoning her shirt.

"Not a one." Her voice hitched when Max's hand slipped from her knee to the middle of her thigh. "Can we agree eight years is long enough to wait?"

"It's plenty enough time to craft a good whiskey, but way too long when it comes to you." Max stood and cradled her. "We can talk later."

"Yes, so much later. Right now you need to remind me how good your hands feel on me."

"Anyplace in particular you want me to start?" Max said after she laid Hayley on the bed and finished taking her shirt off. "My hands are getting twitchy."

"Surprise me." Hayley knelt at the center of the bed, reached back, unzipped her skirt, and wiggled her hips to get it to slide down. She took it off before sitting on the edge and crooking her finger at Max. "Come here."

"Aren't you going to finish?" Max pointed to her bra and cocked her head. "This time around I'm going to touch where I want until you scream my name."

"I am." Max watched as Hayley unbuckled her belt and unzipped her pants. If there had been a certainty in her life, it was that Hayley wasn't shy about what she wanted in bed. At least, she'd been assertive about that after realizing the results it got her. "Does that mean you aren't hard as a rock? I won't believe you if you say yes." Hayley smiled up at her.

"Son of a bitch." She had no choice but to curse when Hailey reached in and squeezed her clit so hard between two fingers her legs weakened.

"It's good to know not all of you forgot me," Hayley teased as she pumped her fingers a few times.

"Believe me." She had to grit her teeth for a moment while Hayley drove her mad.

"Believe what, baby?" Hayley rested her feet behind Max's knees, her touch softening.

"That low-cut blouse you wore the first day was a good reminder to some parts of me how much you were missed. I was pissed, shocked, and horny all at once, and it confused the hell out of me."

"Which one won out?" Hayley licked her nipple as she peered up at her. "I'm guessing pissed, since you left."

"When it comes to you, horny always wins, and you're distracting me from my goals." She moved her hands into Hayley's underwear and squeezed her ass.

"What goals?"

"The *I'm going to hold out until I make you come* goal." She smiled as her pants fell to the floor and Hayley laughed. "That sounds like you think I don't have the willpower." Hayley laughed again, making her exhale so forcefully, her nostrils flared. "That's not helping." Hayley had wet her fingers and stroked her until she couldn't say anything else.

"Know what I think?" Hayley pulled her hand free, and that made her groan louder than all the touching.

"What?" She watched as Hayley reached back, unclasped her bra, and held it in place one-handed, then snapped the fingers on the other hand to get Max's attention.

"I know you want to get naked and lie down so I can put my mouth somewhere that'll make us both happy." Hayley slowly lowered the bra, and the sight made her want to agree to anything. "If you do that for me, I promise I'll give you whatever you want."

Max got naked as she nodded but stopped when Hayley started crying. It wasn't the reaction she was hoping for, and comforting Hayley took precedence over everything else. "What's wrong?"

"I forgot how much fun you are, and how much you make me feel." Hayley put her arms around her shoulders when she hugged her. "How could I have forgotten that and left you?"

"Hayley"—she had no choice but to hold her once the tears started again—"please don't cry." The feeling of desire she'd experienced so acutely just minutes before was replaced by the ache from Hayley's pain, so she moved onto the bed and lay down. "I was thinking that first night outside the distillery that I've never seen you cry."

"I seldom do," Hayley said, taking some deep breaths as if trying to calm down. "But I saw you again and it broke me. Now I'm an emotional mess, so lucky you." She wiped her face and laughed. "Sexy, huh?"

She rolled over to be able to look at Hayley while she spoke. "I like to think of it as your head finally catching up to your heart about wanting to be here."

"I do, honey, more than anything. Maybe we can start from where we left off, but believe I want to be here with you." Hayley smiled but she still appeared sad.

"I hope we don't start exactly where we left off. That would suck," she said and winked. "But I would like to start fresh."

"You would?" Hayley's smiled widened.

"I do, because what I said about that head and heart connection is something I have experience with. You own my heart, Hayley Wyatt, and I've been waiting on you to either fully claim it or give it back."

Hayley put her arms around her and pressed their bodies together. "I want all of you."

"I love you, and it's something I didn't want to admit, but I never stopped."

"I love you too, and that's not something you ever have to question again." Hayley rolled with Max and rested her head on her shoulder.

"Does this conclude the emotional part of our evening?" She placed her hand on Hayley's butt and slapped it gently.

"Yes. I promise my tears from now on will only be from happy times. *You*, though, might start crying when you have to move me and help me find a job. If my father doesn't calm down, I doubt he'll let me work remotely, so I'll be an unemployed squatter in your house."

"You can work for me, and my mother will be the first to volunteer to pack you up and give your father a lecture."

Hayley laughed, then quieted as she made random patterns on Max's abdomen with her fingers. "I'm exhausted, but grateful you forgive me."

"Family is why you left, and family is something I understand. Hopefully you'll be happy once you get a full dose of mine in a city that's not as exciting as New York."

"The city is something you don't have to sell me on, but it could've been Bumfuck USA, and I'd still be thrilled if you were there."

"What?" She was totally confused now.

"It's something Josie told me."

She laughed. Ah, Josie. "I'll just bet."

"Hey, she told me that while trying to convince me to tell you the truth about how I felt." Hayley rested her weight on her elbows and gazed down at her. "You changed my life the day you walked into that classroom, and I've never been the same. There'll never be anyone else for me." She placed her hand on Max's chest. "You're it."

"Then we're as good a pair as whiskey on the rocks." There was a limit to her ability to be this close to a naked Hayley and not touch her. "I have ways of making you believe me."

Hayley might have been upset, but she was also wet, and she bit her bottom lip when Max touched her clit. "I'm starting to."

"Are you sure? You seem to need some more convincing." She loved Hayley's expression and just how beautiful she was. "I thought now would be a good time to remind you that you're mine."

Hayley nodded as she moved on top, giving her room to maneuver Max's hand down where she wanted it when she spread her legs wider. They'd made love often, but Max would never get tired of the look of ecstasy on Hayley's face.

"I need you." Hayley moved her hips, rubbing her clit harder against Max's fingers. "So much, baby." She stopped talking and groaned when Max put the tips of her fingers inside. "Please…oh, please. It's been so long." Hayley sat up as she pleaded and came down on her hand.

There was nothing that would keep her from giving Hayley everything she wanted, and she didn't stop when Hayley leaned down and kissed her. God, she'd missed this connection and the freedom to show how much she cared. Sex had been simply sex for way too long, but this act with this woman would never be that.

"Oh." Hayley sat back up as if to move better and held Max's free hand as her moans got louder. "I'm coming…Jesus, I'm coming."

She watched as the orgasm swept through Hayley and prayed she was serious about staying. "You okay?" she asked when Hayley collapsed on her, trapping her hand in place.

"You have no idea, and stop trying to move—I might not be finished." Hayley lifted her head and kissed her. "You're still a sexy beast, and I'm so glad you waited for me."

"Waited for you?" She didn't understand the statement.

"I told Josie you were probably married with a couple of kids when she asked about you." Hayley stopped when she moved her fingers slightly. "I'm lucky you're not."

"All in good time, but right now, we need to finish with the reconnecting part of our evening." She rolled them over wanting more freedom to touch Hayley like she wanted. "There's plenty I want, but right now all I want is you."

"Sweet-talker…yes, like that. Just like that."

EPILOGUE

Two Months Later

"Stop moving—I said it was perfect just like that," Hayley said to Roger. They'd arrived early to set up their space at the World Whiskey Competition, and he was worse than Josie when trying to get his way. She moved the sign back to the side table where the information about Traditions was set out.

The marketing campaign had rolled out the week before, and from all accounts, everyone had fallen in love with the ads that featured Carter, Dale, and Preston. She picked the ad with the two men standing behind Preston, who sat on a stool at On the Rocks holding a glass of her new whiskey. The sight of Max and her smile still made her shiver.

"If we put it out front, it'll draw a bigger crowd." Roger sounded a wee bit condescending.

"Percy is delivering the ones that'll go out front, so sit and let me finish." She'd actually never done anything like this, but she was having fun.

She and Max had picked up from the day *before* she'd left, and it had been two months of making love, family dinners, and working. Max had talked her into keeping her apartment, and into splitting her time between Cinclair's and her father's firm. Her father had, of course, complained at first, but Max's charming personality worked on more than one Wyatt.

"So we're done?" Roger asked.

She nodded. "We'll be swamped once the judging is over and we get a mad rush of people wanting free booze, but we're ready for them. And here comes the last piece now."

Percy pointed to the corners of the space where the two signs with the Cinclair bottles printed on them went. "Where's the bootlegger?" he asked, using the nickname their father had coined when he thought Hayley was running away.

"Don't call her that." She slapped his arm. "He should be glad this thing is in New York this year. Max brought enough booze to get your guests drunk three times over at your wedding next week."

"I'm just glad you won't be pathetic without a plus-one." Percy kissed her temple when she slapped his arm again.

"Can I have my girl back?" Max asked as she arrived with Major, of all people.

"Hey, Daddy. Come to check on us?" She put her arms around Max's waist after hugging her dad.

"I came to help out." Major's declaration made everyone's mouth but Max's open in surprise. "You have an appointment to get to."

"I do?"

"You do," Max said, shaking Major's hand before leading her outside. Her father's driver was waiting for them and took off when the doorman shut their car door.

"Where are we going?" They were leaving the large hotel in Times Square behind and heading toward Central Park. "Did you have a sudden urge to take a walk, honey? It's snowing and I'm in heels."

"Not a walk—a drink." Max sounded completely serious.

"A drink? We have loads of alcohol where we just left, and it's ten in the morning." They came to a stop at a restaurant she knew well, and she snapped her mouth shut with an audible click of her teeth. "You know this place?"

Max held her hand as she got out of the car, and they walked to the door one of the waitstaff held open. "I've come a few times when I was in the city, but it's the first time I'm bringing a date."

"I don't think they're open yet, but I don't mind waiting if you don't."

She wanted Max to promise they'd come back in the spring so they could sit outside. How Max knew the Loeb Boathouse in the middle of the park was one of her favorite places was a mystery, but Max was always full of surprises. That'd been true for the last few months, and all those good times had made her fall deeper in love.

"Ms. Cinclair, welcome," the maître d' said, bowing his head slightly. "And Ms. Wyatt, welcome back."

"Thank you." She doubted he knew her but followed him to the back and almost hesitated when he took their coats and opened the door to the outside seating.

"Trust me, Ms. Wyatt, you won't freeze."

When it wasn't freezing, this place was one of the most romantic spots in the city with a view of the lake and the gondola and rowboat rides, but even in winter, this was picture-perfect. The snow and the early hour gave it a peaceful surreal feeling that made her think they were miles away from the craziness that was New York.

"Thank you," she told him, "and thank you for bringing me." She kissed Max before sitting in the chair Max held and looking out at the water and park. "My parents come here often."

"They do?" Max nodded and a waiter brought out a bottle of Traditions with two glasses and a bucket of ice.

"My father proposed to my mother here, and she loves telling people about it." She watched Max pour two small drinks and place a cube of ice in each glass. "That might've been the last romantic thing he ever did."

"I don't believe that, and that's not what he told me." Max handed her a glass and held up hers. "According to him, he's plenty romantic, but you, my love, will never complain about that. To us."

She tapped her glass to Max's and gazed at her. "To us, and to the universe for giving me the biggest romantic of them all."

"Eh, I do all right," Max teased her. "All I wanted was to have you all to myself for a bit."

"Believe me, you do better than all right in the romance department." She leaned in and whispered in Max's ear, "It's why I'm constantly wet."

"Ms. Wyatt, you are something, but right now I want to talk to you about traditions."

"Oh?" She sat back and tried to concentrate on work.

"Not what's in the glass." Max put her drink down and took her hand. "More like family traditions and the history they mark in our families."

"Is this a new idea for a campaign?" She smiled when Max laughed. She loved that laugh.

"Not exactly a work campaign." Max pushed her chair out and dropped to one knee. "See, your father told me where he proposed, and how happy he was Percy chose the same spot. It's become a Wyatt family tradition of sorts."

"It has?" All she could do was stare into Max's eyes and pray she wasn't misinterpreting this.

"It has, and he followed that up with what he expected of his daughter-in-law before he gave his blessing." Max reached into her suit pocket and took out a box. "I gave him my word I would love you, take care of you, and do my best to make you happy."

"I love you so much."

"I love you, and I'm going to spend my life showing you. You'll never doubt how much I want forever with you. Hayley, will you marry me?"

"Yes." It was all she could say before she started crying again as the box creaked open.

"This was my grandmother's ring." Max took out the two-carat square-cut solitaire and placed it on the end of her finger. "She would've loved you and the dreams you've inspired in me. Gramps said she wore it for a lot of magic-filled years, but its job isn't done." Max slid it onto her finger and kissed her hand. "Thank you for saying yes."

"My heart gave me no other choice." She kissed Max until she heard retching noises from the door.

"Good Lord, you two are so damn sappy," Josie said.

"It's why I'm not single," Max said without turning around.

"I still say it's because you're richer than shit," Josie said as Max stood and helped Hayley to her feet as both their families came in.

"Why do you think I agreed to this?" Major said, putting his arms around both of them. "I'm kidding, and I'm happy for you both."

There was plenty more teasing and congratulations before everyone had a glass in their hand and Carter lifted his in a toast. "To Hayley and Max, may all your days be filled with love and good times, and may the bad times be easily handled over a glass of good whiskey."

"You're stuck with me now," she said when Max pulled her aside.

"You make that sound like it's a bad thing," Max said and kissed her. "You do realize all those Cinclairs come as part of the package, right?"

"As long as I get a few who are all mine, I'll be fine." She kissed Max again because she couldn't help herself, and as usual her feet came off the floor.

"You get whatever you want," Max said as she put her down.

"Then let's get to it."

And they did.

Author Bios

Jenny Frame is from the small town of Motherwell in Scotland, where she lives with her partner, Lou, and their well-loved and very spoiled dog.

She has a diverse range of qualifications, including a BA in public management and a diploma in acting and performance. Nowadays, she likes to put her creative energies into writing rather than treading the boards.

When not writing or reading, Jenny loves cheering on her local football team, cooking, and spending time with her family.

Carsen Taite is a recovering lawyer who prefers writing fiction to practicing law because she has more control of the outcome. She believes that lawyers make great lovers, which is why she includes so many of them in her novels. She is the award-winning author of over twenty novels of romance and romantic intrigue, including the Luca Bennett Bounty Hunter series, the Lone Star Law series, and the Legal Affairs romances.

Ali Vali is the author of the long-running Cain Casey Devil series and the Genesis Clan Forces series, as well as numerous standalone romances including two Lambda Literary Award finalists, *Calling the Dead* and *Love Match*, and her 2020 release, *Face the Music*. Ali also has a novella in the collection *Girls with Guns*.

Originally from Cuba, Ali has retained much of her family's traditions and language and uses them frequently in her stories. Having her father read her stories and poetry before bed every night as a child infused her with a love of reading, which she carries till today. Ali currently lives outside New Orleans, Louisiana, and she has discovered that living in Louisiana provides plenty of material to draw from in creating her novels and short stories.

Books Available From Bold Strokes Books

Entangled by Melissa Brayden. Becca Crawford is the perfect person to head up the Jade Hotel, if only the captivating owner of the local vineyard would get on board with her plan and stop badmouthing the hotel to everyone in town. (978-1-63555-709-1)

First Do No Harm by Emily Smith. Pierce and Cassidy are about to discover that when it comes to love, sometimes you have to risk it all to have it all. (978-1-63555-699-5)

Kiss Me Every Day by Dena Blake. For Carly Jamison, wishing for a do-over with Wynn Evans was a long shot, actually getting one was a game changer. (978-1-63555-551-6)

Olivia by Genevieve McCluer. In this lesbian Shakespeare adaption with vampires, Olivia is a centuries-old vampire who must fight a strange figure from her past if she wants a chance at happiness. (978-1-63555-701-5)

One Woman's Treasure by Jean Copeland. Daphne's search for discarded antiques and treasures leads to an embarrassing misunderstanding and, ultimately, the opportunity for the romance of a lifetime with Nina. (978-1-63555-652-0)

Silver Ravens by Jane Fletcher. Lori has lost her girlfriend, her home, and her job. Things don't improve when she's kidnapped and taken to fairyland. (978-1-63555-631-5)

Still Not Over You by Jenny Frame, Carsen Taite, and Ali Vali. Old flames die hard in these tales of a second chance at love with the ex you're still not over. (978-1-63555-516-5)

Storm Lines by Jessica L. Webb. Devon is a psychologist who likes rules. Marley is a cop who doesn't. They don't always agree, but both fight to protect a girl immersed in a street drug ring. (978-1-63555-626-1)

The Politics of Love by Jen Jensen. Is it possible to love across the political divide in a hostile world? Conservative Shelley Whitmore and liberal Rand Thomas are about to find out. (978-1-63555-693-3)

All the Paths to You by Morgan Lee Miller. High school sweethearts Quinn Hughes and Kennedy Reed reconnect five years after they break up and realize that their chemistry is all but over. (978-1-63555-662-9)

Arrested Pleasures by Nanisi Barrett D'Arnuck. When charged with a crime she didn't commit, Katherine Lowe faces the question: Which is harder, going to prison or falling in love? (978-1-63555-684-1)

Bonded Love by Renee Roman. Carpenter Blaze Carter suffers an injury that shatters her dreams, and ER nurse Trinity Greene hopes to show her that sometimes love is worth fighting for. (978-1-63555-530-1)

Convergence by Jane C. Esther. With life as they know it on the line, can Aerin McLeary and Olivia Ando's love survive an otherworldly threat to humankind? (978-1-63555-488-5)

Coyote Blues by Karen F. Williams. Riley Dawson, psychotherapist and shape-shifter, has her world turned upside down when Fiona Bell, her one true love, returns. (978-1-63555-558-5)

Drawn by Carsen Taite. Will the clues lead Detective Claire Hanlon to the killer terrorizing Dallas, or will she merely lose her heart to person of interest urban artist Riley Flynn? (978-1-63555-644-5)

Lucky by Kris Bryant. Was Serena Evans's luck really about winning the lottery, or is she about to get even luckier in love? (978-1-63555-510-3)

The Last Days of Autumn by Donna K. Ford. Autumn and Caroline question the fairness of life, the cruelty of loss, and what it means to love as they navigate the complicated minefield of relationships, grief, and life-altering illness. (978-1-63555-672-8)

Three Alarm Response by Erin Dutton. In the midst of tragedy, can these first responders find love and healing? Three stories of courage, bravery, and passion. (978-1-63555-592-9)

Veterinary Partner by Nancy Wheelton. Callie and Lauren are determined to keep their hearts safe but find that taking a chance on love is the safest option of all. (978-1-63555-666-7)